John Spencer Curwen

Memorials of John Curwen

John Spencer Curwen

Memorials of John Curwen

ISBN/EAN: 9783337399061

Printed in Europe, USA, Canada, Australia, Japan

Cover: Foto ©Raphael Reischuk / pixelio.de

More available books at **www.hansebooks.com**

MEMORIALS

OF

JOHN CURWEN.

COMPILED BY HIS SON

J. SPENCER CURWEN.

WITH A CHAPTER ON HIS HOME LIFE, BY
HIS DAUGHTER, MRS. BANKS.

"Let the people praise Thee, O God; let all the people
praise Thee."—PSALM lxvii. 3.

LONDON

J. CURWEN & SONS, 8, WARWICK LANE, E.C.

1882.

INDEX.

IN MEMORIAM.

—

JOHN CURWEN.

Sung at the Annual Meeting of the Tonic Sol-fa College,

AT EXETER HALL, MAY 30TH, 1881.

Weave a strain of mingled tone
   Praise and joy with mourning blend,
Life so lived, and work so done
   Lives and lasts, and knows no end.
While grief her song is raising,
On yon sea, with glory blazing,
He now, the highest praising,
     Sings evermore.

Still, though dead, he speaks on earth
   To a vast increasing throng ;
Faith, and love, and guileless mirth,
   Teaching still to speak in song.
Boys in the school-room singing ;
Hearts that feel new joys upspringing ;
Pure souls, their worship bringing,
     He blesses still.

Yet we mourn who loved him well,
   Missing here his kindly face,
Still in saddened tones we tell
   All his gentleness and grace ;
O brother ! from us riven,
Though all joy to thee is given,
We, looking up to heaven,
     Still mourn for thee.

              W. F. CALLAWAY.

MEMORIALS OF JOHN CURWEN.

CHAPTER I.

1816—1832.

THE roots of John Curwen's character must be sought
in the characters of his father and mother. His father,
Spedding Curwen by name, was born at Whitehaven
in 1790. Here his grandfather, Thomas Curwen, was at
the time in business with a Mr. Spedding, as a corn
merchant, and he seems to have named his son after his
partner. Both Spedding and Curwen are Cumberland
names, the Curwens having been settled for several
centuries at Workington. Thomas Curwen belonged, no
doubt, to one of the numerous offshoots of the family
which has still its head-quarters at the old castellated
building known as Workington Hall.

B

When Spedding Curwen was nine years of age, his parents moved to Middleton, near Leeds, where his father pursued the occupation of surveyor of mines to a nobleman whose property was adjacent. His parents were strict members of the Church of England, but there was at that time no "live" ministry in the parish church, and Spedding often carried the lanthorn by his mother's side to light her to the Methodist prayer-meeting. Through listening to a Christian lady at his father's sick bed, Spedding was stirred to a sense of religious responsibility. Through the same lady's influence he began attending the ministry of Mr. Parsons at Leeds, and at last found himself preaching at Middleton and other villages near at hand. The nobleman already mentioned, when this turn for study and preaching discovered itself, wanted the young man to go to Oxford, and offered him one of his own livings when he should be ordained. But Spedding had parted company with the establishment, and was committed to the Independents. He entered their College at Rotherham, and remained there four years. Subsequently he was Independent minister at Heckmondwike (where John was born), Cottingham (near Hull), Barbican Chapel (London), Frome (Somerset), Newbury (Berks), and Reading, where he died in 1856.

Spedding Curwen is described by friends who remember him well as very fertile in conversation,

dependent on mood and sympathy for success as a speaker,
but in his best moments 'abounding in thought and
imagery, expressed in the happiest way. Men of wit and
taste came to listen to him, and an old Somersetshire man
at Frome bore this testimony to his preaching :—

"Ha didd zeem ta I, as iv ha didd stand under the
dree a life, a pluckin' the vroots, and vlinggin them out
into the buzzums o' the peeple."

Translation : "He did seem to me as if he did stand
under the tree of life, a plucking the fruits, and flinging
them into the bosoms of the people."

He was a man of firmness as well as sympathy, and,
as in the bitter discussion on Catholic Emancipation, did
not hesitate to take the unpopular side if he was convinced
that it was right.

Spedding Curwen was twice married, and the student
of heredity will naturally enquire about the mother of
John Curwen. She was Mary, daughter of Mr. John
Jubb, of Leeds, and the two were married soon after Mr.
Curwen's settlement at Heckmondwike, 1814.

Mrs. Curwen, the mother of John, was a woman of
education and culture. She seems to have been engaged
in teaching before her marriage. In the spring of 1813
she accompanied a friend in a carriage drive from London
to Penzance and back, lasting three months. The
diary which she kept during this tour is preserved,

and shows quick perception for scenery and men, and some power of description. She seems to have been a strict Nonconformist, and a devout Christian. The diary is full of outpourings of religious thought, self-examinations, &c. She resumed her teaching at Heckmondwike after her marriage. Mrs. Oldfield, an octogenarian lady, who was a girl at Heckmondwike at this time, says that Mrs. Curwen did much to raise the tone of the girls who attended her school. It was the first attempt at a middle-class school in the village. Some sacred verse composed by Mrs. Curwen is before me, which shows devotional feeling and good diction. It is written in a small, neat hand that seems to suggest her character.

John Curwen was born at Hurst House, Heckmondwike, Yorks, on November 14th, 1816. The plain old house where he saw the light is still standing. A big co-operative store towers at its side, and the two buildings tell the tale of old and new Heckmondwike. The blanket-weavers, working at hand-looms in their own cottages, have given place to "factory hands," the power-loom, and its accompaniment of gaunt factories and screeching locomotives. Heckmondwike is more prosperous if less picturesque than it was in 1816. The village has become a town. Men, however, change less than their surroundings, and these Yorkshire folk have still the rough heartiness of their ancestors. The picture which Mrs. Gaskell, in her life of Charlotte Bronte, draws of the neighbouring village of Haworth, may be taken to describe Heckmondwike as it was in the early part of the century.

John Curwen, as the records show, was baptised March 11th, 1817, by Mr. Hale, minister of the Upper Chapel. An elder sister, Mary Jubb Curwen, had been born a year previously, but she died a few months after her brother was born. The Rev. Spedding . Curwen resigned the pastorate of the Lower Chapel at the close of 1817, and moved to Cottingham, near Hull, where he was called to a similar office. Here, after a long illness, his wife died, leaving her husband and two little boys, John and Tom (who was born at Cottingham) to mourn her loss. She chose as the text for her funeral sermon, words which aptly spoke her own experience and told the mother's heart:—" The God which fed me all my life long until this day, the Angel which redeemed me from all evil, bless the lads; and let my name be named on them." A tablet in the chapel records that she died September 27th, 1822, aged 37 years.

The memory of his mother was peculiarly sacred to John Curwen. When she died he was six, just old enough to retain the impression of her face and the recollection of her dying blessing. Writing to his brother fifty-six years after, he says:—

" Remember, our mother's blessing is on us two. It was in the text she chose for her funeral sermon."

And in a letter to his daughter, dated from Hull fifty years after, he recalls his early impressions of the place :—

TO HIS DAUGHTER.

Hull, April 3rd, 1862.

It was a very beautiful morning, and after I had called on Jane Gregory—to whom my dear father used to teach Hebrew, and who used to bother me (when a boy like ——) with fine scraps of poetry—on the Rev. Mr. Jukes, and on old Mr. and Mrs. Newlove (who kept a farm at Beverley Park, where I played at five years old), with whom I prayed, I went with Mr. Winch and kind and happy Mr. James Sibree (a minister) to Cottingham.

We entered the village, through the churchyard, by the house where I first went to school. We passed along the street (unaltered), where I remember meeting my precious mother once—the only time that I remember her walking. I could not see the house were she died, for a new one is built. But there was the garden by the chapel where dear father planted the apple trees and where the thunderbolt fell. There also was the little vestry where my sainted mother taught the little Sunday School, and in the chapel I stood over her grave, and prayed that God would answer her prayers for me fully. I remember that she was seized with one of her fits while I stood by her knee, and her hands were on my head, and she was praying. I was only six when she died, yet how dearly I love her fragrant memory! I often thank God that He has spared to you and the dear boys just such another precious mother. His blessings— His highest blessings of spiritual life be with you all.

A letter from the Rev. Spedding Curwen to Mr. (afterwards Sir) Charles Reed, written in 1839, says :—

You are quite correct in regarding John's devotedness as the result of the prayers of his glorified mother. He inherits her natural temper, which was that of an active tranquillity very seldom ruffled. He was much with her in her last long affliction. If you had entered the room suddenly her hand would be seen resting on his head, and her lips uttering prayer. He was too young to receive any mental impression then; but the Lord answered her supplications by his early conversion. He was at that time only five and a half years old. At the age of twelve he was put under the care of a second mother, whose kind and affectionate watchfulness trained my children to what they are.

Chiefly in consequence of this loss, Mr. Spedding Curwen moved, at the beginning of the year 1824, to Barbican Chapel, London. He took a house near London Fields, Hackney, and the motherless boys were sent to a boarding school at Ham, near Twickenham, developing a taste not only for study, but for gymnastic exercises.

In the summer of 1828 Mr. Spedding Curwen moved to Frome, in Somerset, and became the pastor of Zion Chapel. Here he remained for eleven years, which covered the most formative and impressionable period of John's life. Of Frome and its people John always spoke with great warmth, and he retained to the last the friendships which he formed there.

In a speech delivered at Frome in 1876 he said :—

This afternoon I have been going over some of the scenes of my boyhood. I know I am a better man for having lived at Frome. I might have lived under the same circumstances of parentage and yet lacked many advantages elsewhere. The beautiful scenery in the neighbourhood has had a power over me all through my life; it has influenced my thoughts, and has helped to mould my character. My wanderings in Vallis Vale are as fresh in my recollection as though they were but of yesterday.

In a short piece of autobiography read at the entry upon his ministry at Plaistow in 1844, Mr. Curwen said :—

A little before the age of sixeen I was united to the church of Christ to which my father then ministered, at Frome, in Somersetshire. I shall never forget the sweet fellowship I enjoyed with them in meetings for prayer and worship, and in works of usefulness.

Dr. E. G. Monk, organist of York Minster, who was a contemporary of Mr. Curwen's at Frome at this time, writes :—

I distinctly remember him as a very young man, of ready speech, and bright intelligence, evidences of which I repeatedly witnessed at meetings of the "Young Men's Debating Society," of which I was a humble member, and he was an occasional visitor and speaker. I have never forgotten his fluency and animation, or the fact that the side into which he threw his weight of argument and rhetoric proved ever the winning side! My impression of his amiability was as high as that of his intellectual level.

Mr. J. Poulter, whose school at Frome he attended, still survives, at the age of 78. He spent a day with

Mr. Curwen shortly before his death. Mr. Poulter writes :—

At this distance of time I cannot call to mind any incidents to interest you, as my dear boy came up to us as a day scholar, so that he was less under my cognisance than if he had boarded with me. But this I can say of him, that I never knew any boy for whom I felt an equal affection, and I am sure all his schoolfellows were similarly affected. I can remember well his endeavours to keep at the top of his class in the face of a very vigorous opponent, both boys animated by an emulation quite free from ungenerous influences. On one occasion I was astonished to see the ability with which he delivered a lecture on "Dreams" to a very large audience at Frome in his school days. Such as he was then, in disposition, in looks, in energy, I found him fifty years after.

Of his training at this school, Mr. Curwen himself writes in his "Teacher's Manual:"—

It would be impossible for me to calculate what a long train of advantages have accrued to me through life, from the discipline and pleasure which was given me in two lessons from the Rev. J. Poulter, of Frome. In one of these he made his pupils thoroughly apprehend the first proposition of Euclid, and in another he carefully developed to us the meaning and power of the letter x in algebra. These lessons not only made us clearly understand the subject before us, but left us stronger for the work of understanding other subjects, and gave us an inclination to renew the pleasure of understanding things.

CHAPTER II.

1832—1838.

ENTERS WYMONDLEY COLLEGE—DIARY—COWARD COLLEGE—
UNIVERSITY COLLEGE—HIS TEACHERS THERE—REMINISCENCES
BY FELLOW STUDENTS—REV. ANDREW REED—REV. H. M. GUNN
— REV. H. GRIFFITH — REV. J. B. JOHNSON — REV. W. H.
GRIFFITH—HIS STUDIES AT COLLEGE.

IT was not long before John Curwen was called away
from Frome for the greater part of the year. 'A letter
from the chairman of Wymondley Independent College
to the Rev. S. Curwen, dated September 8th, 1832,
informs him that his eldest son has been accepted as a
student, and is requested to enter forthwith. A private
diary kept at this time shows that he entered the College
December 16th, 1832, being then in his seventeenth
year. There is nothing in this diary which it would be
profitable to print. It deals exclusively with the
religious life, and is introspective to a degree which
would now be thought unnatural and unhealthy. The
theme is ever the same—disappointment and self-reproach
at the non-attainment of an ideal. A form of self-
examination, to be used every day, is given.

Wymondley is a village in Hertfordshire, where,
at the time of which we write, there existed an Academy

for Independent Ministers. A few months after Mr. Curwen's entrance as a student the Academy was, however, removed to London, and its name changed to "Coward College." Here the students attended the newly-founded University College, Gower Street, for classics and mathematics, and studied divinity under their own tutors. This was in every way a gain. The men mixed with the larger life of an unsectarian college, and gained in toleration and culture. Mr. Curwen always looked back upon these student years with delight. He remembered especially the debating class, at which John Stuart Mill and other men of note were occasional speakers, and the vigorous atmosphere of the new college. In the "Teacher's Manual" he writes :—

I wish to express my gratitude to the late Professor White, of the old London University, Professor T. H. Key, of the same University, and one of my fellow students, the Rev. Henry Griffith. Mr. White used to make the most complex subjects of mathematics plain to the understanding by realised instances and illustrations, before he would even allow us to proceed to practice. Mr. Key not only taught us Latin, but showed us how to investigate, on principles which were not only applicable to language, but to everything else. Mr. Griffith took a special delight in setting his young friend thinking on almost all questions under the sun. Many of my other teachers in early life were learned and faithful men, but they spoke *to* me rather than *with* me. A large portion of their valuable lessons have long ago passed from my memory, but the lessons of these men whom I have mentioned are living powers with me now.

Several reminiscences of Mr. Curwen during his College life, contributed by fellow students, now follow :—

THE REV. ANDREW REED, B.A.

My first knowledge of John Curwen was at Coward College, where we were fellow students. He was one of the seniors when I entered. Curwen was beloved by every one for his cheerful sympathy and amiable sociality. He was the soul of honour and of generosity; methodical and precise in details, even to the dotting of his "i's," and crossing of his "t's" in writing, but what he began he stuck to with invincible tenacity. He was very resolute in matters of principle. In our debating society I recollect his declaiming on the theme "that principle must be carried out to its furthest length without the least heed to expediency." He was full of Jonathan Dymond's books on the Quaker views of peace and non-resistance, and if he was not a fluent speaker, he stood by the chimney in the midst of us all, with Gunn, as president, in the chair, and with Joseph Fletcher, W. H. Griffith, Philip Smith, Joseph Smedmore, Benjamin Kent, and C. Peter Mason, and Baldwin Brown, and my brother Charles, who had come in as visitors to the debate, and there he illustrated his views profusely, ever and anon thumping the chimney-piece and reiterating "no heed whatever to expediency!" "vile, disgraceful, disastrous expediency!" Nor though Porter with his cutting satire carried out his extremes to the *reductio ad absurdum* amid our general laughter, could the orator be moved, but remained, the apt emblem of his own principle, like a rock, without the least swerving to his hated "expediency." He was sometimes visited by his brother Tom, whose quieter and gentler manner covered a no less firm and righteous spirit. Both the brothers carried into useful and honourable lives the characteristics which made them agreeable as young men. I had the misfortune to catch the small-pox at college, and then I had occasion to learn what Curwen could be as a friend in trouble. I felt miserable, but he established himself in my room, and was like a woman in tender care. Heedless of danger to himself, he gave me warm water to promote sickness, attended to my food and medicine, treated me with every attention, read amusing stories to keep up my spirits; all this for a day or two he kept up till the doctor ordered me to be wrapped up and taken home in a carriage. Even my mother, though devoted to my care, could hardly be more kind or effective than my student nurse had been. Thus he carried out his principle without heed to expediency.

Curwen was intensely interested in children, and attached to Sunday School work. He inoculated us all with his zeal, and we often discussed with him his favourite ideas of teaching to read by the "look and say" system, putting everything for children into a picture form, and systematising lessons for them. He used to go to the Barbican Sunday School, which was under the able superintendence of the genial Alderman Challis. He engaged us to deliver addresses there. One of my first efforts in speaking was an anxious pictorial address on Elijah at Carmel, which I read to Curwen beforehand, profiting by his criticisms. He was everywhere acceptable in his addresses to the young.

THE REV. H. MAYO GUNN.

It has been a happiness to me to have been intimately acquainted with John Curwen since the year 1834, when I entered Coward College for theology and University College for general knowledge, and received kindness from him, who had been admitted a year or two before, which was valuable to a junior. All through life, his character has been distinguished by a rare union of noble and practical excellences, both in private society and in public work.

Residence in the same college gives students thorough knowledge of each other, and leads young men to form close and enduring friendships, and there could be no doubt in anyone about John Curwen, as he was familiarly and affectionately called. His nature was most open and transparent, while he was always the same kind, free, and cordial companion. With much intelligence and benevolence, there were blended deep piety and great perseverance. Though not robust in health, care enabled him to keep up with the hard work of the classes, in cheerful, good spirits, that brought the charm of his bright, genial smile and the ring of his hearty laugh into every circle.

Reminiscences of special interest will relate to any signs or traces of the lines along which he afterwards worked with eminent usefulness and distinction. His two favourite and predominant occupations may be said to have been the training and singing of the young, and some foreshadows of these tastes can be remembered during his college life, though developed subsequently beyond all expectation. Of these two tendencies the appreciation of good singing appeared before his attention to the instruction of the young. For as soon as our acquaintance was formed, I found his musical talent, early impressed in his father's congregation at Frome, had received a great attraction in the best congregational singing then in London—at almost the only place of worship where it was cultivated—led by a large choir

gathered by the influence of Dr. Liefchild, in connection
with his powerful ministry at Craven Chapel. Interested
also by friendship with the Doctor's only son, who retains
a lively remembrance of it still, John Curwen induced
some of his fellow students to attend the large and
crowded services, where the charm of superior psalmody
was followed by the study and practice of sacred music at
home. The worth of such knowledge to young ministers
was not then thought of, though now fully recognised,
but to some it has proved a means of unexpected utility.
In the impulse then given may be discovered the early
conviction of the power of music for good, as well as the
first study of its elements, that contributed with Mr.
Curwen's high sense of duty to urge him on in the plans
and labours he pursued with such devotedness through
life. The valuable and extensive results of his work
remain an enduring monument of a noble heart; conse-
crated to religion, and adorned with the trophies of music.

Of the other line of philanthropy to which he devoted
himself for some years, an indication appeared in the
latter part of this college course, as I have a distinct
recollection of much attention being paid by Mr. Curwen
to the Sunday School at Tonbridge Chapel in our neighbourhood. This was done in his last year, when not away
for preaching, on Sunday afternoons, when several of us
were accustomed to visit the mews around the squares
with religious tracts for the working men and their
families. His sympathy with children impressed me the
more from being familiar with the efforts of relatives
in the same object. His conviction of the need of
improvement increased afterwards, and showed itself in a
series of addresses in various parts of the kingdom,
continued with persistent fidelity to the welfare of the
young of all ages.

THE REV. H. GRIFFITH, F.G.S.

When John Curwen entered Wymondley College he was quite a beardless youth, decidedly grave, though cheerful in manner, and of a singularly modest and winsome appearance. It is no exaggeration to say that he soon made himself the pet of our whole fraternity. I believe no one in the house at the time was more truly respected, or so universally loved.

It so happened, that while his study was contiguous to mine, we had the same district (Highfrolity) allotted to us for tract distribution and visiting the sick—a labour of which he never seemed to grow weary. We therefore necessarily saw a great deal of each other, and had nearly all our out-door work and exercise in common. The result was that we became specially intimate friends, and I am thankful to add, that friendship continued unbroken till the end.

Like most other earnest searchers after truth, he had not a few intellectual difficulties to contend with at the outset, but so far as I could discover, he never allowed them seriously to discourage him, or in any way to lessen his interest in the great cause to which he had con-secrated his life. I fear I cannot recall any of his religious utterances with sufficient distinctness to warrant my attempting to repeat them, but I well remember being very solemnly impressed with the purity of his character, the warmth of his heart, and the enviable reposefulness of his spirit. He had early learnt to *trust*. Like Luther's "Innocent Robin," he could tuck his head under his wing, go to sleep, and let God take care that the sky did not fall !

From the first he was seen to be a steady, hard-working student, systematic and careful in all his move-ments, though not accredited with any extraordinary brilliancy of genius. I never heard what school he attended as a boy, but his home training, both intellectually and morally, must have been good, as he had a fair share of healthy ambition, and was scrupulously correct in his habits. In classics, if I mistake not, he stood considerably above the average of his fellows, but for mathematics he had no genuine passion, and concerned himself about them little more than was required to pass muster in the lecture room. *That* I always regretted, as I knew he had a strong liking for physical science, with quite a gift for mechanical contrivances and combinations.

After our transference to the London University, our immediate special pursuits were so different that we saw nothing of each other during class-time; but in the evenings and on Sundays we were as much together as ever. His views of men and things had now become more decided and settled, but his child-like disposition had lost none of its sweetness. Of selfishness in all its forms he had unquenchable detestation, with a sovereign contempt for mere dilettantism and the love of display. He was not, however, insensible to the charms of general culture, though his heart was else-where. His chief delight was in sacred literature—especially in the writings of our semi-Platonic divines. I cannot tell how far or how long the feeling lasted; but he was then an enthusiastic (we used to say idolatrous) admirer of Bates, John Norris, Jeremy Taylor, and Dr. Thomas Brown, &c. Many a midnight hour of "stout talk" did we have over those old worthies. In poetry we read comparatively little together, the taste of one leaning to the idyllic or pastoral, and of the other to the dramatic and impetuous. The first drew the line at Wordsworth, the second at Coleridge or Byron and Shelley.

c

This brings me to a chapter in Mr. Curwen's history which probably will be new to yourself, and is sure to surprise not a few of your readers. Up to February, 1834, when he must have been above eighteen years old, he knew absolutely *nothing of music.* It was generally said that he could not distinguish the Old Hundreth from the National Anthem! There was doubtless some exaggeration in that, but not as much as you would be apt to suppose. In the bravado of after-supper discussion, a challenge was thrown out to " compel him to master the gamut," if he would only pledge himself to give to it twenty minutes per day for a stated period. It fell to my lot to lead the forlorn hope. After almost incredible difficulty I managed to evoke the sounds C, G, C, to the Welsh words *Bara, Berem, Berw.* We next had some trouble with E, but that once conquered, the battle was virtually won! Our friend, the late Rev. Thomas Parry, of Dover, then took the matter in hand, and between us we succeeded in getting him to sing several simple tunes, with commendable accuracy! It was thought a grand triumph; and we may justly call it so now, though we little imagined at the time what was ultimately to spring from it.

In our debating societies, though a constant attendant, he seldom took any prominent part, as he much disliked obtrusiveness, and did not consider himself a ready speaker. We always attached great weight to his judgment, but did not ordinarily look to him for a speech. Of his power in the pulpit I never had an opportunity of forming any opinion, as I left college just as his name was placed on the preaching list. The only occasion on which it was my privilege to hear him in public (if *public* it can be called) was a short address to a ragged school in a cottage at the back of Fetter Lane.

THE REV. G. B. JOHNSON.

Deeply did I love him. It was love at first sight too, and its only change was that of growth. He was quite a senior when I entered college. Well do I recall the kindness, the gentle brightness with which he ever greeted us juniors. His whole relationships then and ever after seemed to me invested with the rarest beauty. Seldom have face and voice so perfectly expressed the heart as his; neither was complete without the other. A cheerful piety was the charm of his being; the secret of a fine and tender sympathy that was prompt for enterprise or for comfort. I imagine that outside of his direct family circle he was never happier than when he and his dear wife entertained the Coward students. All valued his friendship as one of the jewels of life; he had the happy art that comes of so finely-strung natures of uniting his guests in their truest and deepest relations, and of individualising each one as if his history and character had been a particular study. John Curwen was and remains a synonym of all that is high and holy in principle, of all that is upright and tender in affection.

During his student life, which lasted six years, Mr. Curwen spent his holidays at Frome. Here his father married, as a second wife, Mrs. Davies, daughter of the late Mr. John Spencer, of Oakhill, Somerset. The Rev. W. H. Griffith, of Clifton, who was not only a fellow student with Mr. Curwen at Coward College, but lived at Frome, and saw much of him in these holiday times, writes :—

I remember Mr. Curwen being invited to speak at a meeting held by one of the candidates for the borough,

and being received with great applause.   He was also one
of the prime movers in starting and supporting a Young
Men's Mutual Improvement Society in Frome, a thing in
that day not so common as at present.   Before I became
acquainted with him he had distinguished himself as a
writer in the *Youths' Magazine*, and, I believe, some other
publications, and was looked up to by his young friends as
a prodigy.   I have a very vivid impression of the great
kindness and goodness of his temper and disposition, which
made him a general favourite among his fellow students
at Coward.   There was certainly no want of manliness or
power, but tenderness and gentleness were perhaps the
most striking features in his character.   Mr. Curwen was
a diligent student at college, and distinguished himself in
some of the classes—the Hebrew and English, and
probably some others which I do not remember.

Mr. Curwen always spoke of mental philosophy as
his favourite study; he regarded it indeed as a relaxation.   It was no doubt this study of the methods of the
mind which formed in him those radical notions of
teaching which were the key to much of his after work.
He passed through life a methodiser, a graduator, an
educationist, having no special skill in any one subject, but
maintaining the attitude of the learner, and pointing the
way.   Every subject that he touched yielded to the
charm.   His orderly exposition, his power of seizing upon
main facts, his enthusiasm, and his sympathy with the
learner were the sources of his power.   He always
thought clearly, and never assented to anything he did
not fully understand or agree with.

CHAPTER III.

1838—1840.

APPOINTED ASSISTANT MINISTER AT BASINGSTOKE — FORMS A HABIT OF GIVING—SCHOOL FOR BOYS AT BASINGSTOKE— RECOLLECTIONS BY TWO LADIES—HIS POWER IN ADDRESSING CHILDREN—ITS SOURCE—ANECDOTE—REV. W. ROBERTS — ALDERMAN THOMPSON — A LADY—HIS EARNESTNESS—MR. CURWEN ON SPEAKING TO CHILDREN—THE VANNERS—"NELLY VANNER"—ITS SUCCESS—REV. H. M. GUNN ON THE BOOK— MR. CURWEN AT BASINGSTOKE—REMOVES TO STOWMARKET— BIBLE CLASSES THERE — BEGINS TO LECTURE ON SUNDAY SCHOOLS—SIR CHARLES REED'S RECOLLECTIONS.

IN 1838 Mr. Curwen was appointed assistant minister at the Independent Chapel, Basingstoke, Hants. The salary attached to this appointment was fifty pounds a year. Mr. Curwen here began the habit of giving away one tenth of his gross income, a habit which he maintained through life with scrupulous care, until from 1862 until his death he doubled the proportion. Any denial which this rule may have caused counted for nothing beside the pleasure which he had in giving. At the beginning of every new year the income of the last was estimated, and the amount available for "giving" was fixed. The money was then set apart.

At Basingstoke Mr. Curwen, in addition to his ministerial work, kept a little school for boys at his lodgings. He writes of this in the "Teachers' Manual"—

When at twenty-one years of age I kept a little school of boys I became very successful in teaching arithmetic. The reason was that I did not teaze my pupils at first with the abstract ideas of the tables, but followed Mr. Horace Grant's plan. I had a box of peas, a box of beans, a box of shells, and a box of wooden bricks. With these I made the little children work out sums in adding and taking away, and multiplying and dividing. When they had worked out a sum with the shells, they worked the same with the bricks, and the same again with the beans and peas, and so gradually formed for themselves abstract ideas of number, and prepared their minds for a real enjoyment of the tables.

The work of Froebel and other educators has made us familiar with this method, but forty years ago it was much more radical and original than it appears to be now.

Two ladies who remember as girls Mr. Curwen's manner and influence at Basingstoke have written interesting sketches of it. The first says :—

Mr. Curwen's stay at Basingstoke will always be remembered with feelings of the keenest interest and love. Whenever he entered our school the faces of both teachers and scholars lighted up with unusual pleasure. One had only to see him with young people, and one felt to be in the presence of a man who lived for children, and who, by every word and look, won their love, and gave them instruction and delight. His manner of communicating thoughts and ideas was perfectly unique. I shall never forget a service, one Sunday afternoon, when the chapel was filled with children. It was an intense joy when he entered to see their faces beam with delight. As soon as he spoke there was perfect quietude. He took the text " Commit thy way unto the Lord ; trust also in Him, and He will bring it to pass." First he taught them to sing it a few times. Then he explained, in a beautifully simple story which the children could understand and appreciate, what committing our way is, the trust that should accompany the committal, and the promise of our Heavenly Father to bring it to pass, not always in our way, but for our best. He related to them the circumstances in which Paul Gerhard was placed when he wrote the hymn " Give to the winds thy fears," and very pathetically told the incident of his being exiled from his country on account of his firm adherence to his religious principles. Mr. Curwen rendered great assistance in helping to establish the British School in Basingstoke.

The second writes :—

My first introduction to Mr. Curwen was on his coming to Basingstoke, when he threw a great amount of energy into the work of the Sunday School. I became one of his first teachers, and he taught me himself how to conduct the infant class, even to the actions for attracting attention while they learned a hymn. In giving a lesson himself he would say " Now all look at me—fold arms— now let us hear a pin drop," and you could invariably hear it ; in fact, with my own children it became a household word, " Now let us hear dear Mr. Curwen's silence." I have never before or since seen his equal with children. His nature was so simple and loving. I remember being sent for once after school. Mr. Curwen had come to have tea with us, and he was at the piano trying to make out a tune. " My dear child," he said, " Why will not this sound correctly?" " Oh, Mr. Curwen," I replied, "You have forgotten F sharp." We had many little consultations over the " Child's Hymn Book," and I remember playing him many of the tunes to see if they would do for hymns. I was also at what I believe was his first meeting to try the Sol-fa method, and he gave me one of his first books.

Both these letters speak of Mr. Curwen's power in addressing children. This, indeed, was one of his strongest points, and his fame in this department spread in a few years throughout the country. The growth of the Tonic Sol-fa movement compelled him in after years gradually to retire from this work, which he dearly loved, but the impression he left never died away among those who heard him. Up to the end of his life, when he had given up Sunday School meetings for twenty-five years, he used to receive every spring a crop of invitations to them from all parts of the country. In his journeys he met with people constantly who recalled, across a space of thirty or forty years, addresses which they had heard from him as children. The impression was still vivid; they would repeat the text and the anecdotes with much enthusiasm.

The power was partly natural, but partly also the fruit of study. Sympathy was its first source, but Mr.

Curwen had read all the books on education he could lay hands on, and formulated to himself the method on which he proceeded. His bright and kindly manner won the children to him, his method made his subject attractive, and he succeeded to a wonderful extent in keeping their attention alive. He had a fine power of dramatising and picturing a scene, stooping to the simplest words, proceeding by the easiest steps, so that nothing might stand between him and his purpose of moving his audience. His children well remember how vividly he would sometimes describe, for their amusement, the use of the " ferule " at one of the schools he attended, striking one hand with the other to show how the leather struck the boy's hand, and starting back with supposed pain. The action was so graphic that Mrs. Curwen, with a shudder and a cry, would beg him to stop. This dramatic power served him in his addresses, and was the secret of much of their force.

One anecdote, which Mr. Curwen was fond of telling in his Sunday School addresses, was characteristic. It was about a very unruly class of boys who had been given up in despair by all the teachers in the school save one. This one volunteered to try them, and determined to make an example of the first boy who misbehaved. After several plans for punishment had been tried, and had failed— these were described in detail—the teacher hit upon a plan which he was sure would be effectual. He provided a cage, large enough to hold a boy, and popping the first offender in, hauled it up to the ceiling. The hauling of the rope, hand over hand, was imitated perfectly, and the imagination of the children, kindled by the vividly-told narrative, saw the boy looking through the bars upon his comrades below. Of course this failed, like the other schemes, and, as it was the teacher's last resource, he broke down completely. ' "Boys," he said, "I must give you up, as others have done, but, boys, I *do* love you." The boys were more softened by these words than by all the punishments ; they became tractable and attentive, and soon were the best class in the school.

Several friends have put upon record their impressions of Mr. Curwen's Sunday School addresses. The Rev. W. Roberts writes :—

His successful musical career notwithstanding, John Curwen will always be best remembered by his relation to children. Even his musical exertions bore preeminently upon the interests of children. His addresses to children, I have always heard, were inimitable. I never heard but one of these, and that was given in his father's chapel when I was a youth. I remember his trying one or two positions, first about the pulpit ; he stood at last on the table, in the table-pew. He wanted the children to see him, and to speak to them with his whole body, as well as his voice. He chose a short text : " Wilt thou not from this time cry unto me, My Father, Thou art the guide of my youth ?" (Jer. iii. 4). He first taught the children to chant these words, till they completely knew them. He then gave them the simplest conceivable address, in the simplest possible manner. There was hardly any action, any motion, in the delivery of it. He held both hands up, pretty steadily, almost stiffly, but the children were spell-bound. At the time, I remember, I thought it rather wanting in substance. I was at the hungry age for *thought* then, but as I reflected on it, I saw the clear decision underlying every tone, and I felt the sweetness of spirit that breathed through every syllable. John Curwen was a man with whom, probably, no child would think of taking any liberties, for children feel the presence of force of character where, to elder people, it is sometimes veiled by gentleness of bearing, but he was also a man whom every child would love.

Mr. Curwen's nephew, Alderman Thompson, J.P., of Manchester, writes :—

As a small child I heard him deliver an address to the scholars at Rusholme Road Chapel, Manchester. The subject was " Moses lifting up the brazen serpent in the wilderness." Though so many years have passed away since that event, and although I was very young at the time, I have a very distinct impression of the clearness of the story, and of its application to our Saviour's death. Mr. Curwen's admirable faculty of telling his stories clearly and picturesquely, of making his hearers see and hear the events themselves, and of drawing from the incidents the moral that was to be taught, was his special gift, and continued with him through life, although in later years he shrank from such efforts, and thought that his power had gone.

A lady who heard Mr. Curwen give an address to children at Frome, writes :—

I attribute the vivid impression which remains entirely to the mode and manner of Mr. Curwen's address —his pleasant voice, fine presence, wonderful clearness of style, and freedom from conventionalism, while keeping up, at the same time, his dignity as a speaker. He first fixed the words of his text in the minds of all by making them repeat it phrase by phrase, and setting it to a little chant which he taught us. He then enforced the lessons by a story or two. One of these I remember perfectly from the amusing and graphic way in which he told it. I need scarcely say that the interest of the audience, amongst whom were some hundreds of children, as noisily disposed as English children in a factory town could be, was kept up without flagging.

Much has been said of the source of Mr. Curwen's power in speaking to children, but the ultimate source was intense earnestness. "It is a sacred work," he wrote many years after, " to get near the soul of a child, and to be permitted to plant a seed of God's truth there."

The following is an extract from an article which Mr. Curwen wrote in the *Independent Magazine*, 1842, on the subject of which we are speaking. It is important as showing the distinction which he drew between child*like* and child*ish* talk, and as betraying the fact that his addresses were studied in form and detail :—

All that is said of the art of writing for children applies with full force to the art of speaking to them. The power to write fittingly is only one part of the power required for speaking with success. For this there is also necessary a certain assumption, or rather, re-assumption of naturalness ; a certain putting off of one's own conventional dignity—that thing which children entirely despise among themselves, and quite disrespect in their elders ; and these are very difficult things to do indeed, until the teacher has once tasted the pleasure of becoming unreservedly a child.

But wherefore do we quote these difficulties ? To discourage? No, to encourage; but first to rouse. Ministers and other intelligent men we would rouse, who strangely imagine that anyone will do to feed the lambs ! The teacher we would rouse, if such a one can be found, who teaches no better this year than last. We would rouse energies worthy of a great task ; for when an attainment is meanly thought of, no one will bestow labour to gain it.

Some persons appear to have entirely mistaken what simplicity of thought is. Poverty and commonness are not simplicity. Simplicity is the very pure essence of a thing presented in some form of unpretending beauty— a beauty which requires the thoughtful eye to see its charms, but to such an eye discovers all its loveliness.

During his life at Basingstoke Mr. Curwen became acquainted with Mr. T. Vanner and his family, and to one of the daughters of this gentleman, Fanny Vanner, he became engaged. She, however, died of consumption before the engagement had long continued, her death having been preceded by that of a younger sister, Nelly. It was the short sweet life of Nelly Vanner, and her tranquil death, that tempted Mr. Curwen into his first serious effort at authorship. " The History of Nelly Vanner " was a great success. It is a child's book, and was written at a time when there were few books for children.   The story is simple and uneventful; there is neither plot nor agony.   The diction is transparently clear, tranquil, and natural.   The art is so entirely concealed that a careless reader is apt to wonder what can make the story so interesting to children.   There is none of the self-conscious simplicity of " Alice in Wonderland " and books of its class, which seem written for grown up people who like, for amusement, to imagine themselves children. ' The child's point of view is taken, but this is done so naturally that the reader hardly notices it.

In his preface to " Nelly Vanner " Mr. Curwen says :—

Those who have not much studied how to tell a tale to a child, should they read this book, will no doubt make the discovery that it is full of what they will call unnecessary repetition and over-plainness of speech. From such unskilful attacks an easy refuge is found in the example of those Scripture stories which, with great plainness and frequent repetition, have yet been ever found more attractive to children than any others ; and that not only for the stories themselves, but greatly because of that simple, truthful Hebrew style they are told in.   Translate them into a different style, and, for a child at least, half their interest is gone.   Others may object that the topics themselves are childish.   They should be so, for children are the class addressed.   An orator, at the bar or on the hustings, reckons it not a condescen-sion, but a triumph of his art, to show a knowledge of all those habits of thought and modes of life which are familiar to his auditors.   It is thus that he makes himself one of them. A smile, as of recognition, is seen on their countenances. It is thus that he stirs the secret springs of deep sympathy. Why may we not use, with children, the same honourable artifice ?"

One or two letters of Mr. Curwen's to children, printed in subsequent chapters, display that patient eye for detail which so pleases children ; a minuteness almost worthy of Defoe. "Nelly Vanner" is forgotten at the present day, but it passed through fourteen editions, and a competent reviewer said that there had been nothing like it since "The dairyman's daughter."

The Rev. H. Mayo Gunn writes :—

After Mr. Curwen had left college he commenced his ministerial work at Basingstoke, and he was not long there before he tried his plans of benefiting the children. Of his work there I am able to testify from the fact that it fell to my lot to succeed him after he had laboured there two or three years. This circumstance gives me another opportunity of tracing his early choice of methods, as tracks or signs of the paths in which he was led by the providence of God, "In works of faith and labours of love" to exceeding usefulness "above all things he could ask or think." After assisting the Rev. D. Gunn at Christchurch for some months I was invited to Basingstoke, and found much interest awakened by him in the instruction of the young, both in the Sabbath schoolroom, doubled in size, and a large day school, built during his residence. At Basingstoke Mr. Curwen printed his first little hymn book with a few of the recent favourites not in other collections, and this was the beginning of the penny hymn book so widely circulated still. This necessitated

his first small selection of tunes to fit them, and one of
the early copies, printed by T. Ward, is now beside me.
The work he had commenced it was a pleasure to carry on
for a similar period, until both the school and chapel were
filled.

Mr. John Curwen's connection with the old church at
Basingstoke became suddenly famous from the popularity
of his wonderful child's book, the charming and touching
memoir of Nelly Vanner. He tried the plan of writing as
a child would think and talk, and his effort was rapidly
appreciated, for the first edition, in 1840, was soon sold,
and a second printed in the spring of 1841. The life-like
sketch of a sweet little lady was drawn in an original,
simple, graphic manner, and introduced a fresh style of
writing. His defence of a childish book for a child has
the authority of one of the ablest writers, who confesses,
" When I was a child I talked and I thought as a child,
but when I became a man I put away childish things,"
or thoughts and words. Nelly Vanner was a rare child of
rare parents, whom it was my privilege to know for some
years. There happened to be the right artist to draw and
hold up the portrait of such exceeding childlike graces as
to charm all who see it into wishing to be more like
it. Had Mr. Curwen written nothing else, this would
have enrolled his name among the truest friends of
children, as in it he has left a legacy of moral and spiritual
power for good, beyond the richest endowments, as long as
our language will last, and as wide as it may spread.
This striking book made Mr. Curwen widely known to all
persons interested in Sunday Schools, and occasioned his
being invited to meetings and conferences, until he was
induced to devote himself to a series of lectures. In his
autobiographical sketch at the grand and enthusiastic
meeting held in Exeter Hall to present him with a

testimonial of public gratitude and admiration, he traced back his mission to a conference of teachers in the autumn of 1841, just after his first visit to Norwich, and discovery of Miss Glover's plan of notation in singing. The "struggle" he described was worthy of the triumph he won, and all the more that he ascribed the credit to every one but himself. While he had striven to press on in the path marked out by Providence, with the courage and meekness of the leader of old, "he served God and his generation," until he "fell asleep in Jesus."

The Rev. Andrew Reed, writing of this period, says :—

After leaving college I settled at Norwich, and he at Basingstoke. There I paid him a visit, and found him carrying out his theories among a very attached people. He had published his beautiful and successful memoir of Nelly Vanner, and I went with him to visit her home. I was delighted to see how her parents loved and honoured my old college mate for his attentions to their daughter in her last hours. I visited his Sabbath Schools, and found them in excellent order, and full of life. He was superintendent as well as pastor, and was making them models in instruction, in the quality of the singing, and in the introduction of many original devices. He had infused his own spirit into teachers and classes.

In 1841 Mr. Curwen removed to Stowmarket, in Suffolk, taking the post of co-pastor at the Independent Chapel there. A lady, who was then a girl in his congregation, recalls his influence over children. When Mr. Curwen came there was but one children's hymn in use in the Sunday School—" Oh, that will be joyful." Mr.

D

Curwen introduced new ones. His Sunday evening sermons were always for the young. This lady continues :—

He had a happy way of utilising friendly visits. I remember him one day out at tea with a child on each knee, and another on a low seat near him, teaching them to sing the hymn " Sweet spices." Then his Bible classes —they stand out as the Bible classes of my life. We took the Gospel by Mark, one or two paragraphs at a time. He knew that many of us were young Sabbath School teachers, almost children ourselves, and he taught us to make the Bible narratives bright, real, and instructive to the little children in our classes. Through 40 years of Sunday School teaching the help and influence of those Bible classes has been working for good with me.

The Rev. T. Fison, B.A., of Hendon, writing of this time says :—

A vivid impression is left on my mind of the quiet ardour with which he was even then devoting himself to what has since proved the great public mission of his life. Some, probably, were surprised and puzzled at this, having no foresight of the immense good which would result. But he must have been sustained by strong inward conviction, and a clear perception of the work to which he was called.

In the autumn of this year (1841) Mr. Curwen began to lecture publicly upon Sunday School methods and plans. He made a tour in Yorkshire, in company with his friend Mr. (afterwards Sir) Charles Reed. An account of this tour is given in the following notes by Sir Charles Reed, to which a touching interest attaches. He had promised to write an account of this early public work of Mr. Curwen's for the present volume, but the pressure of public work interrupted the duty, and death prevented its fulfilment. The following fragment, written on scraps of paper, and evidently meant as a rough copy, was found after Sir Charles's death in his locker at the House of Commons. Though it refers to events both before and after the time of which I am writing, it is best to insert it here entire.

The tenderest-hearted man I ever knew was John Curwen. His father and my father were friends, and when I was at the London University he was a student of divinity in Coward College. Of all cozy rooms his was the coziest, and though his range of library literature was small, his books were very select. His talk about these companions, and his willingness that I should share his love for them, led to very pleasant intercourse. Although I was his junior he allowed me the rank of a friend, and he always called me Charles. He was removed to Basingstoke, and I lost sight of him till the publication of his "Nelly Vanner," concerning which we had some correspondence. In 18— he visited Norwich, and there for the first time he met Miss Glover, to whom my mother introduced him. Miss Glover had told Mrs. Reed of her musical taste, and explained her views on a new notation, and its use in the education of children. Mr. Curwen, always deeply interested in children's psalmody, saw at once in this new idea the germ of a new system which he lived to develop, and which has long since connected his name as the founder of the Tonic Sol-fa system.

Before this, Mr. Curwen had resolved to render his schools an example of a brighter and more attractive institution than Sunday Schools generally were. He visited Scotland, met with David Stow, and came home full of interest as to the Training System. There he met with Gall's school question book. He studied the works of Abbott, and Mrs. Reed lent him Gallaudet's little volumes. He carried on his experiments till he settled at Plaistow, and there formed classes in his model school. He published a magazine, and travelled over England to urge a reformation in Sunday Schools. I was then engaged in Sunday School work in Leeds, and was secretary of the Union there. At my suggestion Mr. Curwen was invited to Yorkshire, and after meetings in Hull, he addressed a large meeting in East Parade Chapel, Leeds, teaching a class of children on the platform in the presence of a large congregation. His lesson was upon the emblem " we all fade as a leaf," and it will never be forgotten. The picturing out of " leaf " and " fade " was full of charm and instruction. He called conferences, and was invited to meetings all over the West Riding. While at Heckmondwike he was alarmed by violent palpitation. The place was crowded, and the writer conducted the service for his friend. That attack he accepted as a warning, saying: " I shall walk softly through the rest of my days, and I think they will be few." In this he was wrong, and he often referred, in grateful terms, to " the Heckmondwike lesson."

In 1840 a new edition of David Stow's Training System appeared, and it quite captivated John Curwen. He wrote to me about it, and sent a copy. He entered into correspondence with Mr. Stow, and with him he urged that moral training, which had not been regarded in education, should henceforth have a prominent place. Mr. Curwen asked me through the Town Mission Agency at Leeds to make enquiries, as he was doing

in London, and as Mr. Stow had done at Glasgow.
The result was that we agreed that there had been
a rapid declension of morals in large towns. He
dwelt much upon the power of Bible training carried on
in all schools through the week, and after considerable
study he gave model lessons in picturing out, and he
showed by teaching large classes of children strange to
him the sympathy of numbers.

*   *   *   *

CHAPTER IV.

1840—1843.

MR. CURWEN IS DRAWN INTO THE STUDY OF SINGING—STORY
OF HIS FIRST EXPERIMENTS — REV. ANDREW REED'S
ACCOUNT OF MR. CURWEN'S VISIT TO NORWICH — MR.
CURWEN'S POSITION IN RELATION TO MUSIC — ARTICLES
IN "INDEPENDENT MAGAZINE"—MR. HULLAH'S MOVE-
MENT — "LOOK AND SAY" METHOD OF TEACHING TO
READ — LECTURES IN MANCHESTER ON SUNDAY SCHOOL
TEACHING—MEETS WITH HIS FUTURE WIFE.

REFERENCE must now be made to the musical work into
which Mr. Curwen was thrown. From the foregoing
chapter it will be seen how it was that he was drawn
into it. Interested in children and in Sunday Schools, he
saw the power of singing, and wished to make it
more effective. His connection with the subject was
not artistic, but moral and religious. His early efforts
and experiences are related by himself in a paper read to
the teachers of the Home and Colonial School Society,
July 8th, 1846 :—

My own connection with the system has arisen in
this wise. I am one who is deeply interested in the
education of children. About eight years ago, I became
anxious to teach a number of them, then under my

charge, to sing, chiefly with the design of making them
love the Sunday School. Having no natural advantages
of ear or voice, I sought help. I learnt a few tunes,
and with the assistance of a friend, taught them to
the children. We had 200 children for two hours twice
a week. By dint of loud singing, we carried the voices
of the children with us, and taught them many tunes.
We endeavoured most strenuously also to give them a
knowledge of crotchets and quavers, and flats and sharps,
and clefs, hoping thereby to give some permanence to the
fruits of our labour; but this was in vain. We succeeded,
however, in producing most delightful results for the
time, although they extended not beyond the particular
tunes which we had taught with extreme labour. I
remember a husbandman telling me that, before the
singing-school was established, he was constantly grieved
by hearing little children, as they wandered along the
lanes and by the hedgerows, disputing, quarrelling, and
swearing, but now he heard, instead, nothing but sweet
singing of hymns, of which they seemed never to be
tired.

For myself, all this while, I could neither pitch a
well-known tune properly, nor by any means "make out"
from the notes the plainest psalm-tune which I had not
heard before. To obtain that moderate ability was the
height of my musical ambition. I therefore sought a
private teacher who, with the help of a piano, drummed
much *practice* into me, but no independent *power*. I
could *run* in the "go-cart," but I could not take a step
alone. I remember being often told that I did not mark
correctly the "half tones" (between the 3rd and 4th, and
7th and 8th) of the scale, and I thought, if those same
"half tones" were but marked plainly on the music
before me, how gladly and earnestly I would strive to

mark them with my voice. But, as it was, I was
continually afraid of these "half tones." I knew that
they were on the staff before me somewhere, but I could
not see them. They lay concealed, but dangerous to
tread upon, like a snake in the grass. No sooner had I,
with great pains, taught my ear an interval, than I found,
frequently, the very next example of what *seemed* the
same, to be quite a different thing by *half a tone!* I
longed for some plan by which these puzzling deceivers
might be *named* and *detected* with equal facility in all
their shifting abodes on the staff.

Some time after this, Mrs. Reed, of Hackney,
kindly lent me the book describing Miss Glover's system.
"Well," said I, after a cursory glance, "if the old notation
is puzzling I am sure this is more puzzling far," and I
laid the book aside. But having occasion again to teach
children, I thought proper to give it a more careful perusal,
and was persuaded to study the science of music itself in the
best works I could obtain, especially those of Dr. Callcott
and Mr. Graham. I soon found that the old methods of
teaching had deceived me with the shell of knowledge
instead of giving me its kernel. The *thing*, music, I perceived to be very different from its names and signs. I found
it much more simple and easy in itself, and incomparably
more beautiful than the explanation of the signs of the old
notation, with which elementary books are commonly filled.
I had easily mastered them all, and had also studied a "first
book" on harmony, but I seemed to have known nothing of
music till then. I now saw that Miss Glover's plan was
to teach, first, the simple and beautiful *thing*, MUSIC, and
to delay the introduction to the ordinary antiquated mode
of writing it, until the pupil had obtained a mastery of
the thing itself. Her method was, beyond all controversy,
more deeply established on the principles of the science

than any other; and, by giving it a fair trial on myself, and on a little child who lived in the same house, I became convinced that it was also the most simple of all—the most easy to teach, and the most easy to learn. The methods of teaching which are truest to the nature of the thing taught, and the least artificial, are always the most successful. In the course of a fortnight, I found myself, *mirabile dictu!* actually at the height of my previous ambition, being able to "make out" a psalm-tune from the notes, and to pitch it myself! It was the untying of the tongue—the opening of a new world of pleasure. A visit to the school under Miss Glover's patronage at Norwich confirmed my impressions.

In a lecture delivered in 1875 Mr. Curwen referred to his early attempts to teach singing by ear as follows :—

Many a schoolmaster has said to me, "How can I teach singing when I am talking all day long? Depend upon it I have no voice left at the end of the day to shout with these children." To which I reply, "Exactly so, if you must shout with them." I have much sympathy with the martyrs of this old system, for some thirty-four years ago I taught 200 children upon this plan. I stood on a platform in the middle of the room, and the children stood around the walls. I sang, and they sang ; and the louder they sang the louder I was obliged to sing. What is the use of leading if your voice is not to be heard above those you lead? So great was the exertion that I had to ask a friend to help me, and I assure you there was a pretty considerable noise between us, especially when the children *marched* and sang! For two hours twice a week we worked at this, and my friend generally had a sore throat next morning! The worst of it was that with all our effort we did not really lead the children, for if I sometimes

stopped to listen I found that some of the children were
going wrong. The man who sings loud sets the bones of his
head into such vibration that he cannot hear.   So when I
came to a new situation, in which I could not give so much
time to singing, I set to work to find some time-saving
plans.   I thought I would teach singing as I had before
taught reading, and as a lady teaches cutting out—by
pattern.   I soon found with my new pupils that by the
help of a little patience in cultivating their *listening*
powers, I could get on twice as fast, do my work twice as
well, and produce twice as good a quality of tone.

In the same lecture Mr. Curwen spoke as follows
of his first visit to Miss Glover's school at Norwich :—

I shall never forget my first impression of the singing
of Miss Glover's school after I had for the two previous
years laboured hard in the ordinary way—beginning with
staff and clefs and time-marks and intervals, and all the
other laborious explanations.   As I stood on the stairs
listening to the music of that upper room I found it soft
and cultivated, such as I had never heard from school
children before.   As I opened the door I saw a little girl
pointing to syllables on a diagram, singing as she pointed.
Stepping in, I saw that she had in front of her a gallery
of children, who were following her pointing and singing
the syllables with her.   I had never been able to get
anything like it in all my hard two years' work !   Here,
this kind-hearted musician, out of love to the children,
had just swept away all my difficulties and gone direct to
the syllables and their sounds!   Let us follow her
example.

The Rev. Andrew Reed thus describes Mr. Curwen's
first visit to Norwich :—

I took him to see the Misses Glover in their school, and he was at once riveted by the astonishing results produced by them. He never forgot to allude very honourably to them, so as to give them due credit, but it was himself who saw the general adaptation of the system—who resolved to spread and make it known —who perfected it in many respects, who bore the brunt of the opposition encountered by every novelty—who took the mercantile risks on himself—and who, by his un-wearied perseverance and pluck, gave it a place all over the world, wherever music is taught, and exalted it into a scientific notation, which more and more competes with the established notation. Thus he found the chief mission of his life to improve the psalmody of our churches and the singing of our schools, and to make it a delightful medium for the easy culture in homes, schools, and churches of harmony wedded to moral and religious poetry.

I well remember his hilarity and profound interest when he came back to my lodgings, saying, " Now, Andrew, I have a good tool to work with," and how we sat up into the small hours with my harmonium, studying the mysteries of Sol-fa, and trying some of Miss Glover's exercises.

Mr. Curwen always disclaimed the name of "musician." He did not play any instrument, and he had no endowments of voice. He was a teacher and X methodiser. Often he remarked that if he had been quick at music he would not have been able to sympathise with beginners and those possessing no natural advantages. It may be safely added that it would have been scarcely possible for one who had fallen into the lines of musical practice and prejudice to construct the Tonic Sol-fa system. At every point he took the view of an educationist. Musical tradition was of no account ; everything was weighed, and nothing that could confuse a beginner was accepted.

Mr. Curwen had a natural fondness for music, but he was hampered in it by his ministerial work. He repressed the feeling as much as he could, and would not allow himself to spend any time upon music which merely took the form of enjoyment. For several years, until his health would stand it no longer, he did his musical writing and study from six to eight a.m., so that his pastoral duties might not suffer. In after years he sometimes, not often, went to a concert for its own sake, and enjoyed a symphony or an oratorio with a keen relish. His interest was intellectual more than merely emotional ; he would come home analysing effects and studying form.

In 1842 he wrote a series of articles on " Singing" in the *Independent Magazine*, which explain the Tonic Sol-fa method, in as far as it was then developed. Mr. Hullah's movement was then in full swing, and apparently most successful. Mr. Curwen's attitude to it was not ungenerous, though it differed *toto celo* from the plans he was describing. He writes :—

But yet we are thankful for it—truly thankful— thankful to the Council for their well-intended efforts in a noble cause—thankful to Mr. Hullah for the skill and unwearied diligence and admirable temper he has shown, and thankful to the London public, who by no other means could have been persuaded to take one tenth of the trouble of learning to sing, which they now submit to patiently "by authority of the Committee of Council on Education." Far be it from us to set one straw in the way of their doing so.

In the same set of articles Mr. Curwen gives a few specimen lessons, applying the method of "Nelly Vanner" and his Sunday School addresses to the subject of music. Nothing of the sort, we may safely say, had been done before. The following is a specimen :—

Now, children, we are going to learn the art of singing a tune. What are we going to learn ? * First, then, you must remember that any musical sound is called a note. What is a musical sound called ? * This is a note. I will sing another note. Now I will sing another note. Could not some of you sing a note ? Hold up hands—those who can sing a note. Do you—— *. And you—— *. I want you now to distinguish the same note from a different one. Sing the same note as this. * Sing the same note as this. * Hold up hands, those who will sing me a note, and I will sing the same. Do you—— *. And you—— *. Now hold up hands, those who will sing me a note, and I will sing a different one. * If I sing a note, which of you will sing a different one ? Hold up hands. * Now I wish you to distinguish between a high note (writing on the black board "high note") and a low note (writing "low note"). Hold up hands those who will sing me a note, and I will sing a higher note. Do you—— *. And you—— *. If I sing a note, can any of you sing a higher one ? Hold up hands. * Who will sing me a note, and I will sing a lower one ? * If I sing a note could any of you sing a lower one ?

Notice here the true teacher, keeping the minds of his class active by unceasingly questioning them, and making them work ; drawing as much as possible from them ; telling them as little as possible ; using no words of which they do not know the meaning ; employing the black board to fix upon the memory facts and signs.

The editorship of the *Independent Magazine* occupied much of Mr. Curwen's thoughts while he was at Stowmarket. A letter about the magazine, written to his friend Mr. Charles Reed, Feb. 17th, 1842, is full of hopes for the usefulness of the new venture.

The " Look and say " method of teaching to read, which Mr. Curwen had invented at Basingstoke, was elaborated in a series of articles in the magazine at this time. Educational methods have greatly advanced during the last forty years, and the principles of this method have been re-discovered and practised by innumerable teachers. It is simply the plan of teaching children to look at a word and read it as a whole, never spelling letter by letter. In " Nelly Vanner " Mr. Curwen describes the troubles of a child learning to read, who, having been taught the names of the letters, not unnaturally thinks that r-a-t should be pronounced ar-a-tee, not rat. He describes how

Nelly learnt to read without spelling out the words, and says :—

When I hear little boys and girls read I never let them spell aloud ; and you would be surprised to find how much better they read without it. I would rather tell them a word than hear them spell it, but when I do tell them a word I expect them to know it again.

In a letter written many years after (1859) during the absence of himself and Mrs. Curwen in Manchester, he describes his plan for teaching to read :—

I shall be very thankful if Mary will give each of the little boys a short lesson in reading once or twice a day. Keep them alive ; have no nonsense, but *attention.* If they don't know a word, tell them directly, while their eye is on it. Only read it again afterwards. Make them read *one* word at a time, and never look at the next till its fair turn comes. These rules, with patience, and two short lessons a day, will make them good readers by the time we come home.

In June, 1842, Mr. Curwen gave a series of lectures to Sunday School teachers in Manchester and Salford. They seem, from the programme, to have been illustrated by lessons given to a class of children present, and they dealt with the various grades of Sunday School work. These lectures led to an interesting and unexpected result. The chairman at the first lecture was Mr. Joseph Thompson, a cotton spinner of Manchester, and a leader in Sunday School work. After the lecture he invited the young minister who had given it to stay with him.

Mr. Curwen used often, in after years, to tell how the thoughts of Mrs. Thompson, when she heard what her husband had done, flew to her two daughters, both unmarried, who were living at home, and how she exclaimed "I *hope* he is married!" Mr. Thompson replied that he did not know positively, but he felt convinced that a man who could speak to children, and of children, as Mr. Curwen had done that night, must have children of his own.

The catastrophe which Mrs. Thompson, with a woman's instinct, foresaw, happened, and Mr. Curwen fell in love with the younger of her two daughters, Mary. Elsewhere we shall speak of the married life of Mr. and Mrs. Curwen. It is enough here to say that the union was opposed for some time by Mr. and Mrs. Thompson, not from any personal objection to Mr. Curwen, but solely because of his slender means; that at length they gave way, and allowed the engagement to proceed, which ended in their marriage in May, 1845.

˙CHAPTER V.

MISS GLOVER'S WORK AT NORWICH—MR. CURWEN'S ACCOUNT
OF IT—LETTERS FROM MISS GLOVER—CONGREGATIONAL
SINGING—MR. CURWEN'S ALTERATIONS IN HER NOTATION
— SOIREE AT JEWIN STREET SCHOOLS — INFLUENCE OF
MUSIC — THE CHEVE SYSTEM — REV. J. J. WAITE —
HEREFORD — MENTAL EFFECTS — PROPOSED REPRINT OF
MISS GLOVER'S BOOK — VISIT OF MR. CURWEN TO
HEREFORD—MISS CHRISTIANA GLOVER.

THE lady from whom Mr. Curwen received his first
ideas of the Tonic Sol-fa notation was Miss Glover,
daughter of a clergyman at Norwich. Miss Glover was,
for a long time, governess in the family of the late Sir
Fowell Buxton, the anti-slavery advocate, by whom she
was highly esteemed.

The story of Mr. Curwen's intercourse with her, and
a few quotations from her letters to him, extending from
1841 to 1867, will be of interest to the reader. Mr.
Curwen has himself described Miss Glover's work in an
article in the *Tonic Sol-fa Reporter* for December, 1867, on
the occasion of her death. He says :—

She must have been about 28 years of age (in the
ripeness of her educated powers) when, in 1812, she first

E

commenced those experiments in simplifying the teaching of music, which have since proved so fruitful.   It was in the effort to train a young man to teach the Sunday school children of her church that her first experiences were gained. For a series of years the church at Norwich, whose choir she superintended, owed much of its popularity and attraction to the beautiful two-part singing of the children whom she trained. Clergymen of her acquaintance, as well as strangers who visited the church, began to enquire about her method of teaching.   She encouraged them to send young women to Norwich, whom she or her assistants might train to teach the choir and the National School in the various towns and villages from whence they came.   In a quiet way this good work went on for many years, but it was not until the year 1827 or 1828 that she first published her "Scheme for rendering Psalmody Congregational."   She would then be more than 40 years of age. All her efforts for psalmody were greatly aided and guided by her natural love for education generally. The labours of herself and sister in supporting schools and promoting the education of the poor were long known in Norwich, and at a time when such devotion to educational objects was very rare. It was one of the infant schools under Miss Glover's patronage that Mr. Curwen (at that time a young minister of about 24 years of age) visited at the close of 1840. Miss Glover must then have been in her 55th year.   Although she retained a remarkable freshness, power, and beauty of mind to the last, yet after that age it was not possible that anyone should give very great exertions to the public propagation of a new method. But what she was able to do, Miss Glover, always assisted by her sister, diligently and lovingly did to the end.   The kindly interest which she took in Mr. Curwen's labours, as they grew upon him, at first slowly, and later on with all engrossing demands, will be sufficiently evidenced by some of the following letters :—

MISS GLOVER TO MR. CURWEN.

Chapel Field, Norwich, Dec. 31, 1841.

It is very pleasant to see how our country promises to be cheered by sweet musical sounds. I have this morning had a pleasing account of the singing of a juvenile party in a poor man's household, which had assembled to keep his daughter's birthday, and how delightful will it be when a "whole assembly" can unite at once in singing the songs of Zion. May the "melody of heart," which is taught from above, increase with the gift of utterance.

In a letter dated March 15th, 1842, Miss Glover describes how the children in the Black Boy Yard, where she had a Mission School, remember the address which Mr. Curwen gave them, and hopes he will some day repeat it. She writes on October 5th, of the same year, urging Mr. Curwen not to modify her system, but to adopt it in its entirety. She says :—

But though you prefer some alterations, yet you keep to the leading principles of the Sol-fa notation, and my pupils would soon sing from your book, and yours from mine. It appears to me that it would be for the advantage of the cause in general that you should not make the variations you propose, on account of the perplexity which might be felt by pupils on meeting with a diversity of signs for the same thing.

Miss Glover proceeds to argue in favour of placing figures in silent pulses to enforce attention to rests, and against giving pulses equal lateral space, which she does not consider practicable in any but the simplest music.

After a soirée, held at Jewin Street Schools, on April 20th, 1855, to welcome her while on a visit to London, she writes :—

It seems to me as if I had been permitted to look down from your platform upon a beautiful land of promise. Some time ago I felt depressed in spirit lest the fruit of years of toil should wither away, but, looking on your field of labour, I take courage. There I find intellectual young men enriching the air with the full tones of their manly voices ; young damsels piping aloft with delight, and yet with a sedate manner that well becomes the trainers of children in the narrow path which leads to a land of sober bliss ; dear youths looking so guileless, so happy, so intelligent, one cannot help supposing that they derive great benefit from the sympathy and co-operation of their seniors in pleasures which elevate and refine the mind.

Several other letters follow, in chronological order :—

Cromer ; about 1855.

Dear Sir,—Here, in Cromer, I have resided ever since May, 1851, with slight exceptions ; and here the post never brought me a letter which gave me so much pleasure as I felt from reading the letter I received from you yesterday. Here I mourned over the declining state, as I fear, of a favourite scheme, which I loved as a child, and now I find that you have been, in the meantime, nurturing it with so much care and skill, that, if you have somewhat shorn its locks, I may well forgive you, in consideration of the flourishing aspect of the creature altogether.

I admire the plan you have pursued of practising individual classes, and of granting certificates of proficiency, &c., and then combining the results of separate industry; it reminds me of the combination of the stones hewn at a distance from the spot where the temple was erected. Surely the unanimity about which you are so justly anxious, may well be prized as a gift from Him who approves "melody of heart" beyond any system of sol-faing, but how grievously scarce it is in general among those who cultivate music. Is it that music is too good a thing for this fallen world? I once observed to a mistress of the workhouse school in Norwich (who was mourning over the silent obstinacy of a boy whom she was endeavouring to render vocal), "Luther says the Devil hates music." "Ma'am," she replied, with gravity, " I believe he does."

Coley Hill, Reading, December 29, 1855.

DEAR SIR,—A happy new year to you and your harmonious troops! I congratulate you on the birth of the "Bell" in the Tonic Sol-fa notation,* I beg you will accept the best thanks of my sister Christiana and myself for the elegant little copies you have sent us of this attractive little work. I am persuaded it will give a charm to many a musical soirée at this interesting season of the year, when relaxation from toil, of a uniform character, and the re-union of domestic, and of more extensive circles, makes it desirable to find employment suited to the buoyant spirits of youth. I have often

* Romberg's "Song of the Bell"—the first attempt to represent classical music in the Tonic Sol-fa notation. It was received with great interest by the small circle of Tonic Sol-faists.

thought of the words of a little girl who said to her mother
in a dame's school, " We can't keep 'em quite (quiet)
unless we give them something to do ; " and what better
conductor can be found for superfluous activity in joyous
meetings than music ?   I confess I am not sufficiently
versed in your method of expressing sol-faing to be able to
do justice to the composition of the " Bell" without the
assistance of the old notation, but then an eight shilling
volume is an expensive interpreter to a publication, price
one shilling. . . .   Have you seen anything of a modification of Rousseau's system of figures by the firm, as it
may be called, of Galin-Paris-Chevé?   It appears to me to
have supplanted Wilhem in the estimation of the French
public. Miss Emily Taylor lent me the volume which
explains the system, and I daresay could procure you a
sight of it if you wished to see it. It seems to me much
more rational than the usual notation of music, but of
course I do not like it so well as Sol-fa letters, and I am
so convinced that the centre place in the heptachord
belongs to *doh* that I cannot call the key-note 1 with good
will.   When you come to Reading again I hope it will be
under less affecting circumstances than when you last
visited your respected father, and that you will then allow
me, if you can spare the time, an opportunity of discussing
this point with you more fully.

Coley Hill, Reading, April 20, 1858.

Accept my thanks for the letter I received from you
this morning, which I intend carefully to preserve ; but
wish you clearly to understand that it is far from my wish
that you should undertake any risk at any time respecting
my little volume. In plain terms it is my request that
you would leave the management of the affair completely in
my own hands. I regret that any loss should have attended

your Sol-fa labours, but I believe amateur publishers seldom make fortunes, and as for reformers, whether musical, or philosophical, or religious, their course is, I suppose, always uphill, and generally thankless during their lives. The performance at the Crystal Palace on the memorable 2nd of September, and the applause it so deservedly elicited, may, I imagine, be considered as a brilliant exception to the common course of events.

11, St. Owen Street, Hereford, Oct. 11, 1864.

I hope that the letter to you which I posted yesterday has very opportunely crossed that which I received from you this morning. I cannot flatly contradict the contents of yours, for I do think you have not acted quite generously in stating publicly (in contradiction to my private opinion) that your modification of my notation is an improvement upon the original. But this is a subject on which I am unwilling to dwell, what I should *now* delight to see is that your skill in promulgating a system, and Mr. Waite's learned powers of investigation, and my long experience and still longer consideration, should co-operate in presenting to the rising generation a notation of music as near perfection as human beings can produce.

Hereford, Nov. 9, 1864.

I feel somewhat puzzled to invent suitable thanks for your bounty to me. Certainly I cannot repay you in *kind*. No steam press teams with any productions of mine ! Nor can I sound your praises on any instrument of the brass band which now does homage to the Tonic Sol-fa flag ! But I hope you will accept my simple thanks for the peep you have just given me into the present state of the Sol-fa world, not only by your new publications for instruments, but by your constant periodical, and by the paper entitled the *Nonconformist*, which was particularly interesting to me from the following circumstance : Towards the beginning of last month a pleasing young lady called on me, and told me that her father had heard my name from Mr. Curwen, and wished to make some enquiry of me about the Tetrachordal system. The young lady was to me a stranger, and the name of her father was almost so. However, shortly afterwards the pleasing daughter entered my apartment leading the blind philosopher, her venerable looking father.* Notwithstanding my ignorance and his learning we soon discovered in ourselves much congeniality of taste respecting the science of music. I have not yet seen his notation of figures, and Sol-fa initials I shall ever prefer to figures, though sanctioned by Rousseau, by Pestalozzi, and by the firm of Galin-Paris-Chevé. You well know that Luther's opinion was that the devil hates music. If so, have we any reason to be surprised if he is very busy in promoting differences and divisions when music is applied to psalmody ? However, let us be thankful that our best friend is stronger than our worst enemy, and is infinitely wise in contrivances for effecting peace and eliciting harmony out of discord itself.

Wishing you and Mrs. Curwen and your olive branches the blessings particularly brought to our mind at the approaching blessed season.

I remain, my dear sir,

Yours with much regard,

S. A. GLOVER.

---

* Mr. Waite.

St. Owen Street, Hereford, Nov. 17, 1864.

In a letter I addressed to the Rev. J. Waite on Tuesday I declined, with feelings of respect and gratitude, the testimonial he had suggested. After some preamble I observed : " I do not suppose that wealth and fame should be regarded in the same light by those who have the honour to be fathers of families, but I think that at 78 years of age *I* ought not to be blamed for withdrawing more than ever into my shell. In justice to Mr. Curwen I ought to acquaint you with his repeated offers to me of a share in the profits of his long and successful labours."

St. Owen Street, Hereford, Nov. 18, 1864.

I hope the letter of mine which crossed that which I received from you this morning has in some measure relieved your mind. While I thank you for the willingness you have expressed to take a long journey this damp and blustering weather to pay me a visit, I will honestly confess to you that I do not consider the proposed visit as favourable to our health. We are both of us by nature of a nervous temperament, and as all the symptoms of age mentioned in the 12th of Ecclesiastes manifest themselves in our infirm persons, we study to keep ourselves quiet, and our desire has been granted. I did not cry

> And may at last my weary age
> Find out the peaceful hermitage—
> The mossy cell—

for that would have been too damp for my taste. But what I like much better has been given ; dry warm apartments, situated in a house that has an airy garden at the back of it, containing a broad gravel walk ; and if you and Mrs. Curwen should like to visit the garden of England (Herefordshire) next summer, I should like to show you the gem of this city, as concerns the beauty of landscape—the Castle Green on the banks of the swiftly-flowing Wye. But the word "landscape" may show you that my pen has been hovering over it while sleep has been gently creeping over my eyelids. So till a more seasonable season let me say farewell to you and Mrs. Curwen. My sister unites in kind regards to you and Mrs. Curwen with your sleepy correspondent.

S. A. GLOVER.

The following letter refers to the theory of "mental effects" which Mr. Curwen originated. In an address delivered in 1875 he described how his attention was first directed to this point :—

This distinct character or mental effect of tones in key was a discovery to me, though others had observed more or less of the facts before. I got a glass harmonicon, by Miss Glover's direction, which had all the semitones, and could be played in any key. It happened that one of these glasses had a decidedly blue shade of colour. In one tune which I played, the effect of the tone from the blue glass was very touching and somewhat sad, but in another tune its effect was quite different. It was rather bright and rousing. This puzzled me. I was careful to strike the glass always in the same way, and I knew that it must produce absolutely the same sound, and yet the effect was different ? I noticed that in the two tunes the key was different, so that in the one case the relationship of tones made my blue glass the sixth of the scale, and in the other case the second. After many experiments I was at last convinced that the mental effect of tones depends chiefly on the tone relationship which is thrown around them, just as the mental effect of a lady's bonnet depends very much upon the colour of her shawl.

Miss Glover writes :—

December 5, 1864.

If I am accused of smiling at the honours which your lively imagination has bestowed upon *fah* and his associates in the diatonic scale, I must hold up my hand and plead guilty. But far be it from me to cast any slight upon the Tonic Sol-faers ! Well do I remember the kind reception they gave me at their pleasant soirée in Jewin Street ! Well do I remember the intelligent tuneful class of boys who sang to me so admirably at sight a German duet in canon style (after translation by one of their teachers into Sol-fa letters), which I presented to them as a test of their vocal and scientific powers. Moreover, I entertain a vivid recollection of the glorious host of youthful faces and youthful voices assembled in the Crystal Palace on the 2nd of September, 1857.

I regret that two leaders of congregational psalmody should not cordially co-operate in their endeavours to benefit society,* but I must not forget that psalmody is here cultivated in an enemy's country, where one must not expect to hear the songs of the spirits of just men made perfect. Yet much has been done, I trust, towards the promotion of "melody in the heart," and I hope still more will be done by Him who knows how to tune all hearts, however discordant by nature.

11, St. Owen Street, Hereford, Dec. 1, 1865.

Though I do not regard you altogether in the light of a faithful disciple, yet I should consider you so valuable an ally (if certain that you would grant me cordial co-operation) that I should be sorry to lose your assistance in

---

*The Rev. J. J. Waite had recently attacked the Tonic Sol-fa system and Mr. Curwen.

consequence of negligence on my part.* . . . I hope I
may soon write with a more disengaged mind ; but I
experience such a decay of strength in mind and body, and
I find that agitation is so injurious to the frail tabernacle
and its invisible tenant, that I will now only add a brief
expression of my desire that the only wise God will enable
both you and me to see and know in what way we
may best help one another and promote His glory.   I
believe you will say Amen to this desire of your senior
fellow labourer

S. A. GLOVER.

December 15, 1865.

I was so much gratified by the letter that I received
from you this morning that I do not like to defer telling
you so.   At the same time, considering my increasing
infirmities and the usual rapidity of your movements,
I should like to reconsider it, so as to state more distinctly
my wishes, before you take further steps in this affair.

January 13th, 1866.

[Copy of a letter addressed to Mr. Bell originally, but
for the sake of dispatch sent straight to the Rev. J.
Curwen].

My Dear Cousin,—I am not too old to be gratified
by the kind and respectful compliment to me, proposed by
Mr. Curwen, but I am much too old to be disposed to
sanction such an expenditure of money upon the preserva-
tion of a resemblance of my withered face.   Besides, what
can serve the purpose better of a portrait to prefix to the
projected appendix than the photograph requested by

---

* This and the three letters following refer to an offer made by Mr. Curwen
(for the second time) to reprint, at his own expense, Miss Glover's book, with
an appendix giving her latest views.

Mr. Curwen some years ago at Reading, when I was about 70 years of age? The design appears to me to be so original [She is represented as holding up her ladder of tune, and pointing to the notes upon it] as to afford some apology for publishing the face of an old woman. . . .   I am glad that Mr. Curwen desires a clear understanding of my designs and expectations with respect to the proposed joint work.   It is difficult to foresee the precise dimensions and foliage of a tree before it is raised, but (if you will kindly communicate this letter to Mr. Curwen) I hope that Mr. Curwen will be furnished with sufficient data to set his Sol-fa press to work without delay.

1st.   I decline (with grateful feelings for the honour designed me) the expensive portrait, but should be pleased if Mr. Curwen liked to prefix to the Appendix the Reading photograph as an engraving, copies of which could be purchased at a cheap rate by such of my former young disciples as may still remember me.

2nd.   I have no objection to Mr. Curwen's commencing the work by a publication of the Tonic Sol-fa as he now uses it, but may I take the liberty of suggesting the omission of the term Tonic in the title of the work, as the word seems to me to imply a distinction where none exists among those musicians who make use of the diatonic scale, whether they consider Doh to reside at the bottom of the scale or in the centre of it.   Am I mistaken in thinking that needless divisions are inimical to the complete unanimity of sentiment which is favourable to outward success, and in no way injurious to that inward "melody of heart" which is enjoyed amongst those members of a congregation who desire to praise God not only with their lips but in their lives, and are, therefore, anxious that music may never engender discordant feelings, but promote peace and goodwill on earth at all times, especially in places of public worship.

I do not forget that Mr. Curwen offered to print my " maturer thoughts " on the Sol-fa notation some time ago ; but I was then fearful that the execution would not accord exactly with my wishes on the subject. I have ventured to express to him this fear ; I am now more sanguine than formerly, that a sincere co-operation might exist between us. But as I am by nature in general a coward, I own I should be thankful if Mr. Curwen would assure me plainly that he will not *stereotype* any part of the Appendix, nor anything else I may send him, and that he will give me the opportunity of revising every proof sheet before copies of it are multiplied. . . . Though I know I am often regarded as needlessly fearful, yet I have often been accused of being unreasonably sanguine. Notwithstanding the commencement of my eightieth winter, I am inclined to the sanguine side, when so powerful an ally as Mr. Curwen offers to assist his decaying fellow labourer.

S. A. GLOVER.

February 12, 1866.

In order to qualify myself the better for framing the proposed Appendix, I sent for the last edition of your " Grammar of Vocal Music." I have not had time to examine its contents composedly, but my general impression of your publications is that dazzling as your proposals of printing for me appear at a superficial view of them, yet my persuasion is that were I to avail myself of them my old age would be embittered by trouble and anxiety unsuited to one who has reason to expect so short a remnant of life as can well be calculated upon by your aged friend,*

S. A. GLOVER.

11, St. Owen Street, Hereford, August 19, 1867.

DEAR SIR,—I wish it may prove as gratifying to your son John to see me as it will be to me to behold my invisible and obliging correspondent from Queensferry. However, if he is imbued with an antiquarian taste he may value the sight of one of those scarce human beings who has accomplished eighty years, especially as she has been rendered somewhat notorious by his father's imaginative pen.

If father and son honour me with a visit on Thursday next I trust they will make allowance for a less hospitable reception than my sister and I should like to have given them under other circumstances. The house in which we are located overflows this week with inhabitants attracted to Hereford by Jenny Lind's vocal powers. My sister Christiana and I are both invalids. She unites in kind regards to you with, Dear Sir, your aged friend, in Sol-fa bonds

S. A. GLOVER.

To these letters of Miss Glover may be added two from her sister Miss Christiana Glover, who survived her sister several years.

Great Malvern, August 27, 1869.

My sister has not left sufficient music sol-faed to serve those who know too much of music to be inclined to

---

* Miss Glover finally changed her mind, and declined to consent to the re-issue of her book.

commence as learners upon a system to facilitate the knowledge of music upon correct principles. Could you furnish me with a book by which they could teach themselves your modified system and go on with it? I am too old at 81½ to undertake the toil of following up my dear sister's labours. You appear to have obtained such marvellous success that I am very glad to follow down your stream. I hope that your health does not fail you in the midst of your career, and that your labour is diminished by your younger associates.

The following letter relates to the disposal of a subscription which Miss C. Glover had sent to Mr. Curwen to aid his projects. It also refers to a renewed offer of Mr. Curwen's to reprint Miss Glover's "Scheme" :—

November 10th, 1873.

I can have no objection to your putting the two pounds to the fund for supplying ragged and industrial schools with books for singing. However blinded by professional prejudice, few dispute the excellence of the Tonic Sol-fa system for the lower grades of society.

If the system be correctly carried into execution, it trains the children to fixed attention and orderly habit. The words which you have selected, and the style of music to which they have been applied, are calculated to encourage right feeling, and also refinement of mind.

As to your kind offer to reprint the "Scheme," I do not think it would answer. It has lived its day, and may its offset long survive all competitors.

CHAPTER V.

1843—1849.

EXPERIMENTS IN TEACHING SINGING AT READING—FORESHADOWS
OF THE TONIC SOL-FA METHOD—SETTLEMENT AT PLAISTOW—
OLD PLAISTOW—DAY SCHOOL STARTED—MR. ALFRED BROWN'S
NOTES—RECOLLECTIONS BY TWO LADIES OF THE CONGREGATION.

Mr. Curwen remained at Stowmarket only eighteen
months, and then lived with his father at Reading for
a year. He speaks of "more than a year's interruption
from ill-health," and of "the mental anguish and harrow-
ing cares to which a dreadful bereavement (the death of
Miss Vanner), followed by the peculiar difficulties of my
last station, have exposed me during the last year and
a half."

While staying in Reading Mr. Curwen continued his
experiments with the Tonic Sol-fa method. An MS.
"Journal of a Singing Class conducted on the method
entitled 'Singing for Schools and Congregations,'" explains
with great minuteness the proceedings of each evening.
The class met daily from October 9th to 31st, 1843.

Notice was given in four of the Sunday schools of
this town on Sunday (yesterday) that a singing meeting

F

would be held on the next and following evenings, to
which those children would be admitted who were fond of
singing. About 70 children assembled in consequence
of this notice, at eight o'clock this evening. An earlier
hour could not be chosen as many of the children do
not leave work till eight.

It is remarkable how clearly the main principles
of the method were developed at this early period.
Mental effects, teaching by chords, the modulator, the
silence of the teacher while his pupils are singing—
these are all dwelt upon. Mr. Curwen was also working
his way to the fact that we sing by recalling the
character of the tones of the scale rather than by mere
intervals. He says, after describing some mistakes made
by the class :—

We were convinced by this experiment that the
difficulty in singing interval does not arise from the mere
distance of the notes from each other, but from their
relative position in the key—that a fourth, for instance,
taken in one part of the key will be found more difficult
than the same interval taken in another part. Thus *lah me*
was found more difficult than *doh soh*, though the interval
between them is the same. This shows the importance of
our attending more to the proper musical effect of each
note as it stands in the key than to " thirds," " fourths,"
" fifths," &c.

The separation of pupils according to their grade
of progress, which is such a cardinal feature of the method,
was insisted upon in this tentative class by Mr. Curwen.
He describes how one evening he went early to the

class-room and reserved some front seats, which he told the children were for those who could sing the first nine exercises of the book alone. Whether each candidate should pass was put to a popular vote. Before the class ended a second examination had been established, and the " little graduates," as Mr. Curwen playfully calls them, were taught by themselves, as well as with their fellows.

On May 22nd, 1844, Mr. Curwen was ordained to the pastoral charge of the Independent Chapel at Plaistow, Essex (five miles from London). He received the call in the previous December, and in reply said he would prefer to take up his abode at Plaistow for a few weeks before giving an answer. He did this, and wrote on January 29th definitely accepting the call. The circular announcing the special services informs the reader that " the Plaistow omnibus leaves Leadenhall Market at a quarter past ten o'clock." This was the only communication with London. Plaistow—Plahstow, as the natives call it—was a rural village at the time when Mr. Curwen came to it. A few large houses, a few cottages ; it was an eminently quiet and respectable place. Elm trees lined the streets, and the old red brick of the houses peeped through coverings of ivy. Two miles away, across marshes that were sacred to a few cattle and the herons from Wanstead Park, lay the river Thames. These marshes are now covered with docks and shipyards and factories of all kinds, and with thousands of labourers' cottages. In

Plaistow itself the old large houses have been pulled down
or turned into asylums, the fields have been covered by
the builder, and an industrious population of artizans,
ministering to the needs of mighty London, is supreme.

Mr. Curwen began his work at Plaistow on the same
lines and with the same spirit as at Basingstoke and
Stowmarket.   Mr. Alfred Brown gives an account of the
establishment of what was the first public elementary
school in Plaistow, of which he is still the master :—

Mr. Curwen came to Plaistow in January, 1844, and
in the course of six months, such was his unselfish
earnestness, he had infused his educational spirit into
the minds of the people to that extent that three
gentlemen were induced by him to guarantee the necessary
funds for three years for the establishment and the
carrying on of the " Plaistow Public Schools."   These
gentlemen did not all at once believe that the school was
needed, or that it would be a success ; but they could not
resist the earnestness of their pastor, who was not only a
thorough educationist, believing in what he taught, but
who also possessed that rare faculty, which it is said that
Lord Nelson was so eminently gifted with, viz., of
infusing his own spirit of enthusiasm into the minds and
hearts of his co-workers, which, like an electric current,
sometimes compelled them against their wills.

In July I was invited to an interview at Plaistow,
and found Mr. Curwen a handsome young bachelor, beaming with benevolence, and filled with bright hopes for the
children of Plaistow.   I dined with him, and his cordiality
and kind consideration (for which he was so eminently
distinguished) won my heart entirely.   I was henceforth

his servant, as long as he wished it. His aims were high, but every difficulty which could be suggested was blown away like a soap bubble in a stiff breeze. His self-devotion was overwhelming. The school was opened on the 11th of August, 1844.

A lady, who was at this time a child in Mr. Curwen's congregation at Plaistow, gives the following reminiscences :—

I feel desirous of giving a slight testimony, from my point of view, which was that of a child when he first came to Plaistow, to his great acceptableness with children. I can assure you that when he paid occasional visits there as a "supply," before his settlement, the announcement that there would be a children's service in the afternoon, conducted by Mr. Curwen, was received with great delight by those concerned. I could, for years afterwards, have repeated the substance of the address on one of these occasions, on "Faith, Hope, and Charity." I could not quite do so now ; but I know that he found a similitude for each of these graces, and I still remember to what he compared " Charity." " It is like," he said, " five rings. You will wonder how Charity can possibly be like five rings. I will tell you. The smallest innermost ring is love to oneself ; the next, a little larger round it, is love to the family, parents, brothers, and sisters ; the next, still larger, is love to friends ; the next love to everybody, and desire to do them good ; and the fifth, largest ring, is love to God. Now, if you begin with the smallest ring, love to self, it will not take in any of the others, but if you begin with the largest ring, love to God, you will find you have all the others in it ; so it is best to try to get that." Of course I cannot exactly give his words, but this was the sense. His beaming eye, and cheerful voice, and kind manner added much to the effect of his words in this and all his discourses to children. The same may be said of his visits to our house, where he was occasionally a guest from Saturday to Monday before he settled at Plaistow. He won a great deal of personal affection in our family; my parents almost regarded him as a son, and we younger ones were intensely interested in him and his ministrations, especially after he became our minister. I remember with what delight my brother Charles and I attended his children's Bible class, held on a week-day afternoon. It was there that we learnt the elements of the Tonic Sol-fa system from himself, and it has been a help to me in singing from sight through life. I had great delight in the hymns, and songs, and tunes in the children's little books, "School Songs" and "School Music," and some of those dear old melodies are sweet to me now, and I make use of them in a Bible class. We enjoyed, also, attending his examinations and addresses to the Sunday school children on Sunday afternoons.

In illustration of his character being, as you say, at once "gentle and resolute," I can relate you one anecdote. On one occasion my father and mother gave a tea meeting in the schoolroom to the people of the chapel, including, of course, the poorest members of the congregation. They provided two or three things to entertain them, such as photographs and engravings, and my sisters played and sang. Among other things they, with my father, sang some passages from a "Mass," I fancy Mozart's 12th Mass, with Latin words. This much distressed Mr. Curwen, who regarded it as making an undevotional use of sacred words, and he came rather pale and trembling to my mother, showing the effort it cost him to make the request, begging her to ask them to leave off, which, I need not say, was done. There was both gentleness and resolution in what he felt was a point of conscience ; and I think there were many such instances. His father, whom I remember as a white-haired old gentleman, said once, in reference to his son's resolution in carrying out his musical publications (of the pecuniary success of which the father had some doubts), "You cannot turn him." And it is well he was not turned from that path in which he was so useful and successful, and by his achievements in which he will be chiefly remembered.

The following letter, also from a lady member of Mr. Curwen's congregation at this time, presents another view :—

Mr. Curwen came, a young man full of hope and zeal, warm-hearted and ardent, and inspired a great deal of interest. A grand stirring up followed. The chapel was repainted and improved, the schools were enlarged and rendered much more efficient. Mr. Brown soon began his career of usefulness in connection with them. The Sunday schools also were revived, teachers' meetings for preparation were started, and it was quite a pleasure to hear the minister examine the children after the afternoon school. The singing of course soon received Mr. Curwen's attention. The Tonic Sol-fa method was already developed, and classes were held for the instruction both of the congregation and schools. Very soon the congregational singing and chanting in four parts was something unusually good. The fresh life that was introduced had other manifestations. You know that Mr. Curwen was a thorough-going dissenter and radical in politics, both ecclesiastical and secular, and tried to manage the chapel and its affairs from this point of view, and also to use it as a propaganda of these ideas. They were much to him—

he thought them taught in the New Testament—and, as you truly say, was both "gentle and resolute" in a very high degree. Now my father, who was trustee of the place, and had the lion's share of providing for it, would have none of these things. He was a man of much culture and refinement, kind and helpful to every one, but democratic equality, either in church or social life, had no charms for him—indeed, his church principles, not perhaps very strong, were decidedly national; the Anti-State Church Society was extremely distasteful to him. The rub was very great sometimes. In looking back to that time, from a middle-aged point of view, I think they were both to be pitied. Young men are so possessed with their theories, and older men, who have lived past many such, and seen both sides of many questions, do not think them so important. Indeed, as a proof of this latter remark, I may mention a circumstance that gave me great pleasure at the time. Some time ago, when Mr. Curwen came here to see my dear mother, he said how much better he understood my father's character now than he did all those years ago, and appreciated the reasons for many things that had once annoyed him.

CHAPTER VI.

THE TONIC SOL-FA MOVEMENT—TONE GIVEN TO IT BY MR. CURWEN—PLAN FOR PROPAGATING IT—FRIENDSHIPS TO WHICH IT LED—LETTERS AND ARTICLES—REFORMATORY AT EDINBURGH—MR. STOW AT GLASGOW—EXCURSION ON THE CLYDE—CHILDREN'S MUSIC—ECLECTICISM OF THE MOVEMENT — ITS RAPID SPREAD — HEALTHY WORDS — RAGGED SCHOOL SINGING—SOCIAL AND RELIGIOUS POINTS OF THE SYSTEM—RETROSPECT—NEW YEAR COUNSELS— RETROSPECT IN 1861 — PHASES OF THE MOVEMENT — REMARKS ON THE CENSUS—LET MUSIC ELEVATE—"HOW TO OBSERVE HARMONY " — DEBTOR AND CREDITOR — TEMPERANCE MUSIC — CHRISTIAN INFLUENCE — LANCA- SHIRE DISTRESS — ORATORIO PERFORMANCES — TONIC SOL-FA BALLS!—FIXED AND MOVABLE DO—THEATRES.

MR. CURWEN originated the Tonic Sol-fa movement, and directed it for forty years. He was thus able to impress upon it a character, and to keep it up to the high level of moral and religious purpose upon which he had started it. This required constant vigilance and often great firmness.

The Tonic Sol-fa movement touched almost all efforts for the elevation of mankind. By simplifying musical notation, the art in its domestic and religious aspects entered thousands of homes which had before been without music. Thus the method was the indirect means of aiding worship, temperance, and culture, of holding young men and women among good influences, of reforming character, of spreading Christianity. The artistic aspect of the work done by the Tonic Sol-fa method is indeed less prominent than its moral and religious influence.

A tired worldling who had exhausted all the pleasures which wealth could purchase and self-indulgence suggest, is said to have sighed for "a new pleasure." It may be said that, in a very true and healthy sense, the Tonic Sol-fa movement brought "a new pleasure" to thousands of homes and lives. It was the consciousness of this that gave Mr. Curwen so deep a joy in his work, and sustained him in the discouragements which he met.

It is no part of the object of this book to explain the Tonic Sol-fa system, but it may be said that the plan which Mr. Curwen adopted for spreading it was one which led to its very rapid propagation among the people at large. He did not address himself to artistic coteries or to the musical profession, but to the clergy, day-school and Sunday-school teachers, temperance and mission workers, &c. He showed that he was in possession of a simple method which almost anyone could teach. He encouraged all who were desirous of cultivating singing to learn a little themselves of the system, and to begin teaching, improving themselves as they went on. Those who took up the system were almost all men animated by philanthropic motives, and using music as a means to an end.

The friendships which Mr. Curwen's work led him to form amongst all classes were to him very gratifying. Now and then came tokens of regard which pleased him greatly, as, for instance, a walking stick made by a working man Sol-faist in Scotland, a barrel of tamarinds from some coloured disciples of the system in Jamaica. There was a nobleman in the troublous times of '48 who said that for his own part he did not care what happened in the way of revolutions, for he had a *valet* in every capital in Europe. The Tonic Sol-fa system put Mr. Curwen in a more enviable position than even this nobleman, for it gave him a friend in every village, and in distant colonies and mission stations. Often in his journeys, giving his name at a shop, a railway station, or a post office, he would be greeted with a glow of pleasure, and with a deference that sometimes amused him, by some humble adherent of the Tonic Sol-fa movement. He had indeed been the means of putting a new pleasure into thousands of lives.

The following passages from letters and articles written by Mr. Curwen during the period when the movement most needed a firm controlling hand, exhibit his pure

and unbending resolution to keep in view the "noble
ends" for which he wished all his colleagues, like himself,
to be working :—

Edinburgh, June 11, 1859.

I saw yesterday 420 young thieves, who are in
a reformatory, with kind teachers to teach and help them.
Mrs. McCallum, the governor's wife, has a prayer meeting
with them once a week, and the boys conduct it themselves. Two hundred of them often come in to it—all of
their own accord, and they pray very earnestly. Most of
them become good boys through the kindness that is
shown them. They forget all their bad street songs, and
learn to love Sol-fa songs. One boy was put in prison yesterday for bad behaviour, and he was Sol-faing all the time.
The boys sang to me, and I told them the story of ragged
Tom. I daresay you can imagine what parts of it they
were most interested in. I made them chant a text. I
was very glad that Sol-faing was doing so much good.

Tonic Sol-fa Reporter, July, 1859.

On Thursday a conference was held at Glasgow,
attended by about 200 men ; and, best of all, David Stow,
Esq., founder of the Training System of Education, was
moved to the chair by Wm. Euing, Esq. More than 20
years ago we first became acquainted with David Stow's
"Bible Training" and "Training System." These works,
throwing some of the great principles of education into
a bold and popular form, and written with the ardour
of an enthusiast for truth and a lover of children, exercised
a very powerful influence on our mind. They soon led to
the study of Jacob Abbott, and Miss Mayo, and Henry
Grant, and Isaac Taylor on the same great subject ; and
this study of educational principles it was which prepared

us to understand and appreciate Miss Glover's system of music.

Tonic Sol-fa Reporter, August, 1859.

To friendship our closing day at Glasgow was given. We were made guests to a kindly company of Tonic Sol-fa friends, who took us down the beautiful Clyde, showed us Greenock, Dunoon, and the Holy Loch, landed us at Ardentinny, on the shore of Loch Long, and led us a pleasant walk to the Braes of Glen Finnart, where, stretched on the grass beneath an oak tree, we sang Bangor and Martyrs in the true Doric Mode, received a gymnastic and voice-training exercise from Mr. Robertson, and gazed on the grandeur of the mountains. While waiting for the steamer on our return, we sat together on a rock looking towards the head of the lake, singing "Row, brothers, row," and holding discourse on the proper use of the bâton. When the steward of the steamer invited our little party to a quiet attack on fresh-caught salmon and a quarter of lamb, our readers must excuse us for saying that we found an appetite. Now an appetite in ordinary cases is a very vulgar thing, but this was an extraordinary case. Try the mountain air, gentle reader, and then you will excuse us. We soon found our place, however, on the hurricane deck, and there sang our way home, singing the finest two-part songs in "Standard Course," "The might with the right," and other pieces for men's voices. Captain Wilson of the *Chancellor* will perhaps remember the gentlemen who sang from the queer-looking notes, though he may not know with what a fine beaming face he looked at them. We were *loth* to part. May each of us be strengthened to do his own life's work aright, and then if we meet no more on earth we shall yet meet again.

Tonic Sol-fa Reporter, September, 1859.

[In reply to a newspaper critic who had urged that at the children's concerts more classical music should be sung].

The critic has probably committed the common mistake of mere musical men; we mean that of supposing that children generally can be taught to sing well with their voices, *without their hearts*, like some poor, miserable, artistic chorister boys in cathedrals, or the fainting charity children in St. Paul's! No; if you want children to sing well you must give them *words which will stir a child's heart*, and *music* which will *suit* a child's voice. Let us, also, remind our musical friends that taste *grows;* we must *train it.* We cannot make it start up into perfection at once. The jingle of the nursery rhyme trains the young idea to appreciate, after a while, the more delicate cadences of Milton and Pope. But Milton and Pope would offer very wearisome cadences to the child at first. The story, the fable, and the parable must first break that virgin soil of imagination which may afterwards receive as seed the refined imagery of Shelley or of Tennyson. The uncultivated mind, which looks uninterested on a picture by Raphael or Turner, might be delighted with some "rough outline" or "plain daub." But the discovery of whatever truth and beauty there may be in the "rough outline" or "plain daub" is the first step, and a necessary step, towards the true comprehension of such complex beauties as are in Raphael and Turner. So many a Tonic Sol-fa youth, who commenced with the music of our dearly honoured friend, Lowell Mason, is now longing for Handel and Mendelssohn.

Tonic Sol-fa Reporter, December, 1859.

The editor of this *Reporter* has his own personal religious convictions, has knowingly chosen that place in the Christian Church which seems to him the rightest; and he hopes that all his readers have earnestly and resolvedly done the same, however much their doing so may lead them to differ from him. He values earnestness and reality in religion above all names, sects, or parties. As editor of this *Reporter* he is neither a Dissenter, a Churchman, a Catholic, nor a Protestant. He takes joy in helping all in their "service of song in the house of the Lord," and it has been a deep delight to him to notice how men, who differ so widely in their manner of worship, their forms of church government, and their church creeds, do come so wondrously near one another in their psalms, and hymns, and spiritual songs. Men are nearest to one another when they come nearest to God. We are, in fact, necessarily allied to *the good* in all parties. Our columns speak sometimes of the usefulness of our method in "surpliced choirs," and sometimes they tell of what is doing in Primitive Methodist chapels. Occasionally we have intelligence from Roman Catholic schools, and very frequently, indeed, from the schools and congregations of the great Presbyterian churches of the North; and although forbidden to teetotalise ourselves, our hearts are glad when we see the "Bands of Hope" using the modulator, and hear the singing of those earnest men and women who set themselves so resolvedly (even if it were also a little mistakingly) against the most fruitful evils of our times. On the other hand, let it be understood that the Editor of this *Reporter* will never publish music which he does not believe in. If, therefore, his Roman Catholic friends wish to publish hymns of worshipful praise to the Virgin; if Mr. Neale desires to put into

Sol-fa language his songs of dissent and schism; if any temperance advocates desire to set forth in Sol-fa music the glories of the Maine Law, these various parties must do the work themselves. Mr. Curwen will give them free permission to use the Tonic Sol-fa notation, for that belongs to "mankind," and not to "a party." But he himself, as *a man*, must hold his own conscience, rejoicing heartily when others do the same.

Tonic Sol-fa Reporter, January, 1860.

Proofs arrive from every side that our numbers are increasing, that our teachers are growing in skill, intelligence, and personal influence; that hundreds of young men and women who possessed no sphere of public influence before, have now obtained a congenial and happy one as teachers of the Tonic Sol-fa method. They never expected to find themselves so useful. Their whole life is quickened by their new and important work. Ragged schools, industrial schools, reformatories of all kinds, are echoing with Tonic Sol-fa music; National schools and British schools are everywhere awakening to the sounds wafted to them by the Crystal Palace choir; parish churches in Ireland and in many parts of England conduct their psalmody by Tonic Sol-fa aid, and Christians of all denominations are following the bright example of the Scottish churches, and using the Tonic Sol-fa method for the revival of a people's song in the house of the Lord.

Tonic Sol-fa Reporter, February, 1860.

Let it be remembered that music heightens the expression of the words to which it is attached. That which is good in the poetry is brought out with tenfold power by the music, and that which is bad receives a tenfold force of evil. No words, therefore, are strong enough to brand with reprobation the unprincipled habits of musical men in singing foul words for the sake of beautiful music. A very large proportion of our best English glee and madrigal music was originally set to words suited to the immoral age in which it was composed. If this music must be retained amongst us let new words be set to it. But it is better to do without the music, however wondrously charming, than to let it administer pollution to our ears.

Tonic Sol-fa Reporter, 1860.

Who will come out and help the Ragged School Singing Movement? To our young Tonic Sol-faists we would say—" Freely have ye received, freely give." Prepare yourselves to become teachers. First take the two certificates. You will then *know* enough to begin teaching. Secondly, cultivate the "power of control" in a class of pupils. The first element of this power is to have *a well-considered will of your own,* and to know how to assert it *reasonably and kindly.* The second element of this power is, to be always *well prepared* for your class (having gone through the lesson alone, imagining the class with its faces and questions before you), so that you may never have to think, while teaching, " What am *I* saying and doing?" Or " What shall *I* say next?" But that your whole attention may be thrown upon the class—with ears and eyes and sympathies fully open for those you teach. You will then say to yourself, " Did the *class* see that point, or must I illustrate it again?" " Was that pattern well imitated?" " Did all take it?" " Who wants encouragement?" "To whom must I administer a gentle reproof?" " Does general attention flag?" " Is a change needed?" " Are any disorderly, whom I must quietly decline to teach?" &c. &c. You could not be

G

thus awake to every need of your class if you had to think
what to say and what to do. Is it not worth a good
amount of work and drill to make a competent teacher—
to gain a new power of usefulness ?

Tonic Sol-fa Reporter, October, 1860.

[Written after a great competition of Tonic Sol-fa choirs
   at the Crystal Palace, which was followed by a united
   performance on the Handel Orchestra.]

This was a great day—in many respects *the greatest*
day that the Tonic Sol-fa movement has known, and
yet for our own personal pleasure we would rather
have been singing "Hagley Church" with the "young
men and maidens, old men and children" of our own
congregation, or shouting, with a room full of boys and
girls, a hearty Sunday school hymn, or singing glees with
a party of friends at a picnic, or round the fire at home.

These are the social and religious fruits which our
movement is intended to bear ; and it is far easier and
more pleasant to our personal feelings to pluck the ripe
and ready fruit than to go through all the dust and
struggle and toil of ploughing, and draining, and harrow-
ing, and sowing, and weeding, by means of which these
fruits are produced.

But we are *workmen*, and not merely tasters of fruit.
We can dig and prune as well as eat, and we know
that the deeper and more thorough our husbandry, the
richer shall be our harvest.

A good education lifts a man to higher walks of
usefulness than he could otherwise occupy. The struggles
of the school and the college quicken the faculty and
confirm the force of men, and make them greater and
stronger for life.

The discipline of the certificate, the drill-parade in the aisles of Finsbury Chapel, the severe training of the competing choirs—these are "the struggles of school and college" to our Tonic Sol-fa movement. They will develop for us *men*—strong men, who will do the work of our movement as it has never been done before. Our Tonic Sol-fa tree will strike its root more deeply, and firmly, and lastingly than ever.

Tonic Sol-fa Reporter, January, 1861.

[Suggested by a concert by Mr. W. S. Young's Tonic Sol-fa pupils at St. James's Hall.]

It is about eleven years since the first concert was given by Tonic Sol-fa pupils. The choir consisted of members of Mr. Curwen's Bible class at Plaistow, with a few children from Mr. Brown's school. The music was of the simplest kind, but Crosby Hall was crowded by the help of free tickets, sent to school teachers and influential persons in every direction. At that time we had not a single psalm-tune book published in the Tonic Sol-fa notation ; we did not even *dream* of printing any of the classics, even the *Reporter* had not been *thought of ;* we had only one little fourpenny book of exercises from the "Grammar of Vocal Music." But some of our best and staunchest friends took their first lesson at that meeting. And now, behold ! "How the little one has become a thousand !"

Associations of teachers and friends have held concerts at Exeter Hall, concerts in all the largest halls of provincial cities, monster concerts at the Crystal Palace, and now a *single* teacher, with his body of friends, is bold enough to risk fifty pounds' worth of expenses and to make his appearance in the very centre of London's musical world.

Tonic Sol-fa Reporter, January, 1861.

A happy new year to every one of you—merry, earnest, singing, loving brothers and sisters of the Tonic Sol-fa family.

To you, who have first learned to sing during this past year we would say, TEACH, not superficially, not pretentiously, but TEACH. Teach in the ragged school ; teach in the Sunday school ; teach in the family circle. You have not found out half the good there is in Tonic Sol-fa till you begin to *teach it !* " It is ever more blessed to *give* than to *receive*."

To our *old* friends we say—with a hearty shake of the hand—THANK YOU. Thank you for using the certificates more thoroughly than ever before. Thank you for dividing your classes by means of them. Thank you for the present self-denial with which some of you have made the certificates *essential !* The rest will soon find out that *that* is the only way to succeed. Thank you for the heartiness with which teachers have clung to their upper classes, though generally the least remunerative. Thank you for your free lectures and concerts without number. Thank you for the ragged schools and reformatories which you have filled with Tonic Sol-fa song. Thank you for the congregations and Sunday schools you have taught. Thank you for Crystal Palace gatherings. Thank you for the great unity of spirit you showed in preparing for the great competition. Thank you for your prompt co-working, now, in the business of the Twelfth Service. Thank you for your triumphant efforts in behalf of the *Tonic Sol-fa Reporter*.

It is a good new year *for us*, which finds us able, for the first time, to issue our monthly number without pecuniary loss. We can assure our friends that this fact gives us a peculiar lightsomeness of spirit. They must surely notice that everything we write is in a cheerful strain. We feel ourselves well rewarded for our six years' toil by such a triumphant result. Any magazine more costly than a *penny* could only be of surface power in our popular movement ; this, we hope, goes down to the roots. It was worth six years' patience on our part, and six years' kindness on the part of many others, to attain this great object of our ambition—a self-supporting penny magazine, clothed with power of usefulness ! May we have wisdom, and humility, and skill to use this power aright.

Tonic Sol-fa Reporter, May, 1861.

[Suggested by the Annual Meeting of Mr. Sarll's classes in Exeter Hall, April 11th.]

One of our enthusiastic friends went, in his Easter holidays, to a country town, and so inoculated his relatives there with the Tonic Sol-fa virus, that they called a meeting in a large schoolroom, and then compelled the young man, whether he would or no, to deliver a lecture, with illustrations, on the Tonic Sol-fa method. He improvised a modulator, wrote out a round or two, and set the good folk singing, first by pattern, afterwards by the Tonic Sol-fa notation. We hope that he left behind him *something that will grow* in the town thus pleasantly visited. Exactly four years ago the great orchestra of Exeter Hall was occupied, for the first time, by a Tonic Sol-fa choir, but it required the united strength of all the Tonic Sol-fa singers in London, aided by the central committee of the Association, to accomplish the task. Now both orchestra and hall are filled by one teacher alone ! Is this explosion ?

At that time the number of our pupils was calculated to be nearly 30,000, under about 150 teachers. Now we number considerably more than 160,000 pupils, with fully 800 teachers ! Wonderful progress for an "exploded system !"

At that time the style of music commonly used among Tonic Sol-faists was of the simplest and humblest character. But since then both the *Messiah* and the *Creation* have been performed entire by Tonic Sol-faists, and at the present moment we have the best reason to know that nearly 3,000 Tonic Sol-faists are studying the *Twelfth Service* of Mozart. Is not this very well for a people who have been long since " exploded ?"

Tonic Sol-fa Reporter, October, 1861.

Like every other public movement our own has seen its various phases and forms of development. We had first the school song era, with its Crosby Hall meeting and its conferences. Then came the era of psalmody effort, with its sixpenny "People's Service," and its monster classes in London, Manchester, and elsewhere. When monster classes had proved to have sown their seed on " strong ground " there followed the new and most successful era of popular evening classes, with their *Tonic Sol-fa Reporters*, and their active [propaganda of introductory lectures, and lessons, and closing concerts. This era had not waxed old before a demand sprung up for more complete and orderly lesson books, and that inaugurated the era of the "Standard Course" with its new system of certificates. ..The *resolute* manner in which teachers are now beginning to *insist* upon *preparation* for the certificate as a term of membership for an Elementary Class, and *possession* of the Elementary Certificate as a term of membership for an Intermediate Class, is already reaping its appropriate reward. A Tonic Sol-fa class was before, like a ship in the trough of the sea, without power of guidance or forward motion. One season it seemed to be progressing forward, but the next, alas, might see it "progressing backward!" The skilful pupils and the dull were alike discouraged. Now, however, the good ship answers its helm, and moves straight on for its port. The certificates have done this.

Tonic Sol-fa Reporter, March, 1862.

[Written after a census of Tonic Sol-fa pupils had been taken.]

In June of the year 1843, the first edition of Mr. Curwen's grammar of vocal music, under the title of "Singing for Schools and Congregations," was published. In the preface, after acknowledging the deep and strong foundations which Miss Glover had laid, and describing the peculiarities and novelties of the system, the following words occur. They seem to us now almost prophetic, so truly have they been fulfilled. And yet, after nearly nineteen years of disappointments, difficulties, toils, and cares, we are tempted to look back on the confidence which these words express as inspired by the temerity of youth! Oh, happy youth which can dare "impracticable" things, which believes in the victory of truth, and sees no difficulties. The words are these :—

"But it may still be asked, 'To what patronage do you look for support, and who will be your agents in making known the system?' For patronage, the editor seeks none better than the kind approval of those who gain benefit from these his sincere and earnest efforts. For agents, they abound in every town and village; lovers of sacred music, for the sake of the worship which it aids,

young men and women who will examine and think, who
will teach themselves that they may teach others. These
are the agents, filled with a noble *voluntary* zeal, which
is more mighty than any other. That 'system' shall be
most successful in the end which commends itself most to
the judgment of such practical thinking men as these."

By the time Mr. Curwen was called on to print the
second and enlarged edition of the "Grammar," in September, 1848, he had begun to taste some of the difficulties
of the enterprise, and although increasingly devoted to the
Tonic Sol-fa method, he omitted from his preface this bold
and confident paragraph. Now, however, looking thought-
fully over the census table, which fills another page, we
feel that it is time to reproduce the sure and trustful words
of younger days. We stand amidst a company of at least a
thousand friends, full of a "noble, voluntary zeal," who
are striving with us in every direction to promote singing
for the people, in schools, homes, and congregations.
From henceforth let no one despair of the Tonic Sol-fa
movement.

It will be seen from our census paper that our movement is not confined to any one locality. We have classes
from Cornwall in the south to Inverness and Shetland in
the north. We have classes from Suffolk in the east to
County Mayo in the west. We have the addresses of about
25 teachers in the colonies, and there are probably as many
more with whom we are not acquainted. From these, of
course we could not obtain returns in time for the census
tables.

*   *   *   *   *   *

One conviction, strengthened by the ample correspondence which this census has originated, inspires us with
great courage. We mean the conviction that, almost
without exception, the teachers and active promoters of

this movement are men of religious earnestness, who take up their Tonic Sol-fa work as a means of blessing and of happiness to the children, the young people, and the congregations around them. Clergymen and other ministers of religion in large numbers are putting their hand to the work. May we ever keep ourselves worthy of this noble religious enthusiasm.

Tonic Sol-fa Reporter, July, 1862.

We earnestly entreat our friends, if they have any value for our method, any regard for those who have been foremost in promoting it, to keep it ever in the paths of sobriety and nobleness. Let a Sol-fa concert always *elevate*, never let it *lower* the tone of sentiment among the young people who are associated with it.

Tonic Sol-fa Reporter, August, 1862.

A musical reformer, who has had the happiness of securing the adherence and fellowship of a number of intelligent men, up to the point which he has hitherto reached, has no right to expect that in any new step he will necessarily secure the same following. Indeed, the more intelligent and independent his friends are the greater will be the possibility of divergence. No other step but one which is clearly and unmistakably *right*, according to the principles already agreed upon by his friends, could hope to secure success. It is, therefore, always with great interest, even anxiety, that Mr. Curwen looks around among his old companions in labour, to watch the reception and first working out of any new plan. He feels on this account very grateful for the support which has been so freely offered to his little work "How to Observe Harmony." To write a work and publish it is one thing, but to get it read and thoroughly well used, is quite another! Many books have been written with as long labour and as anxious

care as "How to Observe Harmony," but have fallen almost
dead and useless on the field of literature, and if "How to
Observe Harmony" does not fall dead in a like manner, it
is because Mr. Curwen has the good fortune to possess
many friends and co-workers who will not fail to sow its
seeds and reap its harvests. This is great happiness to
him, not merely because he likes harmony for its own sake,
but because he sees that this study will strengthen our
teachers, and will give a new and mighty impulse to our
movement.

Tonic Sol-fa Reporter, October, 1862.

Mr. Curwen has great pleasure in the fulfilment
of an old promise to let his friends know when the Tonic
Sol-fa cup began to overflow.   For eighteen years he has
kept account of cash expenditure and cash returns in
connection with this movement; and now his midsummer
balance-sheet shows, for the first time, cash *returns* from
the beginning, overweighing cash *expenditure* from the
beginning.   There remain to him also his stereotype
plates.

He is grateful to the providence which enabled
him to make the outlays ; and grateful to his friends,
whose kindly help has brought him through many risks
and some dangers.   He is thankful, also, to be placed
in a position which enables him to make the several
proposals for the convenience of the Tonic Sol-fa movement contained in the present *Reporter*, and to carry
on the further enterprises which *he now has in hand*.

Tonic Sol-fa Reporter, January, 1863.

The temperance cause, in Great Britain, has long been
sustained by noble sacrifices and noble work. Great is the
multitude of its preachers, and largely already has it
blessed the land.

Shall not our Tonic Sol-fa movement help on this apostolic work? Let our Temperance Tonic Sol-faists boldly answer "Yes." Let all who have taken even the Elementary Certificate "try their hand" at teaching. Let them only use well the Modulator, and follow the instructions in the books, and they cannot go far wrong.

Tonic Sol-fa Reporter, July, 1863.

[Written after the Crystal Palace Meeting, June 17th, 1863].

More than twenty-two thousand people testified, on Wednesday last, their sympathy with our Tonic Sol-fa movement. Among the crowds which united to form that vast assembly, we were rejoiced to notice a very large number of ministers of religion of all denominations. It was plain, too, that the people generally belonged to that more serious and earnest class of society which does not commonly now make its appearance at the Crystal Palace. These indications strengthen our hope that the Tonic Sol-fa movement is now gaining favour with the vigorous, self-denying, devoted men who move the world.

Tonic Sol-fa Reporter, January, 1864.

There is nothing we more desire than that our Tonic Sol-fa classes should be connected with the social influence of Christian Churches everywhere. Without that influence there is always danger of too much solo-singing, too much concert-giving, and not a little vanity. It is always happiest and best when our young people's classes can work in harmony with church efforts for the promotion of psalmody. The Christian life of England is that to which our Tonic Sol-fa life must cling. No year has ever ushered in a better promise in this respect than that which now opens before us.

*   *   *   *   *   *

During the past year large contributions were sent by Sol-fa classes to aid the sufferers in the Lancashire distress, and books were supplied to our friends in Lancashire at nominal prices, so that they were kept singing even in the midst of their trouble. We thank God that they are not likely to have such another winter of sorrow. Nor do they ask for any great effort of our liberality. But the ragged schools, the reformatories, and the various refuges for the outcasts and the despised, do need our help.

Tonic Sol-fa Reporter, January, 1864.

Mr. J. W. POWELL,

MY DEAR FRIEND,—I rejoice with great joy in your preparing to sing the *Messiah* at Burslem, and am very pleased to know that our worthy and honoured Mrs. Stirling Bridge is to accompany you on the organ. The practice will elevate the musical taste among your pupils, and will, I trust, cultivate in them the loftiest feelings with which music can be associated. But I "rejoice with trembling," because I know the tendency of youth and musical taste to forget the solemn, the glorious, the ever-blessed *words*, and to think only of the musical effects. There is no piece that so truly deserves the name of *sacred* music, in all the world, as Handel's *Messiah*. I hope that Tonic Sol-faists will try to strip it of everything like mere "performance;" especially that they will take care to avoid everything in dress or manner that would be inconsistent with a place and a season of worship.

On this point—the sacredness of sacred music—a friend writes :—

A vivid recollection I have of Mr. Curwen is the devoutness of manner with which he listened to a Tonic Sol-fa performance of *Messiah* at Exeter Hall.   Although the applause was abundant I don't think he made any demonstration till the end, and then he let the singers see, in the plainest possible way, how much he appreciated their efforts.

Tonic Sol-fa Reporter, March, 1865.

Tonic Sol-fa Balls !   We can scarce write the words. It is a pain and distress to us to place the two names together.   We have laboured all these years to make the Tonic Sol-fa movement promotive of social happiness, as well as religious benefit.   We have rejoiced exceedingly that it has brought young people of both sexes together under good moral influence, and taught them mutual respect without discouraging pure-minded and noble love.   We rejoice to think that it has done this for many years, that it has been the killer of balls, the destroyer of evil associations.   But tidings come to us from the far distant colony of Victoria, of the first Tonic Sol-fa Ball.   Polkas and low dresses are not only painful to the Christian mind, but are repugnant to the true instincts of humanity, and disgusting in the eyes of good taste.

Tonic Sol-fa Reporter, June 1st, 1872.

When we gave a name to our method we did not call it the " New Notation Method," but the " Tonic Sol-fa Method."   The *fixed* Sol-fa method had just been introduced from France by Mr. Hullah, and we wished to contend against what we regarded as its false educational principle.   Our new explanatory and concurrent notation was to us a secondary thing.   We did not then know half its value.   We saw that music was being made difficult to the people of England by the fixed *doh*, and we wished to make it easy by the movable *doh.* How far we have succeeded in this struggle of nearly thirty years is well known. Many who were alarmed at our boldness in using a new notation (concurrent with, not opposed to the old) have been stimulated to adhere to the old English principles of sol-faing from the Tonic ; and many of them have also adopted our modulator with its trinity of keys. We regard them as our brethren. We chiefly differ from them in carrying their principle of the movable *doh* much farther than they do. We teach the staff notation as well as they ; but we introduce it at the end of a course of instruction, while they load themselves with it at the beginning. It is well known that this question of fixed or movable *doh* is the principal question in teaching to sing. To use an illustration which we heard from Mr. Barnby the other day :—If the sol-fa syllables may be regarded as a foot rule measuring intervals, the movable *doh* is an uniform and unchangeable foot rule, and the fixed *doh* is a very elastic foot rule which may be squeezed or extended at will—in fact, no foot rule at all. There can be no possible agreement between the two systems. They are irreconcilables.

Tonic Sol-fa Reporter, September 15, 1872.

It was very pleasant to us recently to meet a company of some ninety persons, the teachers of reformatory schools in and around London, and very pleasant to find that the Tonic Sol-fa method was bearing abundant fruit of usefulness in these schools. But it was very painful to read, the next day, the following advertisement, which appears in a Glasgow newspaper of the 27th ult. :—

THEATRE ROYAL, GLASGOW.—To Amateur Vocalists.— Wanted, a Number of Male and Female Voices, for " The Lady of the Lake," produced Monday, Sept. 9th, and for the forthcoming new play " 1679," produced Monday, Sept. 23 ; those accustomed to the Tonic Sol-fa System preferred.—Apply immediately, personally or by letter, to Mr. E. L. Knapp, Acting Manager.

In the one case we saw our humble labours made helpful in leading young people on the right road ; in the other case it seemed to us as though our efforts had only brought some of our young friends to the edge of a dangerous declivity.

When we first heard that some of our Glasgow friends had been singing operas without scenery or action, we hoped that pleasure, without evil, might spring from the attempt. We knew that some operas were as innocent in their story as the " Lady of the Lake," and we thought that the City Hall would be far removed from the immoral atmosphere which hangs around the theatre. But we are quite sure that those good friends of ours, who carried out the plan we have described with a view of drawing thousands of people away from public-houses on Saturday night, and were so remarkably successful in accomplishing that purpose, never dreamt that the young men and women whom they trained to sing were thus placed within the reach of a dangerous temptation. We know that the *ideal* theatre may be a good thing, but the *real* is very different. Henry Ward Beecher somewhere says that the entrance to Satan's door is always made to look beautiful, pleasant, and pure, in order that all the young people passing by may say, " surely there's no harm in it." That phrase, " What harm is there ?" has ruined many a soul. We ought to ask ourselves " What good is there" in the thing we are about to do ? But there are very few theatres in reference to which the question, " What harm is there ?" may be seriously asked by those who know them well. There is harm outside a theatre ; there is harm in the gallery ; there is harm behind the scenes, even if there is not harm on the stage itself. Those who, led by their artistic tastes, have become most familiar with all that relates to a theatre, would be amongst the first to rescue a sister or a friend from taking an engagement as singer on its boards. We heard only recently of a Tonic Sol-fa lady singer who was once tempted to sign an engagement as singer in a theatre, and, indeed, made her first appearance with great success; but who has since then, not once, but many times earnestly thanked a friend who persuaded her to withdraw from the engagement, and assisted her in doing so. We hope, therefore, that this advertisement will find no response from the Tonic Sol-faists of Glasgow. We have, in fact, no further reason than the one we have mentioned to fear that it will.

In 1878, when Mr. Curwen was in the deepest anxiety as to how to raise funds for the Tonic Sol-fa College, he issued a circular to his friends in view of a public meeting at Exeter Hall, asking for subscriptions, and begging those who could not send money, to send a word of sympathy. The result was an enormous number of letters, from which a few passages are appended :—

The fact is (and I am only now saying what I have said many, many times), your notation has been a power in the country second only to the influence of Christianity itself, if we consider the assistance it has given to the millions who unite in praising God from week to week, the millions who have been taught to sing in harmony, who never would have been able to sing a note from the old notation.

I feel that this—the *people's* method of singing—has been of the greatest blessing to me, as it has been to thousands of others. It has introduced me to many friends that but for the passport of Sol-fa I should have never known, but best and greatest of all, it has been the means under God of bringing about the salvation of my soul, for it was for the singing I first went to chapel, and through thus going found peace with God.

Music has been to me a hundredfold more charming since you have made its enjoyment so easy of attainment. I owe you a delight I never expected to know.

Up to the time of becoming acquainted with Sol-fa, I was floundering about in the mysteries of the old notation, but now I can enjoy taking part in praising my Lord; and what a pleasure it is, after business is over, to pick up a piece of music and sing it over ! I have derived great soul good from Sankey's hymns ; but had I been ignorant of Sol-fa I should have lost the great pleasure I have felt in singing them.

You have done a noble work, for you have been the means of putting music into many lives which but for you would have had little pleasure.

Many of my boys went to sea [the writer lives in a seaport town], and there is now a sea captain here, just home from Hobart Town, who tells me that every time he arrives there, he goes to see an old school-fellow, a resident, and they sing over together the old school songs they learnt twenty years since in my school. I may also say that I have known instances in which men who have been to sea for years remembered their Sol-fa, and taught their shipmates what they knew.

Believe me, sir, Wales highly appreciates your noble services in the interests of " Music for the People." You

H

have revolutionised the science in this music-loving country of ours ; and there is hardly a village, much less a town, of all those I visit, in the course of my calling [the writer is a minister], in which I do not find a Tonic Sol-fa class ; which, like an oasis, sends forth its streams of song to the thirsty land around. I have attended many Eisteddfodau, concerts, literary and musical entertainments, &c., during the past year, and find, in all such gatherings, that by far the greater part of the effective work has been done by the aid of the Tonic Sol-fa method. Choirs, classes, and societies, in which the method is studied, are being formed on every hand. The programmes of our monster psalmody festivals are printed in your notation. It has found its way into our weekly and monthly magazines, and our printers are adopting your type everywhere.

I thank God that, though young at present, your system has been the means of giving me a knowledge and love of music, which otherwise, perhaps, I should never have had the opportunity of gaining. Through it I have spent many a happy hour, which might have been spent in the pernicious amusements to which young men resort, having nothing else to amuse their minds.

Our household is brighter, our home is happier because of *Sol-fa*. The choirs of two churches are assisted by the young folks of our family, thanks to Sol-fa. The 70 girls at the industrial school here (who are my pupils) are losing some of their sadness and gloom because of Sol-fa, and the singing-class night is looked forward to as the happiest in the week. So, dear sir, you see your work is lighting up the hearts of thousands, and if they could be at the meeting to-morrow they would say " God bless you."

CHAPTER VII. .

1849—1854.

"THE PEOPLE'S SERVICE OF SONG" — "CASSELL'S POPULAR EDUCATOR"—THE EDUCATIONAL VOLUNTARIES—SIR EDWARD BAINES—CHURCH RATE STRUGGLE—ECCLESIASTICAL POLITICS — PUBLIC WORK AT PLAISTOW — MR. CURWEN'S METHOD AS A SPEAKER — INFLUENCE AS A PASTOR AND A COUNSELLOR — ABSTINENCE — THE GIRL WHO RANG THE BELL — THE SCHOOL BOY — "CHILD'S OWN HYMN BOOK" — GROWTH OF TONIC SOL-FA—JACOB ABBOTT—LOWELL MASON—LETTER TO HIS DAUGHTER.

MR. CURWEN was now married and settled at Plaistow, in Essex, busily occupied with his congregation and his new musical system. The book which first engaged his attention was " The People's Service of Song." In an address at a Psalmody Conference of Tonic Sol-fa teachers in 1864 Mr. Curwen looked back upon the purpose and origin of this book, as follows :—

MY DEAR FRIENDS,—I thank God that I see you here to-night in such large numbers, and in such a spirit of vigorous earnestness. It is a sign that our Tonic Sol-fa movement is drawing nearer to the accomplishment of its great aim than ever before. We have been beleaguering this citadel of Church Song for many years.

More than twenty years ago we attacked it by direct assault and were severely repulsed. Neither Mr. Waite nor the proprietors of any other well-known psalm-tune book would allow their books to appear in the Tonic Sol-fa notation on any terms whatsoever. I appealed to them earnestly to let our Sol-fa movement help their psalmody, but in vain. We had to retire within our first lines, and intrench ourselves in the schools. Here we raised up a new host of Tonic Sol-fa singers, who are now young men and women, Sunday school teachers, and workers in every field of Christian labour. But during all the time in which our army was thus recruiting its strength, we did not neglect to employ another kind of tactics, which I may call " sapping and mining." We provided a book of psalm tunes (" The People's Service") in the established notation, which might, to some extent, compete with our opponents, and, this being our own, we were at liberty to put it into the Tonic Sol-fa notation. The success of this " operation " was so marked as to induce others to follow our example. Dr. William Cooke was the first.

In a letter to his brother, Mr. T. Curwen, written from Herne Bay about this time, Mr. Curwen thus speaks of the new tune book :—

I have decided to prepare the tune book for the pew. My own pecuniary affairs needed it ; the new notation needed it for completion and a fair trial ; and what is, I trust, dearer to me than either, the churches need, for service, a book of tunes containing psalm tunes more lively than Mr. Waite's, a few chants, and a good selection of congregational pieces (if they can be got) to take the place of the favourite old repeat tunes. I have written to give up attendance at the (Congregational) Board of Education till the thing is done. I have also given up the Training College. Thus I earnestly trust that the new undertaking will not hinder my other and yet higher work.

Mr. Alfred Brown writes in reference to the work of preparing this book :—

In 1849 and 1850, when Mr. Curwen was compiling the "People's Service of Song," he often rose before the lark. I was frequently with him at 6 a.m., when we worked at tabulating indices, tunes, experiences of congregations, &c. At seven we had coffee, and soon after eight I left to prepare for school. His brother, Mr. Thomas Curwen, was then residing at Plaistow, and by his sound judgment and practical suggestions greatly helped on the work. The late Mr. George Hogarth (one of whose daughters Charles Dickens married), who composed some pieces for the work, and harmonised the whole, was occasionally at Plaistow in the after part of the day. It was my office and privilege to conduct him to the "Swan," at Stratford, and see him into a 'bus.

At the request of the late Mr. Cassell, Mr. Curwen wrote, about the same time, a series of papers in *Cassell's Popular Educator* on the Tonic Sol-fa system, which spread it far and wide. The frequent re-issue of the *Educator*, and its enormous circulation, made these articles a most valuable propaganda. Through all his subsequent life Mr. Curwen heard now and again from persons who told him that they owed their first introduction to music, and all their subsequent enjoyment of it to *Cassell's Popular Educator*.

About the year 1847 Mr. Curwen took an active part in opposing the Education Bill of Sir James Graham. A number of letters written to Dr. Andrew Reed, the philanthropist, at this time, show the energy which he threw into the subject. Mr. Curwen seems, in 1844, to have been asked by Dr. Reed to become secretary of a society for promoting the formation of day schools among the Congregationalists. He writes enquiring the nature of the duties. The proposal, however, came to nothing. Dr. Reed had noticed Mr. Curwen's vitalising power and vigour of attack. A year or two later he invited him to give up his pastorate, and work with him in organising orphanages and asylums. Mr. Curwen, however, preferred to remain at Plaistow.

Of the position and labours of the Educational voluntaryists, who formed themselves into a party at this period, Sir Edward Baines writes :—

They had no more cordial friend than Mr. Curwen, but he did not publish much on the subject, being so absorbed in the establishment of his system of popular music, in which his success was so distinguished. From the pamphlets which were published you may learn our ardent love of education, the noble principles of self-reliance, mutual help, and religion on which we acted, the difficulties we encountered, the objections which we foresaw to a Governmental system, but the way in which the people were gradually won to that system by numerous concessions and adaptations, and by their generous ambition to have their children and their class educated, at whatever cost of money, and even of economical rules. We had never reason to be ashamed of our principles, which, perhaps, were too high and good to win popular sympathy ; but we ourselves cherished old prejudices, and did not soon enough admit the immense *practical* advantages of Government and rate-supported education, as shown in other countries.

My conditional recantation, if I may so call it, was delivered at Manchester in 1867. I believe I may say that in all that we did we acted on the best information we could obtain, and under the dictates of conscience ; and in not a few matters exerted a salutary influence in modifying the action of Government and Parliament. Many strong opponents have admitted that, after all, popular education owes more to the voluntaries than to Government in all the 19th century.

Mr. Curwen opposed State education partly from that spirit of the old Radicalism which suspected the Government in everything, and sought to minimise its duties, and partly as a religious voluntaryist, opposed to State supported religious teaching. When, in 1870, the Government gave up inspecting or paying for religious teaching, he accepted the system heartily.

Local as well as national politics drew Mr. Curwen into action. At this time church rates, for the support of Church of England worship, were permissive, and could be abolished in any parish that chose to vote them out. Mr. Curwen joined an effort for terminating these rates in the parish of West Ham, in which Plaistow is situated, which was successful. The Rev. T. E. Stallybrass, B.A., who worked with him in this effort, writes :—

I remember, as we read our MSS. to each other, that
Mr. Curwen was very careful to eliminate everything that,
in spirit or expression, should be offensive or painful to
our opponents in the struggle. We owed much to his
influence that the struggle was conducted on our side with
no bitterness of feeling or expression, so that though our
opponents persisted in ascribing to us selfish and sectarian
motives, we used to go home with them personally as good
friends as we ever were.

This literary and public work, added to pastoral
duties, overtaxed Mr. Curwen's strength, and brought on
an attack of rheumatic fever, which probably laid the
foundations of the heart weakness which developed thirty
years later, and caused his death. Soon after this illness
he became an ardent homœopathist, and a patient of Dr.
Kidd, whom he consulted during the rest of his life.

Of Mr. Curwen's interest in ecclesiastical politics at
this time, the Rev. Andrew Reed, B.A. writes :—

When Edward Miall, a former student of our college,
gave up his ministerial charge at Leicester and came to
London to devote himself to found the *Nonconformist*
newspaper and the Anti-State Church Association, while
many questioned the prudence of the step, and shrank
from organising our churches into a combined assault
on the Established Church, John Curwen took a lively
interest in the movement. He became a warm follower of
Miall, with others of us. He defended him from the
attacks of less decided Dissenters. He had no sympathy
with compromise or "expediency" in matters of truth and
right. He preferred going straight to his mark, let
people think and say what they would, he liked to be in

the front ranks of reform. He felt that religion was injured by establishments; that our country was disunited and kept back by establishments, and that the English church itself was the worse for its bondage to earthly Governments, while Dissenters were grievously wronged. He took the bold side of the question, and was not afraid of being in a minority. For an age of persecution he would have been a cheerful sufferer or an unresisting martyr for conscience sake.

Mr. Curwen, though he is chiefly known for his musical work, was by no means a man of one idea, nor did the Tonic Sol-fa method, at any period of his life, absorb all his sympathies or activities. During his ministry at Plaistow he endeavoured to keep the people abreast of the movement of the times. He would give lectures on whatever topic was exciting public interest, or occupying his own mind. These were not formal discourses, but informal talks, with plenty of illustration, and the clear exposition of which he was such a master. He lectured on "Homœopathy," on "Passing Events," on "New Fields of Emigration." Lecturing once on the Californian gold-diggings he described how, in Sydney, it was, at that time, a common thing to see a house closed, and the words "gone to the diggings" chalked on the door. The next morning he found that during the night some wags in the audience had chalked up these very words on his own door! Probably they thought that, from the graphic way in which Mr. Curwen lectured about the gold diggings, he must be intending to go himself. Mr. Curwen had the faculty, both in private conversation and in his public addresses, of making interesting whatever he touched. This was due to the strong conviction with which he always spoke, and to the way in which he arranged his facts, so that the subject often appeared far more simple than it really was. The extempore style suited him best. He wrote out his more responsible and elaborate addresses, but rather as a means of preparation than that he might use the manuscript before his audience. In reading his fervour and vivacity largely forsook him; hence he seldom attempted it. In preaching, as well as in speaking, he thought out his addresses, jotted down the heads or chief topics, and the illustrations he intended to use; his notes, written large, seldom exceeded one or two pages. Mr. Curwen had always great difficulty in remembering poetry, and seldom ventured to quote it in public.

Mr. Curwen's influence as a pastor was, perhaps, deeper and more exceptional than his influence as a preacher. It was the peculiar union of practical good sense and business knowledge with the tenderest sympathy that was remarkable in him. People felt him to be a counsellor who would guide them as well as weep with them. He had a horror of debt, and, with all his generosity, would never *lend* a farthing towards the payment of old debts. He used to say that the tradesmen, who often culpably encouraged people to run into debt, deserved to be left to their chance. People who came to him in difficulty often went away with a gift, but never with a loan. " I learnt from Mr. Curwen," writes a lady who was in his Plaistow congregation, " scrupulous carefulness in money matters." He often took the affairs of an involved member of his congregation in hand, found out his or her real position, and then gave his advice, making his appeal to conscience and duty.

We talk against confession, but there is a sort of confession that is founded deep in human nature, and will last so long as sin, and remorse, and sorrow can meet with purity and love. Mr. Curwen was, throughout life, the involuntary confessor of many a soul burdened with sin or with a secret grief. " We have no letters from Mr. Curwen," writes one of his congregation. " He came to us, or we went to him, for the kind, wise counsels he was always ready to give, and they were wrought into our lives. So that to tell of his influence would be to tell a great deal of one's personal history, which is impossible."

A friend to whom he gave counsel and practical help in the darkest moment of contrition writes : —

I was struck particularly by his evident desire to be mercifully faithful in reproving sin. He knew how to give *loving* reproof, and in such a way that the erring one was irresistibly impressed with the feeling that he could not do better than follow the dear speaker's advice. He spared no trouble in helping the wanderer's return to the right path, and gave much of his valuable time for this object. In this respect he was the most Christlike man I ever knew.

It is a rare gift to be able to reprove tenderly, and to convince the erring one that the very earnestness of your reproof springs from your love for him. Mr. Curwen could do this. He had no fondness for the post of candid friend, and he had none whatever of that coarse make which enables some men to say anything to anybody. But he had an intense conscientiousness, and saw duty in the smallest acts. He often did what is, perhaps, the most difficult duty of friendship — warned intimate acquaintances in whom he thought he saw a fondness for intoxicating drinks that might become dangerous to them. A friend to whom he once thus spoke, writes :—

The most vivid recollection I have of Mr. Curwen, one which I shall always think of with pleasure, was a long walk we had at Plaistow. He was warning me against the dangers of intoxicants. I am afraid I had rather a bad reputation amongst you abstemious people. His manner was, of course, most kind, but his sensitiveness made him very much afraid of wounding me, and I shall ever remember the affectionate manner in which he pressed my arm, earnestly assuring me over and over again of his regard and desire for my welfare. The incident was so eminently characteristic of Mr. Curwen's kindness of heart that I can never forget it.

It may be added that Mr. Curwen, who was through life, as the writer just quoted says, "an abstemious man,"

became a total abstainer about eight years before his
death, in order to help a friend who had given way to
drink, and whom he desired to influence in the strongest
manner possible. He never regretted the change, and
often wished he had made it earlier. During the last few
months of his life, when heart disease had made his
circulation languid and his resisting power feeble, he took
wine at the urgent mandate of Dr. Kidd, and declared that
he found much benefit from it.

Instances of Mr. Curwen's happy manner with
children, and his insight into child nature, could easily
be multiplied. One amusing incident of his early life at
Plaistow has been recalled.

For several days in succession the door-bell of his
house was rung at dinner time, and when the servant
went to the door there was no one to be seen. At last the
servant lay in wait at the proper time, and caught the
runaway in the act. It proved to be a girl. Mr. Curwen
directed that she should be taken into the parlour and
asked to sit down. She was led there, sobbing and in
great terror. In a few minutes Mr. Curwen entered,
bearing—a large slice of pudding! Without saying
another word he asked the girl to eat some. She sobbed
and shook, and declared she couldn't. However, after a
time Mr. Curwen prevailed, and left her eating the
pudding. When she had done he returned, entering the
room with a pleasant smile, and saying, "Now I am sure

you won't ring my bell again." The girl, overcome with shame, took his proffered hand, and said "No, sir, I'm sure I shan't."

In travelling up the Rhine by the slow passage from Rotterdam a few years later, Mr. Curwen met with an English boy who was on his way to a German school. He entered into conversation with the lad, and soon knew all his heart. The boy said he had got a box of tools with him, which he meant to keep locked up, and to allow no one but himself to use. Mr. Curwen listened to what he had to say, and then said, "My boy, you are going amongst strangers, and you want them to be kind to you. Now if you want this, you must remember the proverb, 'He that would have friends must show himself friendly,' and I advise you to lend your tools sometimes to the other boys." A year or more later the boy wrote to thank Mr. Curwen for his advice, and to say he had followed it, and found that it made him friends everywhere.

The "Child's Own Hymn Book," of which the first edition was published in 1841, met with a remarkable success, and carried Mr. Curwen's name everywhere. Since its first appearance the book has been several times remodelled and added to, and its popularity still continues. Mr. Curwen always spoke of the lesson he had learnt from Charles Knight as to the "power of cheapness." Good and pure cheap literature was, at the time of which we write, a new idea, worked out first by Knight, closely followed by Chambers and Cassell. Mr. Curwen threw himself heartily into the movement, and in all his works studied cheapness, knowing that it was a condition of popular use. At a time when penny hymn-books may be counted by the dozen, we can scarcely appreciate the novelty of the first penny hymn-book, which Mr. Curwen was privileged to bring out. Of his own contributions to this book, "O what has Jesus done for me" has been widely popular, and " I'm a little pilgrim " is a universal favourite. The origin of this latter hymn is curious. A hymn with a similar first line was inserted in the book pending a reply from the author granting permission for its appearance. The reply came at the last moment, when the index was stereotyped and the book was about to be printed. The author refused, on any terms, to allow the insertion of his hymn. As an escape from the difficulty, Mr. Curwen took the first line and wrote the following, which is known to almost every Sunday scholar in England and America :—

I'm a little pilgrim,
  And a stranger here ;
Though this world is pleasant,
  Sin is always near.

Mine's a better country,
  Where there is no sin ;
Where the tones of sorrow
  Never enter in.

But a little pilgrim
Must have garments clean
If he'd wear the white robes
And with Christ be seen.

Jesus, cleanse and save me,
Teach me to obey,
Holy Spirit, guide me
On my heavenly way.

I'm a little pilgrim,
And a stranger here ;
But my home in heaven
Cometh ever near.

The chorus which is often sung to the hymn is not Mr. Curwen's. It is an American addition. He afterwards adopted it in his book.

In the autumn of 1853 four large meetings of Sol-faists were held in Finsbury Chapel, Moorfields, at which a choir of 150 pupils sang, and Mr. Curwen gave addresses. His lectures at Crosby Hall, in the same year, were attended by many educationists, and first called public attention to the system. It was estimated at this time that 2,000 persons were learning the system in London, and an equal number in the provinces.

In the same year Mr. Curwen had the pleasure of entertaining, at his house, Dr. Jacob Abbott, the American educationist, with whom he had previously been in correspondence. Mr. Curwen was an enthusiastic reader of Abbott—not only of the " Young Christian " and " The Corner Stone," which drew forth such warm praise from the late Dr. Arnold—but of his books for children. At Christmas, 1852, when his Plaistow congregation raised a little more than his regular salary, Mr. Curwen spent the remainder in buying a complete set of Abbott's works, which he highly valued, and used in the education of his own children.

Dr. Lowell Mason, the founder of popular music in America, whose work for congregational singing is so well remembered, was another of Mr. Curwen's guests about this time.

The following letter to his daughter (eight years old) written at this time, shows Mr. Curwen's method of speaking to children :—

Plaistow, June 22, 1854.

Yesterday afternoon I went to Miss Dale's, and there, in the middle of the room, was a very large box. A number of little girls that belong to Miss Dale's missionary working party were standing round it. The top was ready to be nailed on when the box was filled. Miss Dale was putting some paper all round the sides and at the bottom of the box. A great number of things were on the table ready to be put in. There were copy books, slates, pencils, pincushions, bobbins of thread, needles, pins, pinafores, dresses, a morning gown, bonnets, and a number of papa's hymn books and tune books were to go in at the top. So we began packing. One little girl put in copy books, another gowns, and so on till the box was nearly full. We shall have to get some more things to fill it quite up, and then the top will be nailed on, and it will

I

be sent in a ship to Mrs. W. Gill, who was once a girl in the Plaistow working party, but is now a missionary's wife in Mangaia, an island in the South Seas. Won't Mrs. Gill be delighted when she sees it ! And how the little dark-coloured children will dance round it for joy when they see how many things the Plaistow children have sent them ! After we had put all the things in we stood round the box and sang "Who are they whose little feet." You know there is something in it about "islands of the main" (sea). And then papa prayed to God to bless the little children that would receive the box, and those who sent it.

CHAPTER VIII.

1854—1856.

OVERWORK—VISIT TO GERMANY—RESIDENCE AT ZIEGEL-
HAUSEN—LETTERS OF MR. AND MRS. CURWEN—CHILDREN
IN CHURCH—LUTHERAN SERVICE—SINGING—SHOEMAKERS
SINGING AT THEIR WORK — EXCURSIONS — LETTER TO
PLAISTOW SUNDAY SCHOLARS — SUNDAY — PATERNAL
GOVERNMENT — MISSIONARY MEETINGS.

MR. CURWEN continued his pastoral work at Plaistow,
although the growing claims made upon his time and
energy by the Tonic Sol-fa movement hampered and
perplexed him, and did much to shake his health. At the
end of 1855 he was driven into a strait by feeling the
strain of work upon his health. In a letter dated
November 6th, he resigned the pastorate at Plaistow,
speaking in affectionate terms of his work there, but
adding that a new chapel was needed, and it was better
that he should not enter upon this new responsibility
without the certainty of being able to carry it through.
The people were much distressed at the prospect of losing

Mr. Curwen, and asked him to take a long holiday. This, after some consideration, he determined to do.

In April of the following year (1856) Mr. Curwen took his family to Germany, where he remained seven months. He went first for a month to Langen Schwalbach, in Nassau, to drink the waters; the rest of the time was spent at Ziegelhausen, a village prettily placed on the bank of the Neckar, above Heidelberg. Here a house was rented, furniture hired, and housekeeping set up. Mrs. Curwen had brought two English servants with her, and she fell very easily into the simple German life. The following extract from a letter written by Mrs. Curwen to a relative, describes their new German home :—

The hills rising on each bank of the river are grand in the extreme. They have their sides covered with rich grain or vineyards, and their tops crowned with woods. The air is vocal with the songs of birds whose names I am striving to learn. The cuckoo we hear at all hours of the day from our window, and the bullfinch we see quietly feeding its young in the street as we walk along. We have a very comfortable house, containing ten rooms, with two small gardens and two orchards, for which we pay five pounds a month, rent and taxes included. Then we have to pay for furniture besides. Food is, however, remarkably cheap. Meat is not nearly so good as in England, but it is excellent for Germany, and for it we pay fourpence or fivepence a pound. Bread is excellent. Black bread, which we all like now, and of which we eat more than white, is fivepence for a loaf which, I think, will correspond in size with the large loaves you use in

Lancashire. White bread is just double the price. Vegetables are moderate. Butter, beautifully fresh, ninepence a pound. Fruit begins to be abundant. Wild strawberries and bilberries we are supplied with in quantities, and cherries are now a penny a pound, and they say will be cheaper.

You understand that we have not a bit of carpet in our house, nor a curtain, except in our drawing-room. Really, I begin to think, if these Germans know very little of comfort, we know rather too much about it ; and I find I can dispense with a good deal that I deemed necessary before. Our children are learning German, French, and drawing. We are often amused at ourselves, and at each other, with our attempts at German. I have not got much beyond dealing with tradespeople, and now and then I have to call my dear husband from his study to explain to me some mysticism concerning various articles of merchandise. The money puzzled me a little at first, but now I keep all my accounts in German money most easily.

Mr. Curwen himself draws the following picture of Ziegelhausen :—

We are in a most enchanting place. From my study window I look over the Neckar on to a steep hill-side crowned with wood. Beneath me, across the road, is a little garden, and, through that, an orchard sloping down to the river. There, by the river's bank, on warm days, sits my dear wife, under the trees, with the children around her, and plenty of "work" in hand. We can walk up the pretty mill-stream valley, which opens into this, or mount the hills into the woods, or stroll along the Neckar, listening to the swift stream, watching the swallows, stopping to hear the workmen's song as they go home from their work, hearkening to the students' merry glees, as in their oarless boats they ride the current to Heidelberg, picking wild flowers and strawberries amid the noise of frogs and crickets on the banks ; and often, very often, thinking of home and you.   But our days are very busy ones.   I make as many hours' work as I can.

Mr. Curwen's letters to the Plaistow congregation, to the Plaistow Sunday scholars, and to the Tonic Sol-faists through their *Tonic Sol-fa Reporter*, were collected on his return in a little volume, entitled " Sketches in Nassau, Baden, and Switzerland."   This was published in aid of the new Plaistow chapel.   A few characteristic extracts may be given.   In his first Sunday at Langen Schwalbach Mr. Curwen's thoughts were about the children :—

On either side of the " altar " are seated the children of the congregation—boys to the minister's right hand, with the elders and schoolmasters in raised pews behind them—the girls on his left hand, with ladies, perhaps relatives or friends of the elders, for there are no female teachers here, on the raised seats behind them.   There, in the place of respect and tender love—there, in the very bosom of the church, are the children of her care.   And better behaviour in children I have not known anywhere. Why should it not be so in England ?   Why should we poke the little ones away in heated galleries and ugly corners, and then scold them for not loving the church ? But, better than all, these children have, through nearly the whole of their eight years' schooling, one hour a week for practice in psalmody.   No wonder that every one can sing in Germany ! So much practice of psalmody must also necessarily give fulness and steadiness to their voices.

The following is a description of Lutheran congregational singing :—

On the first Sabbath morning we were early at the Lutheran church. The time of commencement is nine o'clock. As the seats seemed to belong to no one in particular, and there were happily no signs of pew-letting, we took the first convenient place. The congregation soon filled up the seats around us, when, to my surprise, I found myself in the midst of a goodly company of bonnetless, and, for the most part also, capless matrons —the only man in that part of the church. However, my dear wife and children were with me, and I was not afraid !

Soon the organ gave a prelude, and then, while it paused entirely for a moment, a first tone was given out by the *voice* of the organist. It was upper D. Immediately followed, not any sound of the organ, but a mighty out-streaming of 600 or 700 voices, on that same high note, carrying the tide of song swiftly and brilliantly onwards. Presently you could hear that the organ was following. Its ever-varying tones seemed to dance on the crests of the waves. Every man, woman, and child in the place seemed to sing, and all sang in unison. The women around me sang with such a vigour of lung, and such an evident enjoyment of the physical exercise, as was itself inspiring. But there were also many tokens of the heart's interest in the subject of the song. The whole effect was very unexpected and thrilling. It was interesting to notice how well prepared everyone was. The number of the hymns was announced on a black board by the side of

the pulpit.* Every hymn-book was open at the place.
The voices began not only on the first tone, but also
on the very first part of the first tone. It was like
the clear striking of a good clock. In England most
people would excuse themselves from singing so high
a tone as D at the opening of a tune. They would leave
it to the precentor, or send after it a trembling falsetto.
But falsetto—falsetto in a country church of the Duchy of
Nassau! Falsetto is not believed in. It is all healthy
chest-voice here. And yet they neither stand up to sing
nor open their mouths. In this I do not commend them.
But, oh! if English people would but begin at the
beginning, and " sing out " as they do,—if they would
but make the service of praise into *a hearty work*—then
should I greatly rejoice.

Between every line of the words, whether long or
short—and they differ most curiously in length—there is
a little organ play, occupying the time of about one beat,
and then out flies the people's song again. So that there
is none of that rhythmic balance and unity in the psalm-
tunes which we Tonic Sol-faists are always anxious to
observe.

This congregation keep in use, I afterwards learnt,
about fifty tunes, which are adapted to about 300 hymns.
These tunes and hymns they have learnt from childhood.
They know all the tunes, and many of the hymns, " by
heart." And to sing them with the great congregation on
a Sunday morning, after a long walk from a country
village, is evidently a great refreshment.

The advantage of this unisonous style of psalm-
singing is in its vigorous, rugged unity and plain out-

speaking. It is pleasant as a change, but I cannot understand how any one can for a moment prefer it, as a general and constant usage, before the rich and yet simple harmony of each voice to its proper part, which the new era of Psalmody is inaugurating in England. Success to Mr. Waite ! Success to the Tonic Sol-fa Association !

When, on succeeding Sabbaths, I went into the gallery, among the men, I found very little of the same constancy and spirit in singing which the women had shown. At Ziegelhausen, afterwards, the women and children sang well, but not so promptly and vigorously as at Schwallbach. Of the men, some follow the voices of the women ; and others, not able to reach so high, aim at a variety of basses. In a large town-congregation at Heidelburg, nearly all the people joined, but with a feebleness which made me think that there is more heart in the country than in the town.

I shall never forget the first congregational part-singing I heard, after being accustomed, for six months, to what I had then learned to call the rough, heavy unison. It was in Lavater's Church at Zürich. The congregation was small, but all sang, and each took his part. The sense of relief and satisfaction was delightful. It was like getting into a new and purer world.

The following shows how eagerly Mr. Curwen caught any signs or sounds of popular music :—

The mention of Wiesbaden reminds me of "singing at work." We were passing through the open space, where the droskies stand, near the great brunnen, when our cars were arrested by a true concord of sweet sounds. The voices were those of men. The music was fugal, having a complex and refined beauty, but full of life and spirit. We looked around at all the great houses, expecting to see a concert room, and to learn whence the sounds came. But we looked in vain. The drosky men, seeing our puzzled appearance, directed us to an open window in the upper part of one of the humbler houses. We stood and listened, as the sweet music came floating down ; but there came mingled with it occasionally a curious " tap, tap," "tap, tap." This did puzzle us exceedingly, until a good-natured drosky man came to our relief. He placed his hands on the level of his knees, and then moved them sharply away to the right and left several times, exclaiming, with a smile on his face, " Schumacher, mein herr, schumacher!" Why should not English shoemakers rejoice in such harmony as this ? They shall soon.

The following is a description of an excursion to Neckarsteinach, a village higher up the little river :—

M. de la Fite and his young friends walked over mountains and through woods—the *nearest* way, by Schänau. We crossed the river with Mdme. de la Fite; and Herr Hardtmann, from Heidelberg, took us in his drosky by the *best* road through Neckar-gemünd. We had our first view of the great red stone quarries, whose stones we had heard, in the evenings, rolling, and dashing, and thundering into the water. We passed, also, under the furrowed mountain side, where the pine-trees, cut at the top, are made to slide down to the river's edge. At Neckar-gemünd (as afterwards at many other places) we marked high up on a house-side the memorial of the height to which Neckar floods will sometimes rise. Here, too, we stood for the first time on a flying-bridge. This flying-bridge is a barge suspended in the stream, as a pendulum is suspended in the air, by means of a rope or chain passing over little boats, and fastened in the

centre of the river higher up. The water was high and
the stream was strong, so that we had only time to notice
how our barge was *set* so as to catch the stream on one
side, before we heard a little rushing of the waters against
us, and found ourselves quietly touching the opposite
shore. Our brave walking friends had found the short way
longer than they expected. We reached the little town
before them. We mounted the long promontory-like hill
by a pleasant path, looking now into one valley, now into
the other, amused by the little beggars who *would* pick
flowers for us, and scramble down the rocks to get sweet
wild strawberries for the children. The view from " the
Swallow's Nest," of the winding Neckar, far below, and
the long snake-like rafts, fresh from the Black Forest, just
shooting the rapids, and the ancient walled town crowning
the high hill beyond, is very beautiful. Some German
students stood by us quoting Schiller in very eloquent
and poetic style. Descending, we found the foot-travellers
refreshing themselves in the inn garden overlooking the
Neckar. We heard a whisper of their returning by water,
and no sooner had we, with our drosky, reached the mid-
stream on the flying-bridge, than we were greeted with a
right English cheer from a boatful of friends. They came
careering down on the top of the tide. Then followed a
race between drosky and punt, which put the inhabitants
of both into high glee. Sometimes there were windings
of the river, sometimes of the road ; sometimes the stream
was slack, and sometimes the drosky must climb up-hill.
As each party caught sight of the other, a hearty cheer
awoke the echoes ; and, when they went side by side, they
cheered each other by songs,—"God save the Queen"
being loudest and heartiest. But M. de la Fite reached
his own water-gate just as we were paying Herr
Hardtmann his gulden on the other side of the ferry.

The following are extracts from a letter to the Sunday school children at Plaistow :—

The boys have a delightful place to live in here. When they are very little they get whips and help the pig-driver, who gathers all the pigs of the village together every morning, and takes them into the mountains to feed. There is generally a troop of boys after the old man, and they try to make as great a noise in smacking their whips as he does. The pigs go snuffing along, however, without caring much for the little whips. At the proper seasons the boys roam about the mountains and clamber up the rocky places where the sun shines most, to gather first bilberries, then strawberries, then raspberries, then black-berries. They help, too, at haymaking and harvest, for most of their fathers and mothers have a field or two, and when the cherry-gathering time comes, it is wonderful how active the boys are. Then they can play on the river's brink, and watch the fishermen or the bargemen, or plunge in, as they often do, among the beautiful fishes, which abound in these waters. But yet I fear they do not have a very happy life. You scarcely ever see them romp and play with the fresh, free innocent glee of English children. They live on poor bread, and not always enough of it. Nearly all of them are without shoes and stockings. The fathers and mothers are often cruel.

When we were at Schwallbach, I heard of one of the greatest hymn-writers of Germany, named Paul Gerhard, and I mean to close my letter by telling you about him.

Paul Gerhard was, many years ago, a great preacher in Brandenburgh ; and he loved to preach from his heart what he saw and believed in the Word of God. But the "Great Elector" of Brandenburg did not like his preach-ing, and sent to say to him, "Paul Gerhard, if you cannot

preach differently from that, you must leave this country."
Paul Gerhard sent back a message that it would be very
hard to leave his home, his people, his country and his
livelihood ; but he could only preach what he found in
God's word, and as long as he lived, he *would* preach that.
So he had to go into banishment with his wife and his
little children.

At the end of their first day's journey they came
into a wood, and rested at night at a little inn they found
there.   The little children were crying and clinging to
their mother, and she too, who had kept up all day,
began now to weep.   This made Paul Gerhard have a
very heavy heart.   So he went alone into the dark wood
to think and pray.   While he was in the wood, this text
came into his mind and comforted him : " Commit thy
way unto the Lord.   Trust also in Him, and He will bring
it to pass."   " Yes," he thought, " though I am banished
from house and home, and don't know where to take my
wife and children for shelter to-morrow, yet God, my God,
sees me in this dark wood.   Now is the time to trust Him.
He will show me the way through.   He will ' bring it to
pass.' "   He was so happy that he had remembered that
text, and so thankful to God, that he tried to make the
text into a hymn, as he paced up and down beneath
the trees.   Every verse begins with a word or two from
the text, so that if you read the first words of each verse
you just read the text.   When he went into the house he
told his wife about the text, and began to repeat to her
his hymn.   She soon dried her tears (the children had
already gone to sleep), and became as hopeful and trustful
as Paul Gerhard himself.

They had scarcely retired to rest when they heard
a great noise at the door.   It seemed as though some
important person was knocking there.   When the land-

lord opened the door, a man on horseback said, aloud,
"I am a messenger. I come from Duke Christian of
Merseburg, and I am in search of Paul Gerhard. Do you
know whether he has passed this way?" "Paul
Gerhard!" said the landlord; "yes, he is in this house."
"Then let me see him instantly," said the Duke's
messenger. And the messenger handed to the good
man a large sealed letter. It came from the good Duke
Christian, and it said, "Come into my country, Paul
Gerhard, and you shall have church, and people, and
house, and home, and livelihood, and liberty to preach the
Gospel to your heart's content."

So the text was true, dear children. Remember
it as long as you live. "Commit thy way unto the Lord.
Trust also in Him, and He will bring it to pass."

The paternal German Government irritated Mr
Curwen's *laisser faire* notions :—

I was much grieved and distressed the other day
at the manner in which the harvest feast was kept in
this village. It commenced on Sunday, after half-past
ten in the morning, and was celebrated by the most
universal public-house attendance, feasting, dancing, and
playing of music, that I ever saw in my life. By great
numbers the feast was continued on Monday. At twelve
o'clock I heard music on the river. It was a brass
band from Mannheim coming to play at the "Black
Eagle" close by. Going to the bottom of the orchard
an hour or two afterwards, I saw the same band moving
off in a boat, and playing a farewell tune. Lo! the police
had forbidden it! "As many bands as you like on
Sunday, but on Monday the people must not be encouraged to leave their work!" And so these submissive
Germans were going harmoniously away. In England,

such an interference with the "musical liberty of the subject" would have been accompanied with a "barring out" of the police, and a playing of the band inside louder than before; and if at last expelled, the band would have gone away *in silence*, meditating letters to the newspapers, and planning a quiet resistance next time. This sturdy spirit and personal courage among our English people, which never "waits for a revolution" (as the people do here), is the salvation of our liberties. Hateful as revelry is to me, I could almost have joined with these men if they had resisted this meddlesome police.

Mr. Curwen even draws lessons in favour of voluntaryism from the subject of chimney-sweeping :—

The "meddling" of paternal government *can* "go a step further" than I have mentioned above. One Saturday evening when, according to the fashion of English households, the maid had carefully cleaned her kitchen and made it tidy, we were favoured with a visit from the government chimney-sweep! A dreadful apparition to good housekeepers at such a moment! Our kitchen chimney, however, had been swept by a neighbour for us a few days before; so we felt at ease. But our peace was delusive; for the official assured us that the chimney *was not* swept! In vain we affirmed and protested. *He* was *the* sweep for that district! Who could possibly know better than he! Willing to save our poor English cook trouble, we asked whether paying the money would do. "Yes; that would do very well." We thought it best, however, that the man should give an honest testimony to his paternal government that our chimneys were safely swept; so we required him to go through the form of sweeping clean chimneys.

If this important government "department" was established for the sake of preventing fires, it did not answer its purpose at Ziegelhausen, for the house of the dressmaker had been burned down shortly before. Perhaps it had been better if the sweeping of the dress-maker's chimney had been left to her own sense of self-preservation, instead of waiting for the action of "a government department!" I commend these facts to the consideration of those Englishmen who evidently suppose "the government" to be some wonderful wise *being*, capable of an ever-watchful, omnipresent, incorruptible, super-human activity, and imagine that it is far more fit to manage our social affairs than the natural instincts which God has given us for the purpose!

Here we have another picture of a religious service :—

The truest manifestation of religious life I have yet seen in Germany, was the Baden Annual Missionary Meeting, held at Weinheim, about three weeks ago. I went to it in company with my friend Mr. Davis (late of Wandsworth), and Herr Mauch. At half-past five, on a fresh and very lovely summer morning, we watched the mountain pictures on the clear mirror of the Neckar, till Carl, to whom we had called aloud some time before, broke the beautiful images with the paddle of his ferry-boat. The walk to Heidelberg was warm and pleasant, and when we reached the station we soon found ourselves in a third-class carriage, and in the midst of a goodly company of what appeared to be Methodist ministers and Methodist people! I could scarcely imagine myself in Germany. A number of other carriages were soon filled in the same way. In our carriage there were two Protestant "Sisters of Mercy," known by their plain black bonnets. We had not been far on our journey before these sisters started a tune, and soon everyone was joining heartily in a fine old German psalm. As soon as one song was finished another commenced ; and in the intervals of our verses, we could hear that the next carriage, not blessed with so many female voices as ours, was also vigorously sustaining its psalm tune. In this delightful manner we came in view of Weinheim, with its little river, its rock and ruined castle, and its background of mountains. Then what greetings at the station! Christian friends from all parts of Baden had met together. The ladies were very quiet, but the gentlemen "greeted one another with a holy kiss." Such a hearty resounding kiss it was ; and then a shake of the hands to finish it off! Our delicate word kiss, does not at all express the thing. They call it here a "kooss!" About 300 persons had come to this missionary festival by the same train, and many others had arrived the night before. It was a general assembly of the people called Pietists— ministers and others. It was delightful to see the free mingling of rich and poor, and the happy faces every- where. The two churches were crowded. A paper of hymns was handed to everyone as he entered the door ; and wondrously grand was the mighty out-singing of the great congregation. The hymns were very simple, and expressive of religious feeling rather than of doctrine. I never heard anything like it, except at a Methodist missionary meeting, and then, though the voices would not be nearly so strong, and clear, and well sustained, our English part-singing would give a softness and richness to the effect, which I should be sorry to lose. But evangelical Christians make a "melody in the heart," vibrating to the same chords, whether in Germany or in England.

K

CHAPTER IX.

1856—1861.

RETURN FROM GERMANY — BUILDING OF A NEW CHURCH—
STUDY OF HARMONY — LITERARY STYLE — MODE OF
WORKING—MR. ASHCROFT'S RECOLLECTIONS—CORRESPOND-
ENCE CLASSES—GERSBACH'S HARMONY—SABBATH HYMN
AND TUNE BOOK—DR. LOWELL MASON ON EXPRESSION
IN PSALMODY—SONGS AND TUNES FOR EDUCATION—A
LADY'S RECOLLECTIONS—CONCERTS—RESIGNS PRESIDENCY
OF THE TONIC SOL-FA ASSOCIATION.

MR. CURWEN benefitted greatly by his stay in Germany.
He came back fresher and more vigorous than ever,
although to some of his congregation at Plaistow he
appeared to be shockingly changed for the worse, for
he wore a beard! His hair at this time, as a photograph
shows, was still black, not even speckled with the grey
which afterwards turned to a snowy white. He had
worn the beard in Germany as a protection from face-ache,
to which he was subject, and had found its protection most
beneficial. It is a curious contribution to the history of
fashion to put on record that when he appeared among his

congregation in this plight several of them declared that they could not possibly listen to his ministrations. One gentleman, indeed, when the bearded minister ascended the pulpit, walked out of the church, followed by his family. He had therefore to choose between offending these "weaker brethren" and enduring face-ache. He chose the faceache, and shaved off his beard.

On his return from Germany Mr. Curwen plunged into two occupations—the building of a new church for his congregation at Plaistow, and the elaboration of a system of harmony for Tonic Sol-fa students. The labour of collecting funds in a district which had by this time been deserted by "the gentry" was enormous; in fact it is difficult to believe that £3,000 was raised and a church capable of seating 800 or 900 people opened in March, 1860. Mr. Curwen threw all his energy into the task; begged of all the friends he could count; gave up his garden for a bazaar; and by his earnestness inspired his congregation to heroic efforts in the cause.

All this while he was pursuing his study of methods of harmony. Mention is made of this because it was the subject which tried most severely his skill as an educationist, and though his progress in forming a system was slow, he always looked back with pleasure upon the success which at last rewarded him. Mr. Curwen was always a slow worker. His books, especially his later ones, are crowded with detail, and only those who worked with him as amanuenses have any conception of the laborious investigation which he imposed upon himself in preparing them. He would often work for weeks at a point before light came, and his plans of treating it were matured. His literary work was almost all dictated. He found it a relief to sit in his easy chair, surrounded by his books of reference, and speak his sentences to a clerk.

Mr. Curwen's literary style was unambitious, and always subordinated to its end. He used plain words, never spent his wits upon form or epigram, but considered only force and clearness of exposition or argument. There was no parade of learning, and professional cant phrases or technicalities were, as far as possible, swept away. He had a great faculty of assuming the position of a learner, and held that a writer should aim to be intelligible to those who do not understand his subject, as well as to those who do. One of his hobbies was his objection to the use of the words "former" and "latter." He never used them, and struck them out in MSS which he revised. "Why," he used to argue, "should an author, from pure laziness, compel a reader to look back to see which of two nouns he is speaking of?" Friends who read to him their lectures or books before publication often derived much help from his criticisms. He knew how to suggest all the possible misconstructions

which a dull hearer or reader might put upon an
ambiguous sentence.   In lectures and addresses he laid
stress on ending well.   "Repeat your arguments and
clench them," he used to say,—"drive the nail home."

Mr. Andrew Ashcroft, who was for many years a co-
worker with Mr. Curwen in the Tonic Sol-fa movement,
has written the following :—

I first made the personal acquaintance of the late
Mr. Curwen during the last days of the year 1856,
immediately after his return from Germany.

I had joined the committee of the Tonic Sol-fa
Association shortly before.   The arrival of Mr. Curwen at
once gave a strong impulse to our operations.   Although
there were many causes for anxiety, and though we were
burdened with debt, many important operations were at
once undertaken and successfully carried out.   The first
Exeter Hall meeting (31st March, 1857), the Children's
Meeting at Exeter Hall (24th June, 1857), and at last
that extraordinary success, the first Crystal Palace
meeting, held on the memorable 2nd September, 1857,
followed one another with such rapidity as to tax the
powers of all engaged.

I have a lively recollection of our president in all
these, and following these, in a long series of laborious
undertakings, culminating in the choral competition and
performance of " Israel in Egypt " in 1862.

During these six years our intercourse was almost
constant.   The Finance Committee of the Tonic Sol-fa
Association (Mr. Wilmot, the late Mr. Starling, and
myself) formed the chief executive in most of the

important demonstrations which were held. And in those which were not directly the work of the Association, we, as individuals, took an active part.

I thus knew Mr. Curwen intimately in the very busiest part of his public life. I believe that very little of importance in that public life was unknown to me. I was much behind the scenes, and in the 1862 meetings, being one of his commissioners, had very much confided to me which could not be made public. What impression of *him* comes up as I think now ? First—Beyond all doubt there rises the memory of a man of *thorough honesty of soul.* Upright to the very core of his being ; instinctively turning from all crooked ways ; scorning all indirect, doubtful paths ; trusting in truth and in right. And then I think comes the recollection of his genuine *kindness of heart.* Very tender—caring personally for those he worked with, not as means to his ends, not as helpers to the true and good mainly, but as men and women, yes sometimes as children, for children helped us greatly sometimes.

I experienced his kindness very frequently in this way, and notably I remember his care of me when, after the 1862 meetings, I fell into bad health. How he insisted on providing me with the best medical attendance, and the best wine ; more thought of as helpful then by both of us than afterwards.

Perhaps, most of all, when temporary difference of judgment made us take opposite sides on administrative questions, his kindness bore that test and never wavered.

I suppose I should give a prominent place to his well-known *tenacity of purpose.* It was not at all easy for him to give up an undertaking or an idea. He was resolute and courageous too. Indeed, the chief difference of judgment between those who then worked in the cause and himself, was that we could not bring ourselves to undertake some of the large plans which our president proposed. I remember that we at one time had under consideration a series of meetings, one element only ' of which was the performance of Bach's motet "Jesu King of Glory," at the Crystal Palace by some thousands of voices. He was singularly *hopeful*, though many, many times he experienced such checks as would have discouraged weaker men.

He was very *teachable*. However firm in holding to his own views he could and did look on those of others. With all his strength he had a prevailing humility of spirit, beautiful but rare. In a remarkable degree he sought for truth as his main quest, words easy to write, but how hard to embody in life and work !

He was in deed and in truth a religious man. I had many opportunities of seeing how his very heart was touched by anything which showed the value of his movement in spreading the kingdom of our Lord and of His Christ. Nothing was really *separate* from this in his estimation. The closer anything came to it the more interest it had in his eyes.

I have said nothing about him as a teacher, as a philosopher — he was great as both, but to me his intellectual greatness always resolves itself into his moral greatness. He discovered much because he sought "not his own." He taught many because his heart was full of "goodwill."

The following letter illustrates much of what I have written :—

TO MR. ANDREW ASHCROFT.

Brighton, September 22nd, 1863.

We can, *in some cases*, serve a cause better outside an organization than in it, and I think we can more frequently do so in educational matters than in others. But it is far pleasanter to act with brethren, in the same work, and for the same ends, when that is possible. I am sure that I have been more useful to the Tonic Sol-fa cause since I left the Association, but I have often felt very lonely and heavy-hearted in the responsibilities I took upon me. I also think that before that time I was far more useful with the Association than I could possibly have been without it. We must just adopt the plans of individual or conjoint action which will best serve the great purposes we have in view at the time, and in the circumstances in which we are placed. When we cannot do what we *would* we must do what we *can*. Only in the church of Christ are we bound to act conjointly; only there *must* the individual keep with the brotherhood, "walking in fellowship," as John Owen called it. I feel very thankful for the case of hopeful usefulness you name. May the spirit of Christ be more and more among our teachers.

The first step Mr. Curwen took in the teaching of harmony was to gather a small company of disciples from various parts of the country, at Plaistow at Christmas, 1857, and give them a course of lessons. This was largely a tentative course, and suggested more difficulties than it removed. Mr. Curwen's first tract on the subject was not issued for four years (1861). This was immediately followed by the institution of "correspondence classes" for teaching harmony. It is characteristic of Mr. Curwen's organizing power that he should have hit upon this plan for reaching isolated students, which is now so generally adopted, and the " invention " of which, ten years or more later, has been recently claimed by several institutions.

The following, from the *Tonic Sol-fa Reporter*, July, 1861, shows the patient and prolonged thought which was devoted to the subject :—

My present object is simply to promote a more correct singing and a higher enjoyment of the music. These hints for observation are not built upon the ordinary *Grammars* but upon the *language itself* of music. They are offered to my beloved Tonic Sol-fa friends as the *first* fruit of many years' enquiry into the right educational method of presenting the subject of Harmony to the pupil. During all this time I have had invaluable assistance from Mr. James Stallybrass, who first studied in our Gersbach class at Christmas, 1857. He has applied the powers of a cultivated and patient mind, following my suggestions, and also offering many of his own, in analysing every chord in Palestrina's " Missa Papæ Marcellæ," Handel's " Messiah," Haydn's " Creation," and Mendelssohn's "Elijah." But the results of many, many years' labour to *the explorer* must often be presented in a single line, and that line not *new !* It is something, however, to have only begun sifting the *fanciful* from the *real* in musical theory, and to have discovered the relative *practical importance* of various chords, progressions, and accompaniments. Always remember that we do not *make* music simple. It *is* simple. We only remove the unnecessary "trappings" in which grammarians have dressed it.

Mr. Curwen met during his stay in Germany with an MS. work on harmony by Joseph and Anton Gersbach, teachers in the normal school at Carlsruhe. The two brothers had died before their work was published, and Mr. Curwen bought the MS. from the widow. He writes of it :—

"I obtained, two months ago, a very valuable manuscript work, the joint production of the two brothers, which had cost these highly educated men—thorough educationists as well as musicians—many years of thought and practical testing. It teaches the elements of harmony and composition, not by dogmatic instruction, but by making the pupil construct for himself little musical sentences, which are constantly increasing in difficulty and beauty as he goes on. It is the same plan (only with clearer grammar and more science), which Ollendorf has so successfully applied to the teaching of languages. Logier has done, and very well done, something of this kind for music. But this course of Gersbach, which was begun ten years before the publication of Logier's plan, is more scientific, more complete, and more beautiful. Even A. B. Marx's great work does not, in the first volume at least, equal Gersbach. The progress of Marx's pupil in the early steps is like that of a spider on a wall—upwards for a little—then dropping down again—then upwards once more. It really does attain the end, but by a miserable process, as it seems to me. Gersbach goes ever *onwards*, leaving nothing unexplored behind him; like a good surveyor, mapping the country as he goes.

On June 24th, 1857, the Tonic Sol-fa Association held a Juvenile Choral Meeting at Exeter Hall. Intense interest was excited by the success of this meeting, and as the Handel Orchestra was now standing empty at the Crystal Palace, the question was asked, "Why not fill it up with singing children?" This was answered in a month by the announcement that the Tonic Sol-fa Association would venture upon a concert of 3,000 children at the Crystal Palace on September 2nd. The result was an overwhelming success. Says an eye witness :—

The morning broke cold, damp, and foggy, and a drizzling rain fell almost without intermission until towards two o'clock, when it cleared up and became tolerably fine. Notwithstanding the rain, at an early hour large numbers of visitors began to assemble at the London Bridge Station, awaiting the departure of each train; and as the empty carriages were drawn up to the platform they were continually filled by dense masses of infantry, who assaulted the carriage doors amid loud shouts. Fresh carriages continually supplied the place of those which were whisked away ; and still the fierce assault continued with unabated vigour. One platform was found insufficient, and the Brighton Station was pressed into the service, and many trains made up and despatched from its platform. Still, however, the crowd increased ; and not only the platform, the booking offices, and the pavement in front of the station were covered with struggling people, but even the open space towards London Bridge was choked with women and children, who, as the soaking rain descended, groaned under their sad fate and umbrellas ; and, despairing of gaining an entrance into the station, made frantic efforts to sell their tickets at enormous sacrifices, and ultimately departed to their respective homes in tears and a cab. Many hundreds were unable to gain admission, and the scene at London Bridge was absolutely distressing.

When the day closed it was found that no less than 30,000 people had been at Sydenham, and thus, in the words of one of the papers, "It was left for an almost unknown institution to draw a larger concourse of persons than has ever been attracted in this country to listen to a musical performance." As to the singing, everyone seemed enraptured, the critics included. It was said by Mr. Curwen at the time that he believed every newspaper published in the English language contained some account, original or quoted, of the doings of the 3,000 children. The "leading journal" came out with its first notice of the system. So ended a day which lifted the movement to a national importance. In answer to demands on every side for a repetition of the concert, Mr. Curwen wrote : "We—committee, teachers, and conductors—are all worn out. As for the dear children, it would require a large amount of singing to wear them out. But too much exhibition is not good for them or for us. Our end is gained. Public attention is fixed on our method. For the whole winter let us quietly work."

Another fruit of Mr. Curwen's German experiences was the "Sabbath Hymn and Tune Book," which was issued in 1859. He adopted the German plan of placing hymn and tune upon the same page, and he marked the hymns for expression—plans which have since been adopted in " Hymns Ancient and Modern," and a crowd of other books. The "Sabbath Hymn and Tune Book" cost a great deal of labour, but it was not a success. Congregations prefer to chose their own tunes, and besides, the various denominations had begun at this time to issue their own books.

As to the plan of marking the hymns for expression, the following letter from Dr. Lowell Mason, on receiving a copy of the " Sabbath Hymn and Tune Book," will be read with interest. Its argument did not, however, carry conviction to Mr. Curwen :—

DR. LOWELL MASON TO MR. CURWEN.

South Orange, New Jersey, U.S., Nov. 4th, 1859.

How your letter brings up your kind attentions to me and to my wife when we were in London ! Thank you, and your excellent wife, for them ; our visits at your home were very pleasant, not to be forgotten, always remembered with gratitude and love by Mrs. Mason and myself. . . .

And now, dear sir, indulge me in a word or two in relation to congregational singing. I look with sorrow to some of your measures with that professed end in view. I will now mention one—the marking by a notation that which we call musical expression. You cannot work more directly against congregational singing than in this way. Have I not tried it out and out ? Have I not seen

congregational singing driven into the wilderness thus ?
Has not an attempt at the *artistic* been from the beginning
the death to religious influence in song? Surely you
know that history clearly informs us of this. Dear
brother, Christian people need for their religious growth
no such thing. All they want is a plain vocal form of
utterance. Mechanical aids to expression only divert the
mind from the true end. Go into your closet, shut your
door, on your knees offer prayer and praise in song. Do
you want marks of expression ? No. But I cannot
enlarge. With kindest recollections

I am, very truly yours,

LOWELL MASON.

"Songs and Tunes for Education," published at the
end of 1861, was a further result of Mr. Curwen's stay in
Germany, for the book is largely indebted to the
experience and the materials he gained while there. A
sentence from the preface betrays the moral purpose that
lay behind Mr. Curwen's musical work :—

It is not merely musical pleasure or musical training,
but a great Educational purpose, which this book holds
in view. It would have been easy to put together a
number of pretty pieces to delight the children ; but that
would not have satisfied the Editor's desire. He believes
that music in schools and families may be made a mighty
moral agent for developing and elevating the feelings and
sentiments of children. The ordinary school-work may
cultivate well the reasoning powers and the memory, but
it seldom does anything for the imagination and the
emotions. It is vitally important for us that our children
should feel rightly as well as think correctly, that they
should love truly as well as reason deeply.

A lady who was governess in Mr. Curwen's family at this time, contributes the following recollections :—

In one or two cases, where my will came into distinct collision with Mr. Curwen's, the recollection of his looks and words is clear enough. I owe Mr. Curwen a debt of gratitude—for to him I ascribe my power as a teacher, and to a large extent, my interest in educational questions.

The question at issue between us was the method of teaching, and the possibility of my then and there abandoning my old book-method, and taking to oral teaching.

As to the superiority of the oral method, I had even then no doubt; but, nervous and shy as I then was, I held fast to my personal inability to adopt the superior method. Well do I remember how Mr. Curwen, at first simply putting before me the arguments in favour of a change of method, gradually waxed stern and even wrathful, as he perceived the moral character of the opposition, and with unsparing faithfulness laid bare the motives that were holding me back from the discharge of duty. There was no word of duty, as between employer and employed; it was the duty to myself and to God that he urged on me ; and the mirror that he held up to me of my self-indulgence, pride and cowardice, revealed to me secrets of moral weakness that had been hidden from me till then.

Through all, the sense of wrong was what seemed to kindle him; that I should know the good and yet hold back because of its difficulty roused his indignation. And the searching character of his indignation lay in the force of his own moral nature—a force felt by all who came in contact with him.

Equally powerful was he as a stimulator to patient perseverance in work. In this character I learnt to know him before I had been three weeks in residence. I perceived that I had undertaken a charge beyond my power; I knew I had not force enough within me to restrain and develop the passions and intellect I found in his children. I frankly said so, and sought release; but the words of encouragement spoken, stimulated me to try again. Happily for me, for otherwise I should have missed the lessons of the after months; unhappy for the children, for though I yielded to Mr. Curwen's wish, my own judgment was justified by the result.

It was years before I would teach again for *pay*—I had thought I never should. Now I accept pay and know I am worthy of it.

The letter of Mr. Ashcroft, given above, has described the kind of work in which Mr. Curwen was at this time engaged. It was absolutely necessary, in order to establish the Tonic Sol-fa system in public regard, that large concerts should be given, not only of school children, but of adults where classical music could be sung. Mr. Curwen was thus forced into the anxious work of organising these meetings, which involved anxiety, labour, and heavy financial loss.

In 1858 Mr. Curwen had resigned the presidency of the Tonic Sol-fa Association. His reasons for this step are explained in two letters addressed to Mr. S. Linder, the treasurer :—

Brighton, November 13th, 1858.

MY DEAR FRIEND, MUCH LOVED AND HONOURED,—How long and faithfully and patiently and generously you have laboured with me in the Tonic Sol-fa cause! 'Tis hard to grieve you, but I fear I must do so, in telling you how resolved I am no longer to follow our committee in their non-educational, but rather exhibitional spirit and course. It is better for us, in the long run, to make a public failure while sustaining educational truthfulness, than to win a success by educational compromise. Both our Exeter Hall and Crystal Palace successes this year were won by a compromise of thorough educational truthfulness. I am sorry I did not see it so clearly a year ago. Numbers (by universal confession of the teachers) were admitted to the Exeter Hall choir, to whom it was as much an educational injury as it would be to pass a boy on from addition and subtraction at once to decimals. Vast numbers of our last Crystal Palace choir had never passed through any regular course of teaching—were only drilled up to the mark, and so injured like the others. And yet what desperate attempts there have been to continue that Exeter Hall choir! And what an outcry there is just now for another book of pretty Crystal Palace tunes, which may be drilled into the children, instead of the children being trained and developed up to them. No temporary successes, however much fame or money they may bring the Association, will ever reconcile me to this any more. I owe a great duty to the method as a truthful and educational one. I will strive that my name shall be only associated with its elevation. I think you wish to do so also, dear friend, but I am afraid you do not look at it educationally as I do.

Unfortunately the school teachers, who do understand educational points, are not all on my side.

L

You are at the head of a company of generous, disinterested, and devoted friends to our cause on the committee, from whom I feel it very hard to differ. If I were not an invalid far away, I should come and speak to them and you, and tell you all this.

Brighton, November 18th, 1858.

MY DEAR FRIEND,—Your cheerful note was very grateful to me just now. But it shows distinctly the different positions which you and I hold to the Tonic Sol-fa movement. Your position is simply that of benevolence. Mine is that of benevolence also, I hope, but of benevolence pre-eminently governed by true educational principles.

I hope the Association will continue its propaganda. It will, doubtless, win public successes. *I* must go back to foundation work. My one anxiety is that I should not be misconstrued by my friends.

Mr. Curwen's difference with the committee was really caused by his desire for thoroughness. It was not unnatural that others of his friends should be satisfied with the excellent results that were being achieved, without enquiring how far they were superficial. Mr. Curwen wanted to go deeper; he looked at everything seriously, and when his mind was once made up he was impatient of delay. This earnestness, while it was the great cause of his success in life, rather hindered his working with others. He of necessity led, and compromise and postponement were impossible for him.

The work of the Tonic Sol-fa movement at this time involved lecturing and travelling. Mr. Curwen had visited Scotland in 1855, and he continued to lecture in various parts of England as time allowed. In 1862 he paid a visit to Ireland, and he also read a paper on the system at the Social Science Congress in London.

Of Mr. Curwen's pastoral work at this period the following letter from a member of his congregation speaks :—

As a preacher he was powerfully simple. The first time I was really impressed with any idea of *personal* religion was on hearing a sermon preached by him in the old Chapel in North Street, Plaistow. I had been accustomed to a style of preaching which had never touched my heart or claimed my attention, and Mr. Curwen's sermon was, to me, a new revelation. After that I took frequent opportunities of hearing him, and was ever more and more impressed with the reality of the truth as he preached it. Afterwards I came to know him well, and then became a regular attendent and eventually a member of his church.

There was a depth of earnest pleading in his tone, and he had an impressive style of delivery. There was no hurry ; word followed word deliberately ; well and aptly put, and all in simple Saxon English, which adapted itself alike to the comprehension of the youngest or most illiterate of his congregation, and to the understanding of those of higher culture. His manner and language gave weight to everything Mr. Curwen said, carrying his teaching home to every heart, and leaving there the conviction that Christ was, to him, all in all, and that he would fain have everyone of his hearers believe as he himself did, and feel that peace which the full assurance of salvation through Christ our Saviour alone can give.

When he gave up the ministry all his congregation felt that they had lost a teacher whom to know was to love, and who had put the truth before them faithfully, earnestly, and sympathetically, as few others did or could.

For my part I have only met with one or two others who possessed that rare gift of chaining the attention by the manner as well as the matter; a natural, simple eloquence which no mere college training, or even deep learning, can impart.

CHAPTER X.

1861—1868.

AMERICAN CIVIL WAR—SIDES WITH THE NORTH—FOUNDS
THE FREEDMAN'S AID SOCIETY—LETTERS FROM CHARLES
SUMNER AND GEO. F. ROOT—TRIP DOWN THE CLYDE—
GROWTH OF THE TONIC SOL-FA MOVEMENT—FOUNDATION
OF TONIC SOL-FA SCHOOL—CERTIFICATES INSISTED ON—
NEW IDEAS—DR. HELMHOLTZ—INSTRUMENTAL INSTRUCT-
TION BOOKS—SETS UP A PRINTING OFFICE—REMOVES
TO UPTON PLACE—LETTER TO MR. COLIN BROWN—
RESIGNS CHARGE AT PLAISTOW—MR. W. F. CALLAWAY'S
RECOLLECTIONS—LETTER FROM MR. HENRY SMART—
EUING LECTURESHIP AT GLASGOW—JOINS STRATFORD
CONGREGATIONAL CHURCH—FRICTION IN LOCAL WORK—
A REBUKE—DEMONSTRATION AT KESWICK.

WHEN the American civil war broke out in 1861
Mr. Curwen at once saw the issues involved, and enthusiastically took the side of the North, from which he never
wavered. It did not shake his conviction in the least
to find that friends with whom he had all his life coincided in opinion were neutral or opposed to him, but it
gave him great pain. With his usual candour he told

some of his Manchester friends, who had invested capital in blockade runners, that he had prayed that their ships might be captured. The reader has already been told by several writers how inflexible he was; how every opinion and action were based on moral principle, and sustained by religious conviction. He saw that slavery was at the root of the war, and this was enough to decide him. He gave lectures, and got up numerous meetings to inform the people as to the real issues of the war.

Mr. Curwen never did things by halves. At times like this, when he threw himself into some new project, his house would be turned into a workshop, everyone engaged in addressing circulars, &c., and he himself busy with his secretary in letter-writing and pamphleteering.

Mr. Curwen quickly saw that the slaves who had been emancipated by the Lincoln proclamation would be thrown into temporary distress of the severest kind, and he organised the first Freedman's Aid Society that was formed in England. For some months he acted as convener and secretary, and drew up the resolutions that were passed at the inaugural meeting at Exeter Hall, for which he made all the arrangements. Sir Fowell Buxton became the treasurer, and the cheque book shows that several hundred pounds were forwarded to the States. Mrs. Curwen became secretary of a Ladies' Auxiliary. The two following letters, belonging to this period, are interesting :—

Washington, April 14th, 1863.

MADAM,—In any association for the help of the slave I shall be glad to be remembered. It is but little that I can do, I fear ; but I pray you to let me be inscribed among your associates. But permit me to add that, at this moment, the best help to the slave which England can afford, will be the indignant rejection by the Government of the infamous pretension that a new State, ostentatiously founded on slavery, can be recognised in the family of nations. Let this pretension be scouted and blasted as an insult to religion and morals, and all the best traditions of English history ; and then slavery and the Slave Power, obscene and revolting, will receive a blow from which they can never recover.

Believe me, madam,

Very faithfully yours,

CHARLES SUMNER.

New York, October 16th, 1862.

MY DEAR SIR,—I am very glad to get your photograph and to send you mine in return. What you say of my music is very pleasant to me and my friends, but what you say of our torn and bleeding country moves us profoundly, and we give thanks that there is one man in England who seems truly desirous that liberty should triumph.

Yours very truly,

GEO. F. ROOT.

At home Mr. Curwen encouraged the holding of concerts in aid of the Lancashire distress, and several Tonic Sol-fa teachers set to work to hold singing classes among the cotton workers, whose time hung heavy on their hands.

The following extract from the *Tonic Sol-fa Reporter* of October, 1862, describes a visit to Scotland which Mr. Curwen had just paid :—

The Firth of Clyde ! Oh for another month on those shores, with lochs, and seas, and mountains spread before us ! What warm-hearted friends Tonic Sol-fa has brought us ! What beautiful lands it takes us to ! But we return to our work rejoicingly, and dream over the pleasant memories of that summer time. The trip to Loch Goil-head, with Tonic Sol-fa teachers from many neighbourhoods, through a Scotch mist, which we did not care for, the singing on the bridge of the trout-stream, the little fugues from " Standard Course," as we came back to Gourock, the true-hearted adieus, how pleasant they are to the memory ! The crowded Greendyke Hall, the hearty singing of the poor children, Mr. Miller's sharp questioning, and the quick answers they gave him, Mr. Livingstone's address, Dr. Johnstone's humorous speech—our heart was in it all ! Then the Free Church Normal Establishment, with school upon school of children, and nearly two hundred students, all doing credit to Sol-fa, the highest class of students singing in a manner worthy of a Tonic Sol-fa competition—they only strengthened our confidence in Mr. McLelland's faithful teaching ! The Girls' Reformatory, the grateful message of those bright and pleasant children to Miss Glover ! The Boys' Reformatory, some in the school writing descriptions of their trip to gather mussels at Arrochar, others at work wood-cutting, shoemaking, tailoring, baking, and bookbinding (the secret of their reformation being that they always have something to do, are not even allowed to play *idly)* ; the school, which only the magistrates can supply with scholars, which " sweeps the streets !" which glories in lessening its numbers ! Mr. Miller delights to make music do them good ! That quiet brotherly conference in Mr. Miller's spacious rooms ; what courage it gave us ! What plans for future work ! That long talk about harmony with three friends, by the pleasant upper window at Ashton ! The examinations for the advanced certificate, so eagerly and perfectly worked through ! Then the invitation from that fine set of Edinburgh students, which, alas ! we could not accept ! The ebony walking-stick, gift of a harmony analysis student, which will do both for pointer and bâton on all worthy occasions ! Ah ! when will such refreshing dreams come over again !

The Tonic Sol-fa movement absorbed more and more of Mr. Curwen's time. The spread of the system had been very rapid. The following represents estimates that were made of the number of pupils :—

1853	2,000	1862	141,000
1856	20,000	1863	186,000
1858	65,000		

The year 1863 was, in many respects, important in the history of the movement. Mr. Curwen determined to direct his energies to raising the quality rather than extending the area of the work done by Tonic Sol-fa teachers. He announced this determination in the *Tonic Sol-fa Reporter* for January, 1864, as follows :—

Mr. Curwen has, for some time past, seen the necessity of giving his chief attention to the improvement of Tonic Sol-fa teachers, rather than to the spreading abroad of the Tonic Sol-fa method. If an educational method is good, and its teachers competent, every new pupil becomes a propagandist. The propagation of the method will, therefore, take care of itself; that is, it may be safely left to the various Tonic Sol-fa Associations, to the monthly appeals of the *Tonic Sol-fa Reporter*, and to the zeal of its devoted teachers. All the central influence which Mr. Curwen needs to exert should, he thinks, be directed to improvement, rather than to propagation.

Mr. Curwen now formed what he described as " The Tonic Sol-fa School," which afterwards developed into the Tonic Sol-fa College, and concerned itself with training, examining, and certifying teachers, holding normal classes, &c.

Mr. Curwen also began, in this year, a struggle which strained his relationships with many Tonic Sol-fa friends for several years, but which he was convinced was for the right. He resolved not to countenance by his presence or by notice in the *Tonic Sol-fa Reporter* any concerts in which the pupils had not taken a certificate of competency. Slowly, but surely, the leading teachers came round to his view, but the battle was a long one, and it was a pain to him to absent himself from the annual concerts of children at the Crystal Palace, as he did for several years in consequence of this resolve.

The importance which Mr. Curwen attached to the certificates, and the reasons for their usefulness, are fully explained in a lecture which he delivered years after (1875) :—

Untested teaching is disappointing to all—to the teacher as well as to the pupil. If there are any of you who are engaged in the honourable profession of teacher, you will, I am sure, agree with me when I say that " We never know that we have taught a pupil anything till we have got it back again from that pupil." Some of you may have had my experience. I have given a lesson and have thought of it afterwards as one of the best I had given—the points well brought out, the illustration good, and the exercises well done by the body of the class, and then, a few days afterwards, I have fallen in with one of the pupils who has misapprehended my teachings on almost every point, and is quite incapable, of doing the exercises! If that pupil had known that he would meet me and would be so closely cross-questioned, depend upon it he would have given ten times more attention to the work of the class. Now, we ought to put *every pupil* into that position. Every pupil should listen because he is expecting to be examined. Every pupil should work because he expects to be tested. I know some have claimed that it is easy to gather a chorus of good voices, and to prepare them to sing even difficult music for a concert, without any such sifting of knowledge or skill as I have referred to. Yes, this is true except for the word " easy." Any one can thus get up a few pieces, on any system or no system, with certificates or without them. But, first, if the programme is at all classical the work will not be *easy*. I am sorry to say that I once had the weakness to train a class wholly of elementary certificates for so simple a classic as Mozart's " Twelfth Mass." But I was frequently coming upon rhythms far beyond the difficulty of the elementary certificate, and such as would tax the rhythmical perceptions of well practised inter- mediates, and I not unfrequently met with transitions and modulations which the elementary ear had never dreamt of. Every such difficulty was a miserable sticking point, especially as I was never satisfied with only a quarter of the class being able to conquer it, and the disappointing thing was that when by exhausting perseverance we had gained the victory, if the same difficulties occurred again in some slightly different form, we had to go back and fight the same battle over again.   If the singers had previously gone through a proper drill of rhythms and transitions and modulation they would either have felt no difficulty, or would have known how to conquer it easily.   Herr Wieck, in his " Clavier und Gesang," constantly reiterates that the *drill* of the pupil should always go beyond the *pieces* he has to execute.   What he says of the pianoforte will apply also to singing.   Besides this, suppose that by selecting good natural voices and setting the clever singers to lead the rest you do succeed in getting up and performing with good taste a certain set of pieces, what have you done ?   A concert is not the teacher's object in life.   His object is to increase the *musical faculty* of each one of his pupils.   Simply to get together a number of singers who can only perform well as long as *he* is present, as long as *he* gives them the cue, as long as *he* shows them the expression, as long as *he* and his " leaders" help them over the difficult places—to make a number of dependents on one's self—is a very poor and unworthy ambition.   The plan of picking out good voices and setting them to sing by rote—the rote and voice plan—is superficial ; superficial in the know- ledge it gives, superficial in the enjoyment of its pupils, and very superficial for any purposes of usefulness.   It is onesided.   It does not cultivate the musical faculty " all

round." A man under such management may have a
good voice, or he may have a good power of reading at
sight, or he may have a quick and correct ear, or he may
have a sense of propriety in musical expression. He may
have whichever of these faculties comes most easily to
him, but he is not *required* to have them *all*. Good
teaching requires not only increase of one faculty, but
increase of all the sister faculties.

Knowing this we have made the most strenuous
efforts, through a series of years, to establish a system of
graded examination, ascending from the humblest, which
can be passed in a junior school to some which, if not
very high, are at all events very respectable as indications
of musical attainment. It has been a long and resolute
labour on the part of teachers throughout the country
which has given to our set of certificates the general
respect and public recognition which they now enjoy. It
was no small matter to create a public opinion in favour
of true education, but now after some years of labour we
are able to tell you that last Midsummer our College
had granted, great and small, 150,000 certificates !
Think of the number of *genuine* pupils ! It is like the
population of a great city ! Think of the patience and
zeal of the examiners ! Help us, all you that love truthfulness to put honour upon and to sustain the certificates !

Up to this time a knowledge of the staff notation had
been compulsory for every certificated Tonic Sol-fa pupil,
but now the staff notation test was made optional. The
first idea of the new notation as merely introductory to
the staff was modified, and it expanded henceforth into
a concurrent system. Mr. Curwen has been blamed for
not continuing to insist, as he did at first, on the subordi-

nation of his new notation to the old, and making all the pupils proceed to study the musical staff. The rapid growth of Tonic Sol-fa literature, however, rendered it possible to get the results at which he aimed, *i.e.* music in schools, homes, and congregations, without the staff, and the pupils were often unwilling to study it. The tendency of the movement in recent years has been to give more thorough attention to the staff notation, and though the test is still optional in all Tonic Sol-fa certificates, two-thirds of the pupils voluntarily pass it.

Mr. Curwen was always on the alert for new ideas in the teaching or the theory of music, which were likely to benefit his disciples. Almost immediately on the publication of Helmholtz's work "Die Lehre von den Tonempfindungen," he presented a summary of its teaching to the readers of the *Tonic Sol-fa Reporter*. It was not until 13 years later that Mr. A. J. Ellis's English translation of this great work was published, and its author's discoveries became generally known in England. Dr. Helmholtz visited England in 1864, and in connexion with this visit the following letter is interesting :—

London, April 21, 1864.

SIR,—I have received the books concerning the Tonic Sol-fa Society and their methods which you had the kindness to send me, and I beg you to accept the sincere expression of my thanks for them. As the time I had to spend was very short, I was not able to visit another singing class than that at Tottenham Court Road on

Wednesday afternoon. I went there with Mr. A. J.
Ellis. We were really surprised by the readiness and
surety with which the children succeeded in reading
music that they did know before, and in following a series
of notes which were indicated to them on their Modula-
tory board. I think what I saw showed the complete
success of your system, and I was peculiarly interested
by it, because, during my researches in musical acoustics
I came from theoretical reasons to the conviction that
this was the natural way of learning music, but I did
not know that it had been carried out in England with
such beautiful results.

Believe me to be your obedient servant

DR. H. HELMHOLTZ.

Mr. Curwen wrote a New Year's address to Sunday
school teachers in 1864, at the request of the Sunday
School Union. He entitled it "The Teacher's Tools ;" by
which he means certain habits of mind and heart which
the teacher must keep in vigorous use, ready and bright.
Presence of mind is the first tool ; this he describes by
a favourite word, "gumption." It is partly a gift, but
mainly an acquirement which comes to those who strive to
concentrate their attention. Fulness of information is the
next tool ; he urges teachers to be ready upon their own
ground ; to buy books as fast as they can master them,
but no faster. The power of picturing comes next, this
depends on realising the scene you are describing, and
living in it. The teacher who fails to win or keep
attention may learn by heart the published lessons of

skilled teachers, and give them to his class, until he gains
the power he lacks. Skill in probing is necessary ; it is
the art of finding out what a child does not know, and
where he fails to follow the meaning of a word or an
argument. Probing is done by questions, which should
suggest, and set the children thinking in the right way.
Loving patience is the next tool ; the power of personal
sympathy with children, and of individualising them.
Last and mightiest comes a joyful faith both in Christ and
in the possibilities of the teacher's work.

The instrumental hand books upon which Mr. Curwen
was now working, were very interesting to him. He
wrote books for teaching all the different instruments—
organ, pianoforte, harmonium, stringed, brass, and wood.
In the preface to the "String Band Book" Mr. Curwen
explains how he has been pushed into this work by the
activity and ambition of his disciples :—

A good instruction book has been likened to a new
road through some rugged country, hitherto difficult of
access, the interior of which abounds in wealth and
beauty. Such a road once made will last a long time, and
facilitate the travelling of thousands. This simile will
explain my aim and hope, as well as the nature and
responsibility of my work, in this series of Band Books
for Tonic Sol-fa Pupils. I have been drawn on step
by step in this important duty of Road Making. Each
new road made the travelling so easy, that the travellers
wished to penetrate farther into the same country, and by
similar roads. Beginning with Miss Glover's great broad

road of the musical ladder and a keynote notation, I tried to teach children and promote Psalmody. But I soon found that Psalmody could not be promoted alone, that there must go along with it, not only the cheerfulization of the school, but also the healthy and innocent recreation of young people. They were not content to follow a musical road which stopped at Psalmody. I had, therefore, to adapt my musical works to their requirements, and to try to open plain paths into the subjects of Expression and Voice Training, in connection with Part-songs and Glees. But I found that as our pupils' taste was cultivated they would not stop even here ; their desire became intense for the Oratorio and Cantata. Some experiments proved that the Tonic Sol-fa classes most excelling in these studies were exactly those who in their own Churches did the most to sustain the Psalmody, and sought to develop that Psalmody on the simplest and most religious principles. Therefore, to retain their services, it was necessary to provide fresh roads into the subjects of Modulation and Harmony in connection with Classic Music. All this while, however, a cry constantly arose to our ears, " Your simple roads to vocal music are of no use to us when we take a musical instrument in hand. All the instruments are taught in direct relation to absolute pitch. Your great principle of key relationship is worse than useless to us here. It would be quite foolish of us to travel by one road to the music of the voice, and by another to that of instruments. We must, therefore, leave you, for you do not enable us to accompany our voices on the piano, or even to take up Flute, Cornet, or Violin for occasional recreation,—much less do you enable us to supply an orchestra for the great Oratorios and Cantatas which we have learned to enjoy." I was, therefore, obliged to study instruments, and the

M

proper modes of teaching them on Tonic principles. I would gladly have excused myself this labour, but I found that the use and teaching of instruments were so indissolubly connected in the minds of musicians, with ideas of absolute pitch, that it was very difficult, almost impossible, to get them to look at the subject from my standpoint, besides, that very few of them were sufficiently acquainted with our Tonic Sol-fa principles to give me much aid in the earlier steps.

Mr. Curwen's way of going to work at these books was radical. He would first buy and read all the existing books he could find. Then he would hunt up, through an instrument maker or a music shop, some successful teacher,—a man, perhaps, of poor education, but of skill and experience with pupils. He would get him to his house—a smart drum-major or an old 'cello player—turn him inside out, discuss with him, get at the main difficulties of the instrument, and the order in which they should be attacked, try to beat the drum or scrape the 'cello himself, so as to sympathise fully with the beginner. This work was congenial ; Mr. Curwen had a passion for methodising, and the delight with which he saw the fog clearing from an obscure point, or the logical plan of arrangement unfolding itself to him, was very great.

In 1862 and 1863 Mr. Curwen set up a small printing office at Plaistow. The printing of his notation and of his books, which were full of unusual tables, signs, &c., had always been a trouble to the printers, and a trouble to Mr. Curwen. The manuals applying the Tonic Sol-fa notation to instruments, on which he was now working, were specially complex and troublesome to print. He felt that it would be an advantage to have immediate control of the printers, and educate them to his own work. This printing office, which began in a room in a cottage in 1863, gradually expanded until it took in all Mr. Curwen's publications.

Mr. Curwen was at this time much out of health, and felt the need of systematic exercise. He was not one of those men who move by clockwork, and take " constitutionals." Whatever he had in hand absorbed his whole being, and he would remain in his study for days if a knotty point baffled him. He saw that he should never walk unless he were obliged. This was why he determined to do his writing at the printing office, and remove from Plaistow, so as to be compelled to have a walk. He settled in Upton Place, about a mile from Plaistow, and was much benefited by the change.

The following letter to his friend, Mr. Colin Brown, of Glasgow, was written at this time :—

TO MR. COLIN BROWN.

Forest Gate, April 28, 1864.

My Dear Friend,—I am slowly recovering from one of the sharpest illnesses that I have had for a long time. The doctors call it bronchitis. I felt it to be inflammation of the chest. It has about filled up the interval since my last note to you. I am hoping, however, to walk to Plaistow and back to-morrow with the help of my Tonic Sol-fa stick, which has been my daily companion along these lanes, and the silver knob of which talks to me of you and of our noble Tonic Sol-fa work. I often, in these walks, wish that I could get a few quiet hours with you, and secure your true-hearted counsel about the many things which press upon me just now, as well as about a Just Intonation Instrument; our Plaistow Schools, how to build them; my printing office, which partly sharp competition and partly the peculiarity of our instrumental books, has compelled me to burden myself with; my boys, am I obliged also to make them Sol-faists and printers? the brass bands, what *good* can we bring out of them? the wood bands and the string bands, how to melt and mould them into our Sol-fa "method;" how to find a good literature for them; and then how to train players, and how to use them for noble purposes! The instrumental undertaking is four times as costly as I expected, but it is a fine exercise of mind. Indeed, it is very interesting, bringing to my knowledge strange persons and strange things. The reason of my under-taking it (which please do not mention, for it sounds conceited) was to prevent other people doing it *super-ficially* or badly, and so bringing irretrievable disgrace on our method. But at present it feels secularising. I wish it done and done with. It is *necessary* in order to strengthen other parts of our movement, and I hope I shall be able to bring better fruits out of it than I can at present realise. Pray for me, my dear friend, that I may be kept faithful to the great end of our enterprise—God's glory—and that I may be strengthened to do even the humblest and heaviest work which tends to that end.

My joyfullest work, since I saw you, has been in the central psalmody meetings. At the last, and best, I conducted with my Sol-fa stick and its shining knob.

Mr. Curwen continued his lecturing. In the autumn of 1864 he was at Cardiff and Merthyr, and presided over a week of meetings at Bristol. Later on he went to Manchester, Bradford, Liverpool, and Halifax. At the end of the year he addressed a circular to all the Metropolitan Theological Colleges, offering to lecture for them, and circulated far and wide a double number of the *Tonic Sol-fa Reporter*, devoted to the promotion of psalmody.

The close of the year 1864 brought the twenty-first anniversary of Mr. Curwen's Plaistow pastorate. He had enjoyed the help of a co-pastor—the Rev. J. W. Coombs, B.A.—for a year or more previously, but the relief had not been sufficient, and he felt that he could no longer do justice both to his Church and to the Tonic Sol-fa movement. He therefore resigned, and on December 16th was presented by the congregation with a parting testimonial. Many affectionate words were said on both sides. Mr. Curwen, though he ceased to preach, continued to attend the church, and aided in the erection of new schools, which were built at a cost of £2,000, raised entirely by voluntary help, and opened in 1866.

The beautiful sketch of Mr. Curwen's character which follows, is written by Mr. W. F. Callaway, Con-

gregational minister at Birmingham. Mr. Callaway's
recollections of Mr. Curwen begin at this date :—

My personal knowledge of Mr. Curwen began in
1865. I was one of the many persons who, in spite of a
supposed incapability, had learned to sing from note by
help of the Tonic Sol-fa system. I was very grateful for
what seemed to me like the bestowal upon me of a new
faculty, and thought of my benefactor's knowledge and
skill with wondering amazement.

He came to Birmingham, and I met him. Then I
learned to admire the man himself even more than the
work he had done. At the first meeting there was a
hearty cheeriness in his manner which promised much.
He seemed so truly to be glad to make new acquaintances.
This was more apparent the more one saw of him.
He had no suspicion of strangers, no disposition to keep
them in quarantine until he could be sure that a closer
acquaintance was desirable. He seemed to like to believe
in men to begin with, even if his faith had to be qualified
or lessened afterward. He could do this the more safely
that he was able to differ from men, to correct them, even
to rebuke them without any apparent hesitation, and
without any show of temper. Men who doubt their own
courage and strength need be careful what acquaintances
they make on the road. He had no fear, he could afford
to trust men, for he could protect himself.

But I noticed that he was very tolerant of differences
of opinion. He seemed to listen even to blank heresy of
musical doctrine, as if desiring to learn something ; to be
willing to acknowledge it if he could, but if not he would
question or suggest as if deferring judgment ; and then
would speak with great modesty, even when he spoke
most decidedly.

He was remarkably appreciative of the smallest merits in men. He seemed to find out the best thing in them, and to look at that.

He was entirely free from contempt for men who shewed want of breeding or educational deficiencies.

Then he showed so religious an interest in music. He was not carried away by an æsthetic passion ; but he cared for the art as a power ordained of God for high and blessed uses. His religiousness, indeed, showed itself in all things. It shone upon his face and sounded in his speech.

These were my first impressions.

My intercourse with him for some years was carried on chiefly by letters on the antiquities, the history, and the theory of music. The whole subject was new to me, and all facts were about equally interesting.

The born musician usually cares only for results. If a good effect can be obtained he is satisfied. It is of little interest to him how things were found out or grew ; and the experiments and defective theories of explorers are worthy of only a passing thought. He cares no more for the antiquities of the art, or the scientific analysis of sounds, than a successful horse-breeder does for theories of evolution.

Mr. Curwen never professed to be a born musician. He was a student of music in all its roots and branches, and he was willing to encourage all enquiry. He went down for himself into all the old long-disused mines and workings of the art, and noted everything with care. He brought up all that looked at all like ore, and turned it over many a time before he rejected it. It was through the humility of the man. Whatever seemed to have been thought valuable by any, he found it hard to esteem of no account.

Many will remember how long he handled the old disused modes of the scale, and sought to find a use for them. Yet his interest in such things was always secondary to his greater philanthropic purposes. When at intervals I saw him it was usually the case, that while willing to talk of such matters, his mind was more fully occupied upon some practical subject. How to make music help religion or education ; how to get access to schools or factories ; how to make his notation a more correct representation of musical facts, or more easily to be learned and understood, were the chief matter of his talk.

When, in the course of years, I came to be in some small measure a helper to him, his appreciativeness, his gentle forbearance, his wise masterfulness, his loftiness of purpose, and patience in working became more manifest. He talked very moderately of his schemes, and asked for outspoken criticism. Many men ask for criticism—he would accept it. He would speak of the work of others without depreciating it. When he mentioned others he was quick to speak well of them. If in anything he saw faultiness, or had to encounter opposition, he rather regretted than blamed. If any had wronged him he seemed ready and eager to forgive and forget. He was not unwilling to change an opinion, nor to acknowledge a mistake. He was not ashamed to speak of himself as still unlearning and learning, towards the very end of his life.

When one saw him in his own house one saw him, I think, at his best. Eye, and hand, and voice spake kindness and hospitality. He maintained many of the courtesies and gentlenesses, without any of the formality of the generation now passed away. He seemed to have brought a benediction from an older world, which he shed freely on the new. The family life which had shaped

itself under his governance, was very pleasant to behold,
and he, with his manly comeliness, benignly venerable,
but full of cheery interest in all about him, was fit to be
its head.

Next to seeing him in his house, it was good to see
him in your own. He was so homely and so easily
pleased. He seemed so to enjoy things. He made the
best of everything. He so loved children and so understood them. They could not keep their accustomed
shyness before him ; they could not pretend to be afraid.
They gave in at once. Many a child will, through life,
retain a dreamlike memory of "an old man, gray, and
white, and dovelike," who talked to them in a round
pleasant voice, and then passed away.

No wonder he was famous for addresses to the young.
" What ! Mr. Curwen ?" said a working man to me,
looking at the name in a poster on the wall, " Why I
remember him when I was a tiny little boy. He came to
address our Sunday School. I didn't think he was alive
now ; but I have never forgotten him."

When he was addressing an assembly of children, or
even when he was talking to one little child, you saw the
whole man. The love of his kind, which inspired and
ruled his whole life, beamed out then. His eager interest
in little things, while never forgetting those transcend-
ently great, his passion for making something understood,
his genius for illustration, his power of drawing out the
whole faculty of the learner, his genial broad humanity,
ready for laughter or for tears, all showed themselves
then.

Few men set their hands to so great a work as his,
and live to see it so far completed. He was for ever
improving the Tonic Sol-fa system, and writing new
educational books, but I think he had at last finished

nearly all the tasks he had set himself, and the plough was in the last furrow when the night came down upon him, and he went home.

The Tonic Sol-faists were now crying out for better music, and Mr. Curwen had to set himself to supply them. He persuaded several leading English composers to write pieces, both sacred and secular. The following letter belongs to this time :—

MR. HENRY SMART TO MR. CURWEN.

3, Fitzroy Road, N.W., October 11th, 1867.

I have to acknowledge the receipt of your letter accepting my offer to compose you three part-songs. I shall be very happy to leave you with any influence as to the choice of words, only reminding you that in proportion as the nature of words to be set to music, does or does not stimulate the composer's invention, so must it always influence the value of his production. My old friend the Italian poet Maggioni used to say that there were but two subjects fit for music, namely, love and religion. Without going the length of asserting this proposition inflexibly, I must say that I scarcely call to mind a greatly successful vocal composition that is not, however remotely, associated by its poetry with one or other of these subjects.

In 1866 the late Mr. William Euing, of Glasgow, founded a lectureship on music in Anderson's College there, and urged Mr. Curwen to undertake it. Mr. Curwen was at the time developing his plans for teaching musical composition, and the chance of proving them by the help of a band of hard-headed, industrious Scottish students, was too tempting to be resisted. It was difficult for him to leave home, but he overcame all obstacles, and for three months in the winter of 1866-7 he resided with Mrs. Curwen at Glasgow, lecturing twice a week. He always looked back upon this experience as most profitable and stimulating. It came just at the right time. The classes were large and enthusiastic. After the first season he resigned the post, as he had accomplished his object—the lectureship had been successfully started, and the method of teaching had been established. While at Glasgow, having to lecture on musical history and form, Mr. Curwen went, for the first time in his life, to the opera. To one of his training and prejudices this was a new experience, on the very borderland of duty. He fixed his attention closely upon the music. He felt the union of singing and acting to be unnatural, and never went to the opera again.

After leaving Plaistow, Mr. Curwen did not long continue to attend the church there. He joined a new Congregational Church at Stratford, of which the Rev. James Knaggs was minister, and was made a deacon. Amid his Sol-fa work he found time for much activity in the affairs of this church, while Mrs. Curwen continued her devotion to the poor of the congregation. In a letter written after his death the secretary of the church says :—

With their pastor and some of their number Mr. Curwen had until recently been in the active oversight of the church. They will ever retain in their memory the wise counsel, the ardent projects to extend the Divine kingdom, and the help he was ever ready to give.

To us all he has been a noble example of a kind-hearted Christian gentleman, whose open-handed benevolence ever went seeking out objects for itself, not from the motive of self-gratification, but from very love to the Christ who has now called him home.

It must not be supposed that Mr. Curwen's course in this local work was entirely smooth. Far from it. His large schemes frightened little men, and made them oppose him; his intense conscientiousness often laid upon him the burden of saying unpleasant truths to people; his strong purpose, and disinclination for compromise, separated him often even from his own party. These troubles are forgotten, and the impression of his wisdom and unselfishness remains, but they were none the less real at the time of their occurrence.

Mr. Curwen pinched himself at this time in order to contribute one-fifth of a not large income to objects in which he was interested, yet it was now that a rich man in the neighbourhood took occasion to write him a letter on the duty of giving! The incident is merely mentioned to introduce a passage from a letter to Mrs. Curwen, accidentally preserved, which shows the spirit in which Mr. Curwen received this scolding :—

I read your letter first, so I was not so indignant as you were at Mr. ———. Your indignation was a sort of homœopathic medicine for mine. Like cures like. What a blessing, dearest, that we do not *deserve* this rebuke. This shows that we must commend ourselves to God, and not to men. I have constantly to fight against my own love of approbation. I really should *like* not to be so misunderstood by a good man.

The visit of the Tonic Sol-fa Association Choir to Paris in 1867, under Mr. Joseph Proudman, engaged Mr. Curwen's sympathies very strongly. He did not accompany the choir, but he waited with much eagerness for the news of their reception and success. As he read the letter which told him of the prize they had won, and the ovation they had received, he fairly broke down, and handed it to his son to finish. It was very rarely that he betrayed emotion in this way.

In October, 1867, Miss Glover died at Malvern, at the advanced age of 82. Only two months before, Mr. Curwen had visited her at Hereford, and found her possessed of the old spirit of happiness and contentment. When he referred to some recent imputations of plagiarism made by a French musical journal, she replied, " Do not concern yourself to vindicate my originality. Let the question be not who was the first to invent it, but is the thing itself good and true, and useful to the world." When Mr. Curwen spoke of the relation of his labours to her own she answered, "You not only do me justice, but you try to make me famous." In this spirit she passed peacefully away. A resolution of sympathy with her sister was passed at the Christmas Convention of Tonic Sol-fa teachers. "We recognise," it said, "in the late Miss Sarah Ann Glover the founder of our Sol-fa notation, and in Miss Christiana Glover, her sister, the constant companion and sharer of her labours, and we hereby charge ourselves to promote the spread of music among the people for the same high purposes and in the same unselfish spirit which our founder always manifested."

Among the efforts in which Mr. Curwen occupied himself at this time was one for adapting the Tonic Sol-fa system to the use of the blind.

In September, 1868, Mr. Curwen took part in a Tonic Sol-fa demonstration at Keswick, organised by Mr. T. L. Banks, who afterwards became his son-in-law. The following passage from a letter describes the scene :—

Cockermouth, September 10, 1868.

The demonstration at Keswick yesterday was wonderfully beautiful. On a rising meadow at the head of Derwentwater sat two or three thousand people—rich and middle class, with a few of the poor—with the beautiful isleted lake and all its guardian mountains spread before them, and close on the margin of the lake, on a raised orchestra with its back to the lake, four hundred newly-made Cumberland singers. Add to this the crisp pure air and the sunshine and the wind, just breathing out the sound of the singers all up the hill side, and then you can form only a dim idea of the sweet pleasure of yesterday.

CHAPTER XI.

1869—1873.

In 1869 Mr. Curwen moved from Upton Place to a house
about a quarter of a mile further down the same road.
Here he lived till his death, and it is with this house that
most of his friends associate his person and his life.

Mr. Curwen found it hard to disengage himself from
local movements in the district which he had entered
years before in a public capacity. Notwithstanding the
pressure of other work he could not quench his zeal for
the advancement of his neighbours, and for the success
among them of the principles to which he was attached.

In 1869 a large park, situated in the midst of the vast and growing district in which he lived was offered by Mr. John Gurney at a very low rate for public use. Mr. Curwen headed a small band of public-spirited people who advocated the purchase, and he gave up several weeks to the agitation, fighting with much energy. A poll of the parish was taken, and resulted, as was expected, in a crushing defeat of the scheme. The park was afterwards paid for by the Corporation of London, but this solution of the question was not dreamt of at the time of which we speak. To meddle in vestry contests requires a strong stomach. The parochial mind is dense, and its tone is low. Mr. Curwen was assailed in this and similar contests with imputations of every variety, which men of refinement generally shrink from bringing down upon themselves.

The most considerable local work in which Mr. Curwen engaged at this time was in connection with Education. We have seen how from the first he was fond of children, and how his various activities took their rise from this source. The passing of Mr. Forster's Education Act in 1870 inspired the friends of unsectarian education with great hope. Mr. Curwen saw its possibilities, and desired that it should be used in his district for the promotion of schools under public management, in which no distinctive religious formula should be taught. The district was one in which the adoption of the Act was imperatively necessary, owing to the rapidly increasing population.

N

The agitation was a long and wearisome one. The parish
had first to be polled on the question whether it would
have a School Board (*i.e.*, adopt the Act) or not, and then
it had to elect members for the Board. Mr. Curwen,
having come to the front in the preliminary discussions,
found that he was bound to go on the Board. In his
address as candidate he thus referred to the religious
question :—

In reference to the religious question I have noticed,
during long experience, that where religious good has been
done by day schools, it has sprung from the just, and
patient and loving *characters* of good teachers, shown in
their daily life, and not from any sort of dogmatic
teaching. Childhood is not the time for the dogmatic
teaching of any subject. It is the time for teaching
by example. *Indefinite* religious example is far better,
at that time of life, than the most "definite religious
teaching" that can be invented. But I do not look on a
state-aided school as the place for direct religious teaching
in the common sense of the word. The home, the church,
and the Sunday school are the best spheres for that great
work. I would not *insist* on the use of the Bible in
any schools, especially where there was a conscientious
objection to it, as in the case of Jews or Catholics. But I
would not consent to let the Bible be the only book in the
world *excluded* from schools. That would be sectarianism
of the worst kind. Apart from its evangelical doctrine,
which is infinitely precious to me (and which I would not
teach in a state-aided school) the Bible is a book of
history, of morals, and of life-like human character. On
these points the Bible must surely be referred to often.

But the "where, how, and when" I would leave to the teacher.

Mr. Curwen was elected, and served three years on the Board, giving up much valuable time to the work, and seriously delaying the completion of several books on which he was engaged. Of his work on the School Board the following notes by Mr. W. Horn, an artizan, who was one of the ablest members of the Board, speak :—

The education movement of 1870, and the agitation to establish a School Board in West Ham, brought me into close contact and intimacy with Mr. Curwen, and our subsequent connection on the School Board established a friendship between us that only terminated with his death. During these movements many meetings and conferences were held, at most of which Mr. Curwen was a prominent actor. The meetings held especially to discuss the question of establishing a School Board exhibited in striking contrast the divergent views held on education, and much warmth in discussion, bringing out in bold relief many personal traits in the characters of some of those who took part in the proceedings. Within the bounds of these gatherings there were three different sections favouring the establishment of a School Board. One hoped to be able to work it in the interest of denominational schools ; a second, or liberal section, was determined by means of a Board to establish an un-sectarian or national system of education, as distinguished from the sectarian or denominational system ; and a third tried to steer a midway course by declaring in favour of unsectarian teaching, and yet favoured the 25th clause and other objectionable features of the Act tending to perpetuate denominationalism at the nation's expense.

Foremost amongst those of the liberal section stood John
Curwen, earnest and persistent ; pleading for the establishment of a Board, denouncing the provisions in the Act
favourable to denominationalism, and attacking opposing
views with carefully prepared arguments. The Education
Act I remember him describing as having two faces ; with
one face tempting those in favour of sectarian education,
and with the other appealing to the unsectarian or liberal
friends of education. The painstaking care with which
Mr. Curwen applied himself to questions in which he took
an interest impressed me very much at this time. To this
habit of close and methodical examination I think
Mr. Curwen owed much of the success that attended his
efforts to be of use to his fellow men. His expositions,
whether of principles or methods, were always clear, and
although they might not convince an opponent, no one
could listen to his arguments or descriptions without learning something, and feeling that he had spared no pains in
the study of the subject under discussion. Declamation
was not his *forte*, yet I have listened to occasional bursts
of real declamatory eloquence from him. Of Mr. Curwen's
services on the School Board I have somewhat precise
knowledge, and it has always appeared to me that those
services were never sufficiently valued, and indeed I
think his true position on the Board was, by most people,
misunderstood. By those who wished to narrow the
limits of the School Board's operations, and, as far as
possible subordinate them to the advantage of denominational schools, Mr. Curwen was looked upon as a dangerous
man to be opposed and beaten, and, indeed, some of his
opponents treated him on several occasions in such a
manner as almost to look like persecution. By others,
who looked with jealousy upon the Board's expenditure,
he was thought to be reckless of expense in dealing with

the public funds; and even many liberal-minded people,
who at that time had but a hazy notion of what a national
system of education ought to be, thought Mr. Curwen too
extreme in his views. In all matters relating to school
work and school life the comfort of the children was his
first thought. He wisely looked upon their happiness as
a consideration which should never be lost sight of by
those engaged in educational work, and considered that it
was cruelty to place children for so many hours each day
in ill-ventilated and cheerless schools, injuring their
health and chilling the ardour of their youthful spirits.
The more desolate and dreary their homes, the greater the
need for making their school life cheerful and happy. He
never failed to inculcate this when opportunity offered; in
the arrangement of plans for school buildings, or the mode
of progressive teaching advocated by him, the children's
comfort was never overlooked. Hence his courageous
advocacy and defence of a costly system of school
buildings, proposed by him, which made much stir
in the parish at the time. The plans submitted were
for graded schools, and their completeness showed with
what pains he had mastered the whole system. In
explaining the scheme to the Board he exhibited an
amount of educational knowledge possessed by few men.
With convincing clearness he showed the necessity of
adopting an intermediary school between the infants' and
the boys' or girls' school, so that a child leaving the
infants' school might pass by easy gradation into the
sterner methods, severer discipline, and rougher usages of
a boys' or girls' school. How much some children
suffered from being abruptly transferred from the mild
surroundings of an infants' school to the ruder and less
congenial atmosphere of a boys' or girls' school, he
depicted with feeling tenderness. In the earnestness of

his advocacy Mr. Curwen's zeal sometimes outran his discretion, and this particular case was a striking instance. Although the scheme was admirable, yet it was much in advance of a majority of his colleagues, and altogether beyond the grasp of the general public, to whom the outlay appeared to be out of all proportion to the object sought to be obtained. Yet notwithstanding the hopelessness of attempting to carry it out, he was disappointed with those who generally acted with him for not fighting the battle out, although there was not the remotest chance of success.

Methods of teaching, and the character of the education to be given, alike occupied his mind. The mixed system—namely, the teaching of boys and girls in the same classes together, was warmly advocated by him. The array of facts and arguments put forward were clear and forcible, but here, as in the graded scheme, he was unsuccessful in securing its adoption, and this, I have reason to believe, led him to look upon his career at the School Board as a failure. This opinion is not shared by those who sat at the Board with him, and profited by his knowledge. He rendered valuable service in the arduous tasks that lay before the Board in the first three years of its existence ; his minute and careful research in educational matters was on many occasions turned to good account in the discussions that arose. He fought with all his energy on the question of religious teaching, insisting on the simple formula of the Christian faith, and the pure principles of its morality being taught in the schools, but objecting with all his might to everything tending to give that teaching a sectarian or denominational character. Again, on the other " Religious difficulty " question, namely—the payment of fees to denominational schools, his resolute opposition materially assisted in preventing the famous twenty-fifth clause from being put into operation in West Ham.

That he was not unmindful of expense he was careful to explain ; on a memorable occasion he said :— " In proposing so complete a set of graded schools it has not been forgotten that we are using the ratepayers' money ; but no unnecessary expense has been thought of, and it is to be remembered that we are providing for the ratepayers' own children." Mr. Curwen's idea was, that to starve education was something worse than a mistake. He believed that every child was entitled to a good sound liberal education, and that money spent judiciously in making suitable provision for that purpose was wisely spent, and would return good interest in rich blessings to the nation. It gives one pleasure to know that he lived long enough to see the tide of popular thought moving in the direction of his earlier faith.

In concluding this very imperfect sketch of Mr. Curwen I would say he was a many-sided man ; standing fast by that which he held to be true, meeting the bitterest hostility of adversaries meekly yet firmly, braving storms of opposition unflinchingly and ever hopefully, like the martyrs of old ; and possessed withal of a large-hearted philanthropy that gushed with tender sympathy towards the sufferings of his fellow men, and endeared him to all who knew his greatness of heart and open-handed generosity.

It will be gathered from these remarks that Mr. Curwen's career as a member of the School Board was not altogether a success. He did not pull well in harness, and wanted the patience, the willingness to postpone and wait and compromise, which are necessary in administrative work. He gradually came to realise this, and resigned when his term of service was ended, all the more willingly because he saw that the principles for which he had been working were fairly established.

Mr. Curwen had been engaged for several years in re-writing two of his books—"The Standard Course," and " How to Observe Harmony." The following passages from letters to members of his family describe his feelings during this work :—

Upton, July 20th, 1870.

I am only now putting the finishing strokes to step one. But that will be a guide to all the rest. Abolishing the leaning tones as the foundation of a step compels us to take the dominant chord (**s, t r**) for the *second* step, and the sub-dominant (**f l d'**) for the third.

Upton, August 29th, 1870.

I think I am doing great things with my new " Standard Course." I must confess that I naturally enjoy *finding out* things and then *making them plain*. But I want to turn all this to high uses. I should like—if God permits me—when all this educational study is done, to give the end of my life to any quiet work in promoting the usefulness of the method.

The book itself (the new " Standard Course ") closes with the following passage :—

Finally, let us remember two things. First, that even music must be enjoyed " soberly," and the more steadily and soberly it is pursued the more *fresh* will be our desire for its pleasures, and the more keen the enjoyment they bring. And second, that all this vocal culture only puts into our hands a delicate but effective *instrument*. See, reader, that you use it nobly. Exercise yourself to win a humble, true, and joyous soul, and let your heart be heard singing in your voice. Use that voice for social recreation—innocent and elevating. But use it most rejoicingly for "the service of song in the house of the Lord." If the singing at your place of worship does not satisfy you, try to improve it; but first of all show that you mean *cheerfully* to fulfil *your own personal duty* of vocal praise, whoever leads the singing, whatever tunes are used, and howsoever the organ is played.

Here follow two letters, written to members of his family, during the progress of "How to Observe Harmony":—

Tonic Sol-fa College, August 9th, 1872.

Since I got back I have stuck like a leech to "How to Observe Harmony," but have only got to the Fifth Step. I hope, however, I am making a good thing of it, certainly not a condensed thing. Longbottom helps me well. I feel very grateful that I have been permitted to see "Standard Course" done. It opens the door for a great and important series of theory examinations, for which we are making preparations, and enables us to complete the Junior Teacher's Certificate. Thus the whole book will have to be mastered by the time a man is "Member" and "Junior Teacher." I feel filled with joy when I think of and picture to myself the students that "Standard Course" will make this winter.

Southend, November 7th, 1872.

Last night, as I could not for coughing read aloud to dear mother, I wrote "How to Observe." As far as I have written hitherto, I can honestly say that I write *what I have heard.* I wish, however, that my ears were more familiar and acute. The new "How to Observe Harmony" gives me great pleasure, not only because I hope it is a good specimen of the teaching art, but because the subject itself—the esthetic principles of modern harmony—is intensely interesting, and because I am proud to think that we have hundreds of friends ready to use this book as a teaching instrument.

Mr. T. F. Seward, of Orange, New Jersey, U.S., contributes the following impressions, which belong to this time :—

I first saw Mr. Curwen in the summer of 1869, when I called upon him at his home. I had long admired his devotion to the interests of humanity, and the rare combination of qualities which had created the remarkable Tonic Sol-fa movement, but my admiration was not wholly that of a sympathiser. It was modified in no small degree by the conviction that his efforts were largely mis-directed. He was well aware of this, as I was at no pains to conceal it, and the journal I was then editing (the *New York Musical Gazette)* had been out-spoken in its criticism of the new system. Yet the interview was characterised by so much geniality and friendliness, as if his guest had been an enthusiastic supporter of his views rather than an opponent. This could not but make a strong impression on my mind. Yet there was another impression, which was even deeper and more lasting than that.

Here was a man who unquestionably sought the truth for the truth's own sake. He sought it in the highest possible spirit—*i.e.,* in the spirit of a little child.

He evidently cared nothing where it led him, or what the world might think of the new and out-of-the-way paths he followed. Whatever might be my opinion of his methods, I could have but one feeling with regard to the magnificent rightness of the man himself.

Although our various interviews at that time had no effect in changing my conviction as to the needlessness, and therefore the serious mistake of using a new notation to accomplish that which I believed could be as well done with the old, yet during the years that followed, Mr. Curwen's spirit enveloped me like an atmosphere. Though totally unconscious of its influence, it slowly and surely entered into, and gradually took possession of all my processes of thought and methods of teaching. The receptive attitude of his mind, the teachableness of his spirit, the willingness to sacrifice everything of a selfish or even personal nature for the discovery and promulgation of truth ; all this remained with me as a perpetual object-lesson, and did more to melt away the time-hardened walls of prejudice in my mind than uncounted volumes of arguments could have done.

Of the value of the Tonic Sol-fa system it would now be hardly possible for me to speak too strongly. It is, without doubt, one of the most beneficent factors that has ever entered into the problem of human elevation, because it bestows the refining and purifying gift of music upon the masses of the people. It is an easy and pleasant path by which *all* may enter into that beautiful world, the realm of tone, and prepares the way for a realisation of the divine injunction, which was also a prophecy, that all men should sing the praises of God. What more could be said of John Curwen than that he was worthy to be the inspirer and director of such a movement ? Worthy in his spirit of consecration, and worthy in the combination of powers that was needed for the inauguration of such a work.

It is not too much to say that Mr. Curwen has a three-fold claim upon the gratitude of posterity. He instituted a great reform solely for the benefit of his fellow men; he led it with consummate ability to a complete organisation; he left as pure an illustration as a merely human example can afford of the spirit in which the work should be conducted.

Personally, I desire to say that the recollection of my association with him in later years is among the most pleasant, wholesome, and inspiring influences of my life.

About this time Mr. Curwen entertained at his house for a night the two missionaries, Messrs. Moffat and Ellis. Of this visit he writes as follows to one of his sons :—

Upton, July 14th, 1871.

We were very glad to have Moffat and Ellis. There is a wonderful blending of tenderness, simplicity, and greatness in Moffat. He was fifty-four years in Africa. Nations know God and Christ through him. Following religion has gone civilisation. He reduced the Bechuanah language to writing. He translated the whole Bible. He is now, in his old age, revising that translation. Another fine specimen of manhood you have missed is Scott Russell. It was a treat to see and hear him. S——— has enjoyed both the men. H——— listened with open mouth and bright eyes to Moffat's stories about tigers and snakes. Longfellow says " Lives of good men all remind us," &c. So I hope *our* lives will be better and more unselfish for the interviews we have had with these good men. Ellis went out to the South Seas *two* years, and

Moffat to Africa *one* year before I was born! They both rejoiced to see your grandfather's portrait, both knew and loved him. Mr. Moffat spoke very tenderly of his old friend Joseph Thompson.

Mr. Curwen was always happy among Tonic Sol-faists, and often entertained his musical friends singly or in parties at his house. The following letter, to one of his sons, describes his enjoyment of a gathering of the Tonic Sol-fa Composition Club :—

Upton, December, 1873.

We have just had supper. The Club left us at 9.10 in fulness of pleasure. They came with their wives at 4.20, and had tea at 5, sitting down at two tables, one in the dining-room and the other in the library—mother and I in one room, and Lizzie Matthews and the boys in the other. It was very hard work for dear mother and the maids to get such a tea ready after a late lunch. But the Club enjoyed everything thoroughly. Mary Perry said she did not know they were Sol-faists else she would have recommended a larger provision! But the provision was ample. After tea, I made a little speech about *com*-position (putting things together), and illustrated by means of the pictures in the room. I gave them some hints I got from Mr. Ruskin, Mr. Callaway, and Anna Marten. Then we sung or heard fifteen pieces, M'Naught, Longbottom, and I taking notes. When it was over I criticised each piece, giving honestly my general impression of it, and Mr. M'Naught followed with such criticism as the Royal Academy of Music has taught him. At the end of the list Mr. Longbottom, gave some general remarks, saying he had criticised as a conductor, and he was afraid he could not, as such, bring out many good

points from some of the pieces. Two or three he would
have enjoyed conducting. The friendly dicussions which
followed were very enjoyable. They all seemed to go
away very happy.

Mr. Curwen now occupied himself closely in literary
work. In 1872 he produced the new " Standard Course"
and new "How to Observe Harmony," already referred to,
as well as a manual for teaching the staff notation. His
system of harmony had been gradually developed. In
1867, after his "Euing Lectures" at Glasgow, he had been
brought into contact with Professor Macfarren's writings,
and had attended a course of his lectures at the Royal
Institution. Later on, while writing out his " Euing
Lectures " for publication, he had frequent private
interviews with Dr. Macfarren, whom he recognised as
the deepest and clearest thinker on harmony. From
Dr. Macfarren he first realised the difference between
chromatic and transitional chords, which had long perplexed him. He used to describe how, after listening
one day to Dr. Macfarren's explanation, he replied, " Then
a chromatic chord is a transition nipped in the bud!"
To which Dr. Macfarren responded, " Mr. Curwen, you've
hit it exactly."

Mr. Curwen's method of harmony analysis and
composition did not follow Dr. Macfarren in his deriva-
tion of discords from the harmonic chord, a theory which
Mr. Curwen held to be imaginary and unphilosophical ;

but it coincided with Dr. Macfarren's habit of referring every combination of notes to its root in the key.

Mr. Curwen next turned to Acoustics in its relation to music, and produced, in 1874, his " Musical Statics," which works out in detail and applies many of the discoveries and doctrines of Helmholtz. This book occupied him for a long time, and he found the studies into which it led him very interesting. By " Statics " he meant the physical aspect of music as distinct from the esthetic—the source of scales and combinations of sounds rather than the laws of progression and form. During the preparation of this book Mr. Curwen attended some of Professor Carey Foster's lectures on Acoustics at University College, the *alma mater* which he had left twenty-five years before.

" Musical Statics" formed the first part of the proposed " Commonplaces of Music," a large and comprehensive work, embracing all branches of musical study, which Mr. Curwen never completed. The parts which he finished were published at intervals from 1867 to 1874. The preparation of shorter books always pressed upon him, and as the years went by the prospect of finishing the " Commonplaces " grew more distant.

We close the chapter with the following passage from a letter to Mrs. Curwen, written from Glasgow about this time :—

Glasgow, August 3rd, 1874.

On Sunday, after dinner, I went to the Young Men's Service at eight, in a large church. It was crowded, and very impressive. There were as many young women as men. They sang nothing but Philip Phillips' and Sankey's hymns. All joined. They asked me to pray, after announcing a list of those who asked for special prayer. Among the drunkards and others there was this—in a lady's (perhaps the mother's) handwriting—" The prayers of the meeting are requested for the only daughter of a minister, a person of great promise and abilities, who is now walking the streets of this city." Oh! it was heartbreaking. What are all the S—— B——'s and H——'s, and even dear Mr. P——'s teachings when they *come in front of sin?* For this nothing will do but the " Son of man, who came to seek and to save that which is lost."

CHAPTER XII.

1873—1875.

A NEW YEAR'S GREETING—THE JUBILEE SINGERS—IS MADE A
WELSH BARD—CONTROVERSY WITH THE EDUCATION DEPART-
MENT—ZION COLLEGE—JEWS' SCHOOLS—PLEASANT TESTIMONY
—PRESENTATION MEETING AT EXETER HALL—SPEECH ON
THE OCCASION—THIRTY YEARS OF STRUGGLE—COMMISSION
RECEIVED AT HULL—A YOUNG MINISTER—MISS GLOVER—
"GRAMMAR OF VOCAL MUSIC " — DISCOURAGEMENTS —
STIMULUS GIVEN BY THEM—LITERATURE—TAKES TO BUSINESS
—EWING LECTURES—OPPOSITION TO THE SYSTEM—SUCCESS—
CO-WORKERS—OTHER MOVEMENTS AIDED—PEOPLE'S COLLEGE
OF MUSIC—OBJECT—LETTER TO MR. PROUDMAN—"TEACHER'S
MANUAL"—LETTER TO A YOUNG FRIEND.

MR. CURWEN greeted his friends at the opening of the
year 1873 in the *Tonic Sol-fa Reporter* as follows :—

A happy new year ! Yes it will be, it must be, if we
have learnt " in whatsoever state we are therewith to be
content "—if we are trusting our Father's hand, and
rejoicing to do our Father's work. "But," says some
friend, " what has that to do with music !" To which I
answer, the new year will be a happy one to us in proportion as we use our musical faculties so as to please Him.

o

He is pleased with our music for innocent recreations, and for social pleasure. The first miracle of bounty was at a marriage feast. He is pleased with our music for worship when the sacrifice of the lips goes up along with the melody of the heart. But we may believe that He is specially pleased when not for ourselves, either in recreation or in worship, *but for others* we are using the talent—it may be the *one* talent which He has given us. If among young children—if among the poor and joyless we are giving—if in our personal influence with the young we are carrying an earnest, loving, Christian spirit—then it is going to be a happy new year for us. Let us do the humblest work that offers — what " our hands find " to do. Let us do it well, however few may know of it. Good work is a joy in itself. Teaching to sing is not a *direct* form of usefulness, like preaching the gospel or teaching in the Sunday school, but it is a very great and diffusive *indirect* form of usefulness. It gives a new faculty for life ; it places the pupil at once in contact with good social influences in his singing class, and with good poetic influences in the pieces he sings ; and above all, it opens the silent lips in the house of God. It tempts thousands, who were before uninterested, to join in the service of praise. Let us then not despise our gift, however small it is, but let us use it faithfully. And with these thoughts, dear friend, you and I will wish each other a " Happy new year."

Mr. Curwen was deeply stirred, in May of this year, by listening, for the first time to the " Jubilee Singers." All his old anti-slavery passion, all his sympathy with the blacks, and the desire which he had to make the Tonic Sol-fa system known among them, filled his mind. He

wrote an enthusiastic description of the singing in the
Reporter, and did everything he could to help them in
their object.

In August he acted as one of the judges at the Welsh
National Eisteddfod, at Mold. The quaint sights and
customs which he saw there, as well as the ceremony
by which he himself was made a Welsh bard, are
described in the following article :—

Now the time has come, and the little old-fashioned
town of Mold puts on its holiday attire. Flags are everywhere, and crowds stand about all the streets. Carts and
waggons are coming in laden with country people. A
long waggon with two horses can bring in from ten miles
distance quite a little village full of men, women, and
children. It draws up in the middle of the street and
unloads—all but the ample baskets of provisions, which
are kept till the middle of the day. Sober, merry,
kindly Welsh people are everywhere. Every house is
a little hostelry, and homely clean accommodation can be
got at moderate rates. But the great mass of the people
will get their refreshments at the extemporised tea and
coffee-rooms to be seen in every direction. At present the
people are all waiting for the procession of Bards. These
are clergymen, ministers of all denominations, school
teachers, editors of newspapers, and literary and musical
men of all kinds. They have come from all parts of
Wales (north, south, and centre) and from various parts of
England to the Session of their great movable College of
Art. Here is one venerable gentleman in blue gown with
a curious kind of wooden gridiron hanging in front of him.
He is the Arch-Druid, and he is courteously explaining to

an Englishman that this is a specimen of the old Druidical
books, which were the repositories of poetry and art long
before printing was invented. There was writing on each
of the four sides of the wooden bars, so that a great
number of poetical lines could be thus preserved. Several
other elderly and gentlemanly people in academical [caps
and gowns of light blue or light green. The procession is
formed, and some twelve of them march up the street
to the Bailey Hill. There, under the shadow of a lofty
old *cairn* (where the British once hid themselves, and then
came out in Men of Harlech style, to the great dismay
of their enemies) they have twelve great stones arranged
in a circle with a larger one in the centre. The outer
stones keep the circle for the people around, a Druid
standing at each stone, while the two or three who are
speaking or spoken to, stand in the centre. This is the
ancient form of Parliament house ; this is the style in
which our forefathers held their courts of justice, and
celebrated their great religious rites; it is called the
Gorsedd. On the first morning I stood on the top of the
cairn and got a bird's-eye view of the whole scene. I saw
one Bard addressing the Arch-bard, sometimes in Welsh
and sometimes in English. I saw the Undergraduate
Bards (in green) bring first one candidate for honours and
then another, and present him with many Welsh words of
ceremony to the presiding Bard. If the Bards at some
previous meeting have been satisfied of his worth, then he
receives the right-hand of fellowship and is called by his
bardic name. On the last morning of this preliminary
ceremony I received a hint that the literary brotherhood
of Wales acknowledges my musical writings and musical
activities, and would be pleased to confer on me a title.
I, who have always striven to get rid of titles, felt that
this was not a question of title, but of brotherhood with

Welshmen on my part, and of public recognition of the
Tonic Sol-fa movement on the part of these gentlemen.
So I was taken into the circle, presented to a clergyman of
the Church of England (the presiding Druid of the day),
and received the honour with bared head (notwithstanding
the rain), with a great sense of reverence for ancient
customs, and with hearty appreciation of the kindly feeling
which dictated the act. I was obliged to select the name
of a river for my title, and as they did not like the sound
of Thames or Aire I went back to my father's birthplace
and took the Derwent. My Welsh title is, therefore,
" Dyrwent Pencerdd " — or Derwent's singer. I think
that Tonic Sol-faists everywhere will accept this as a
friendly recognition by the Welsh nation of their work in
the world.

The lessons which Mr. Curwen draws from the
Eisteddfod are these : —

Cannot we Tonic Sol-faists learn something from
them ? The enthusiasm of nationality is not a nobler one
than that of thought and method, surely we may learn
from these Welsh Eisteddvodau what great things may be
done by the united and well-directed efforts of the many.
I cannot help thinking our Tonic Sol-fa movement is
about to lift up its head and spread out its arms with new
strength, like a large and fruitful tree. The Tonic Sol-fa
College ought to be essentially the people's college, for
people's work ; not for the aristocracy, not for the higher
walks of the musical profession, but for the common uses
of music among the people. It ought to supply our schools
with competent singing masters, our churches with precentors, with organists, and with choirs, our young people's
classes with Teachers, Conductors, and popular Composers,
so that our homes, our workshops, and even our mines

may re-echo with song. I know that money will be needed for this, much money, but when the time comes for the heart of a people to be united, the many give their little and the few give much ; some give money, others wisdom. I feel confident that that time is near at hand.

In 1873 and 1874 Mr. Curwen and his friends were engaged in a controversy with the Education Department. Since the year 1869 the Tonic Sol-fa method and notation had been accepted on an equality with the staff notation, and the examination papers set at Training Colleges had been given in both old and new notations. In 1872 Dr. Hullah, whose hostility to the Tonic Sol-fa system everyone knows, was appointed Inspector of Music in Training Colleges. Dr. Hullah had frequently availed himself of official opportunities to attack the system. Mr. Curwen saw that a fair treatment of Tonic Sol-fa pupils was practically impossible under Dr. Hullah, not from that gentleman's intentional unfairness, but from his ignorance of the Tonic Sol-fa system, and the unconscious bias of his well-known opinions. He wrote to the *Times* urging this. The appointment, however, was confirmed, and the evils which Mr. Curwen foresaw took their course. In a pamphlet, "The Present Crisis of Music in Schools," issued in 1873, Mr. Curwen told the whole story of the misprints, confusion, and inequalities which had made the Tonic Sol-fa questions and tests unintelligible to the students. He denies that he is animated by any personal jealousy or dislike of Dr. Hullah :—

Some persons who are unacquainted with school music in England, and who do not see the serious nature of the present crisis, have been ready to think that in these protests I was moved by personal animosity to Mr. Hullah. I remember that my honoured friend Mr. Hickson was assailed by the same kind of shameful imputation when, thirty-two years ago, he criticised the Wilhem-Hullah method. I should not have noticed this if the accusation were not widely circulated in private, and had not been suggested even in public prints. Not only is it totally untrue, but there is no ground of excuse for it. I have never sought, nor even desired, official position for myself. I have never asked for the Tonic Sol-fa method anything more than fair play and equal terms. I did not seek the post of inspector of music for a Tonic Sol-faist. For twenty-five years or more, in my lectures in various parts of the country, I have contented myself with expounding musical truth, rarely doing more than refer to Mr. Hullah's educational mistakes—seldom doing that—and never speaking of him but in tones of personal respect. When there was an opportunity for the public generally to manifest this respect, I cordially joined with them. I believed him to be a true friend of people's music, notwithstanding his lamentable mistake in the art of teaching. Even when Mr. Hullah declined to allow a temperance society to use one of his compositions on *the sole* ground that he " could not allow anything of his to appear in the so-called Sol-fa Notation," and in other ways showed his animus, I took but little notice. But when, after all the arduous work of Tonic Sol-faists throughout the country for many years, *our chief educa-*

*tional opponent was made the overlooker, and very largely
the controller of that work,* it was necessary to assume
a more distinct position of hostility—not to him, but to
his method and to his prejudices. Prejudice may in itself
be weak, but armed with Government power it becomes
strong and dangerous every way. As I valued the cause
of popular music, to which the greater part of my life had
been dedicated, I was now bound to protest, as I did in
the *Times* newspaper.

In January, 1874, the errors in the Tonic Sol-fa
papers having become unbearable, Mr. Curwen headed
a deputation to Mr. Forster. The Department of course
defended their servant, but the protest did good. Mr.
Curwen felt the whole action against Dr. Hullah to be
a disagreeable necessity.

Mr. Curwen enjoyed the cordiality with which he
was received at a meeting of clergy at Zion College in
January of this year, to which he was invited. The
discussion was on psalmody, and he replied to Mr. Barnby
and Dr. Stainer, who had advocated unison singing.

He was, however, more deeply stirred by a visit to
the Jewish Free Schools in Spitalfields, which he paid
in March. These schools educate 2,500 children, and the
Tonic Sol-fa system having been adopted, Mr. Curwen
was asked to go and hear the singing. He wrote after
the visit :—

There is a peculiar kind of expression beyond the
mere loud or soft, quick or slow, which comes right out of

the depths of the heart, and that expression these boys
gave. As I passed from room to room I asked what could
account for the marked difference in the style and spirit
and quality of this singing from that of ordinary English
schools. I found that more than half of the children
are of foreign parentage. They come from Poland, from
Germany, and from Holland, and to some extent bring
with them the musical taste of these countries. But,
before all, they belong to that old Hebrew race who
learnt to sing with Moses and Miriam and David ages
before Poles or Germans or Englishmen existed. The
singing of Mr. Abraham's class was certainly exquisite.
I was not surprised to notice that nearly all the teachers
of the girls' school had come to listen to it. As soon
as this was over, I noticed that all the 300 boys had
risen and stood, without books, but with covered heads,
looking seriously towards Mr. Benjamin. Then, before I
was aware, there burst forth the grand ringing tones of
the Hallelujah Chorus in the Hebrew language. It was
wonderful to notice the feeling and the fire with which
the piece was delivered. It quite overcame me. It was
Mr. Angel who had suggested this adaptation of a psalm
of praise to Handel's Hallelujah Chorus. Mr. Benjamin
had arranged the parts for boy's voices, and the boys
had learnt their parts by heart. It was marvellous to me,
when I remembered that only about a year ago there was
no singing taught in the school. These Hebrews must
indeed be a grand old musical race.

This adoption of the system in new and strange
quarters was always pleasing to Mr. Curwen. A letter
which he received about the same time may be taken as a
type of many others :—

I cannot close this letter without expressing my personal gratitude to you for the immeasurable joy you have been the cause of placing within my reach, and that of my immediate friends. The music you have given me has been an angel of light to my home. It *was* anything but a happy home, and it became a paradise when your music came. My father was a reckless and unsteady man, but your music sobered him considerably, and made his dying hours bright and happy. And the sweetest recollections we have of a dead father and a little angel-sister, are those connected with your sweet music. I declare most emphatically that that music has increased our religion, our contentment, and our happiness a thousandfold, and there is not one of my near relations but joins with me to say God bless you. I am not exaggerating, nor too enthusiastic in what I have said. I have not half expressed the thanks I feel, and I never can. I believe there are very many who owe you as much and thank you as much as I do.

A correspondent writing from the Orkney Islands at the same time said :—

Forty years ago there were only *two* individuals in the whole group who could be said to read music, and although several teachers from the south and elsewhere were employed to give instruction, either from the difficulty of the notation, or for want of ability to impart their knowledge to others, little or no progress was made. A few tunes learnt by ear was all that was looked for ; notation was entirely in the shade, reading music at sight was considered equivalent to learning a language, and consequently beyond the reach of common people. Nay, some even ventured to say that there was a certain secret, which if disclosed would unravel the whole thing in a moment. I mention this to show what ignorance at that time prevailed. Twenty years later matters were much the same ; only a few could read music. About this time, however, the Tonic Sol-fa notation was introduced, and although the people were very ignorant, it only required one night's practice to show them that reading music was not impossible, or beyond their reach. The method took, and they took the method, young and old crowded the classroom. A new era had dawned upon them. I may mention, by the way, that Orcadians are fond of music, and wherever it is properly taught the interest is very marked. At present there is not an island in the group where a smattering of it is not taught and well received, and out of a population of a little over thirty thousand nearly one-sixth may be said to read music. Such is a brief outline of music in Orkney. Truly the Tonic Sol-fa notation has proved itself in our experience "Easy, Cheap, and True."

In August Mr. Curwen presided over a week's session of Tonic Sol-fa friends at Glasgow, which was very successful. He was braced for work by the heartiness of his friends, as well as by an excursion to the Gareloch. The following, to Mrs. Curwen, describes the meetings at Glasgow :—

Glasgow, Wednesday.

The meetings yesterday were very fine. The number of precentors from all parts of the country gives a vigour to the affair — makes it an earnest business. Ferniegair came in. He has been teazing the Education Department again, through the Tory M.P. for Glasgow, and has some hopes of their giving the Sol-fa students a syllabus. Mr. Miller's exhibitions of sight singing and voice training with school boys were very good. Several School Board members spoke. In the evening I got on with my modulator lesson better than I expected. The discussion was lively and well kept up. At the breakfast this morning we had forty or more. All were delighted with the idea of "singing for the College," and so raising an endowment fund for scholarships. They are pleased with the idea of Incorporation. Ferniegair—this is the last news — means to pay for an excursion to Gareloch-head to-morrow. Just like him !

Mr. and Mrs. Curwen went to Germany in September, and stayed at Langen Schwalbach, where eighteen years before they had tasted their first experience of German life. Mrs. Curwen was not well, and the waters had been recommended to her. Mr. Curwen studied the manifestations of popular music in the schools, churches, Männergesangvereine, &c., with much interest.

In November Mr. Curwen organised a meeting in Finsbury Chapel for the purpose of stirring up Sunday school teachers to the importance of improving their singing. He spoke with his old ardour on this congenial theme.

On December 30th Mr. Curwen was presented with a testimonial at a meeting at Exeter Hall. It had been subscribed for by Tonic Sol-fa friends in all parts of the country, and took the form of a life-sized portrait and a purse containing £200. The portrait, which was presented to Mrs. Curwen, hung in Mr. Curwen's house till her death, when he presented it to the Tonic Sol-fa College at Forest Gate, where it now is. The money was devoted by Mr. Curwen to the establishment of two " Glover " scholarships in the Tonic Sol-fa College, securing six weeks' training in the system every year to two young teachers.

The sittings which the artist demanded for this portrait were unusual in length and number. Mr. Curwen went ten or fifteen times to the studio at Hampstead. One day he stood for eight hours, with short intervals, in the attitude in which he is represented. The room was perfectly cold—artists object to fires in their studios—and it was the month of December. He used to come home very weary, and when urged to cut the artist short he would say, " My friends are wanting to do me a kindness ; I must do all I can to make their gift a success."

Mr. Curwen had on one or two previous occasions quashed proposals for giving him a testimonial, but he accepted this one for a very practical reason. It came at a time when he was anxiously desiring to consolidate and render permanent the movement to which he had devoted his life, by erecting and endowing a Tonic Sol-fa College. He wanted money for bricks and mortar, and for scholarships, and gladly accepted this means of raising it.

At the Exeter Hall meeting, at which Mr. Hugh Matheson presided, Mr. Curwen delivered a lengthy address, which, contrary to his usual custom, he wrote out beforehand. This was the only piece of autobiography that he ever attempted, and it rightly finds a place in these memorials :—

I am carried back over the memories of thirty years of struggle—struggle to make a useful thing known and to get it used—struggle against popular indifference, against professional prejudice, against the stern weight of government repression —and sometimes also against my own ignorance and incapacity. In all these struggles, including the last, you, dear friends, by whom I am now surrounded, and some like-minded who have passed away from all struggle, have stood by my side and helped me. And now you have come to gird me for new enter-prizes by your sympathy and helpfulness.

A Welsh gentleman—a brother bard—a bard of no mean eminence, well acquainted with his own country, once describing to me the extent to which the Welsh people print Tonic Sol-fa music, and use it in their chapels, their mines, and their homes, finished by saying "you have certainly hit upon a good and useful thing. I suppose it was a fluke" (laughter). Just at that moment the train in which we were riding stopped, and my new acquaint-ance got out. When I got home I consulted my youngest son about the meaning of the word (laughter). I then wished I had said that I did not quite know what a fluke was; but if it meant a lucky accident I did not believe in "flukes." No fluke that I know of ever gave me a lift. I am what Mr. Emerson calls a "causationist." I believe in finding things out and in getting things done, and more than that, I believe in a Providence which helps and stimulates the diligent, the earnest, and the true.

It was at a conference of Sunday School teachers at
Hull, in the autumn of 1841—just 33 years ago—that
I received my commission for this work. I remember
it well. Teachers of all denominations were present.
The Rev. T. Stratton was in the chair. Much had been
said on the difficulties of securing good and hearty singing
in school and congregation. Wonder had been expressed
that an art which, in the word of God, is so clearly
demanded of all, should be really so complex and so
difficult of attainment. I had replied that I did not
believe it could be so, and that what God required from
" young men and maidens, old men and children," from
" the people," from " all the people," must be simple and
easy of attainment if you did but understand the way. I
then described what I had just seen and heard at the
infant school patronised by Miss Glover in Norwich. We
agreed that the method must be easy, for the people have
little time; cheap, for many are poor; true, for the people
love the truth. After a little more discussion a resolution
was passed, charging me, as a young minister, to find out
the simplest way of teaching music, and to get it into use.
Mr. Stratton charged me very solemnly, and I accepted
the charge. So it was not by a " fluke" that I got into
this Tonic Sol-fa work.

I spoke just now of Providence, which sometimes
helps and sometimes stimulates. For some years I " kept
under" this Music Mission, as of third or fourth rate
importance. As a young minister I had—1st, my church;
2nd, my Sunday school ; and 3rd, my day school. All
these came before my duty to music. I was even so
jealous of myself that I would not learn the piano, lest I
should be tempted to waste time. But looking back,
I see that I have been gradually forced, sometimes by
strong encouragements, sometimes by misfortunes, and

more often by the sharp stimulus of opposition, to put music in the front.

My first stimulus was from Miss Glover herself. Very naturally I sent to her the profits of my first Sol-fa publication. But she returned them, saying that she had never received a pecuniary reward for her work, and did not wish to do so. Of course, this made me determine to invest the money in some fresh effort to promote the system. As I was but a young bachelor then it was no sacrifice to add to it all my own little savings—the fruit of other literary efforts—and to write and publish what no publisher would venture on, and what several printers refused to print—the first edition of " Singing for Schools and Congregations." Thus, by Miss Glover's generosity I was committed to a text book on a new system.

And here I should have rested content, thinking my work done, and expecting others to take up and carry on the movement. And thus, indeed, I did rest for five or six years ; for the Home and Colonial School Society had adopted the system, and Miss Matthews (our present much-honoured Mrs. Stapleton) was teaching it there.

But I was destined to receive another stimulus — one of a very different kind from the last. By this time I was married, and my brave wife had seen me lay out all our united savings (and that was a serious thing for a young Benédict with a salary of only £160 a year) — all our united savings in paying for a big book slowly written and slowly stereotyped. It was the now old " Grammar of Vocal Music." When it was finished I asked her whether I should bring it out in an expensive form, so as to be repaid early, or in a cheap form, with the hope of being repaid at some distant period. She comforted me by saying that she did not think it would ever pay (laughter), but she would like me to do all the good I could with it by making it cheap. For my part I hoped that my wife and little child would not be allowed to suffer for my love of music, and so made the book 2s. 6d. instead of 5s.

But, alas! soon after the publication a letter came from Mr. Reynolds, the noble hon. secretary of the " Home and Colonial," saying that their training school was passing under Government hands, and must adopt the system of singing patronised by the Government, but that the committee were anxious that I should not consider this step as a slight on our method, of which they thought as highly as ever, [so that I thus lost at one sweep from forty to sixty school teachers every year going forth to teach a workable method.

Worse than this, another training school (from which I hoped much), 1st, adopted the system in public meeting; 2nd, set it to be taught by incompetent hands ; 3rd, mixed it up with the Wilhem system ; and 4th, cut it adrift as a thing which, after fair trial, had been rejected.

Fairly tried and rejected—weighed and found wanting—was that to go forth to the world after all my labour and study—after my wife's courage in risking our little all ? No. It was surely my duty to prevent that. Minister as I was, I might and ought to give a little time to lecturing, and to such correspondence as might arise, for the promotion of my music mission. I did ; and not a few lectures, conferences, and Finsbury Chapel meetings sprang out of this "heavy blow and great discouragement." Like Jonah, I needed this sudden plunge into the cold waters of rejection to awake me to a new sense of duty—a new acceptance of my mission.

In consequence of that plunge there came ten years of steady work, and marked success. (Cheers.) *Cassell's*

P

Popular Educator, the Tonic Sol-fa Association, with
all its hearty fellowship, Crystal Palace Concerts, the first
books of cheap Sol-fa Psalmody, the introduction of the
method into Scotland, the commencement of the *Tonic.
Sol-fa Reporter*, and the completion of the *Standard
Course.* We had thus got out of the period in which
printers refused to print Sol-fa, and proprietors of the
principal books of Psalmody refused to allow their works
to appear in so queer a dress on any terms.

Some of my other literary work — which was not
connected with Sol-fa—proved profitable, and for about
twenty years my dear wife permitted me to go on
investing these profits, amounting to about £300 a year, in
the Tonic Sol-fa enterprise, before we saw any clear net
return. I often, looking back, wonder that she did not
call it the Sol-fa well into which we were throwing the
money, while our little ones were rising up to make such
things serious. I wonder at her faith, and the remarkable
thing is, that it was not faith in Sol-fa (I have never made
her a great Sol-faist), it was faith in me. (Laughter
and cheers.)

But if it had not been for some resources of this kind
I do not know how the Tonic Sol-fa movement could have
been set afloat. A new notation for a thing in common
use, required nothing less than the creation of a new
literature. How was this to be done ? No doubt others
would have been raised up to do this needful thing if
we had failed, but I am very glad that my brave wife
and I had the beginning of it.

But the close of this ten years brought me to another
stage of this little history—another thrusting forth into
the mission for music. The work I have referred to
added to my ministerial work, and the anxious church-
building enterprise I had taken up was too much for

me. Bodily and mental forces failed me. For several years I felt this humiliation—I thought myself like Nebuchadnezzar sent out to eat grass with the beasts of the field. I wrote no books and could not preach without trial to myself and greater trial to others. What was I to do ?

With the help of my wife's property, and the profits which, after twenty years, the Sol-fa publications were bringing in I was able to live. But it was a poor life merely to live and do nothing. Well I could not give lectures ; I could not write books ; for a long time I could scarcely write a letter ; but I could look after machinery, look after the details of printing, stereotyping, and binding, and so in this dark season of my eclipse I took to business. I have sometimes been blamed for this by those who think that "once a minister always a minister." I do not remember the time when I believed that doctrine. When I went to college at sixteen years of age, I certainly dedicated myself solemnly to the service of what I thought good and right in the world, but I said then as I say now, that there are many ways of serving the holy and the true beside that of the pulpit. I think that indeed the highest service. But a man must serve as he can. If he is shut out from the higher offices he must be glad to take a humbler post.

And this business has proved to me a mighty lever for the propagation of the Tonic Sol-fa method. It has enabled me to produce some costly books great and small, which must necessarily be unremunerative for many years. It has enabled me to keep a staff of helpers, whose daily correspondence has kept alive the Tonic Sol-fa spirit in all parts of the kingdom, and in many parts of the world. In fact, my printing office has in this way been the stimulus and the support of other printing offices which have employed the Tonic Sol-fa notation.

I am glad to say that the number of such offices in England, Scotland, and Wales is constantly increasing. A few years ago I calculated that their Sol-fa publications were as numerous as my own, but now a careful computation assures me that they are twice or three times as numerous. And as my own publications are now, and always have been, steadily increasing year by year, this three-folding of the work by others is a good augury for the future.

My next stimulus came from Scotland. I was taking a quiet month amid the grand scenery of North Queensferry in 1866 when Mr. Colin Brown startled me by a visit, and a message from his friend Mr. Euing. He was about to endow a Lectureship on music. Would I become the first lecturer ? or, at all events, take the first session. It was an opportunity, my friend urged, for propagating what I believed to be true musical doctrine among the people. I should find hearty students in Scotland, and many ready to work with me. I pleaded my inability. A visit to Mr. Euing, however, settled the question, and I tried to think and write and lecture once more. I soon found that the Scotch students demanded something to do. They wanted a text book, and they wanted exercises in composition. I tried to supply their wants. Eminent musicians advised me kindly about a Text Book of Musical Form and Historical Specimens of the development of music itself. I had to work out an Ollendorf system of composition for myself. But these grew into large books, and I was obliged to take my time in getting them through the press, because they were very costly. They have, however, already proved profitable in the sense of being useful, and I am beginning to feel very proud of the little company of young composers which we are raising up. Our students in harmony count by the hundred every year throughout the kingdom ; but Scotland exceeds all. The Euing Lecture-ship which began this movement still stands at its head, and the continued success of Mr. Colin Brown and his co-workers in training those hard-headed Scotch youths to delight themselves in harmony is something marvellous to me. The good and honoured man who established this endowment has recently gone to his rest, but "his works do follow him."

My last stimulus was not a friendly one.* But I recognise in it the hand of a good Providence, for it has been very mighty in its influence, and very useful to our movement. If we get our Tonic Sol-fa College established soon we shall owe it to the stimulus given by My Lords of the Privy Council. It ought to be a very easy thing in a free country like ours to obtain simple even-handed justice, and it would be in this case, if music and the art of teaching were generally and popularly understood. But very few of their lordships know any-thing of either. We had reason to expect that, under these circumstances, they would have submitted the question to competent judges, whose great names appended to their report, would have been a guarantee of honour and truth. But, as I think, to the dishonour of the Department, this was not done. Hence has come to pass what a distinguished friend, writing to me, thus describes :—

"I regret very much the answer of 'my Lords' to our memorial, but more for their sake than for ours. It shows that their eyes are not yet opened to the great work which Tonic Sol-fa has done and is doing, so that they impatiently treat as the groundless complaint of a jealous

---

* Attacks on the system in official papers by Dr. Hullah, the Government Inspector of Music in Training Colleges.

clique a remonstrance which proper investigation would have shown to be not only justly founded, but inspired solely by a regard for the interests of the musical education of the people."

I am sorry to tell you that this unjust treatment of our Tonic Sol-fa students in Training Colleges continues to the present moment. The questions set at the last Christmas examination are undoubtedly such as must necessarily discourage and break down the use of our method in Training Schools. The Department held up the cup of promise to the lip, but they have dashed it from the lip. But in this policy of repression by the mailed hand of Government power our educational opponents have begun at the wrong end. They do not see that the Training Colleges exist only for the schools ; and that whatever the schools demand the colleges will finally have to supply (loud cheers). Now the schools are demanding the Tonic Sol-fa method. Eighty thousand children demand it under the School Board for London, and probably another eighty thousand under the denominational schools, which are equally fond of it. In Scotland and in other parts of our Island this demand is growing. It was to me most remarkable to find in the last Educational Blue Book, that Her Majesty's Inspectors of Schools united in almost a chorus of praise for the Tonic Sol-fa method. The Training Schools cannot long resist this. They will soon be surrounded and will have to yield at discretion. We, as a Tonic Sol-fa organisation, shall not need again to fight the battle of the colleges. They might resent our further interference. They are strong enough to look to their own interests.

In the recent struggle we were looking at the schools far more than at the colleges. Do you think that when a

few of us spent all that long labour and some £300 or
£400 of money in diffusing information we were merely
thinking of My Lords of the Privy Council, or caring
to answer a particular educational opponent ? No ! Not
for a moment ! We were using our opportunity for a
fresh appeal to the people. Much greater issues were
raised than those which touched upon passing events. We
took care whither our arguments went and where they
stirred up discussion. Letters from all parts of our
country, and especially letters from America, show that
our appeal to the people has been a success. I am not
sure that even you would have been here to-day to
greet me so kindly if you did not believe that I had been
fighting for an educational truth which is good for the
nation.

I am anxious to guard you against two errors. First,
that I have been a martyr, or made great sacrifices in this
cause. I assure you that in these later years I have lived
in great comfort. I think it was a witness in the trial of
Thurtle for murder who said that Mr. T. was a
"respectable" man, and being asked what he regarded as
a proof of a man's being respectable, answered—"When
he keeps a gig." Now it is true that I have not been able
to reach that well-known sign of respectability — the
power to keep a gig — but I have not hitherto needed
it. Although for twenty years my Tonic Sol-fa enterprise
was all spending and no return, my friends will be glad to
know that now fully half of the capital with which
our Tonic Sol-fa business is carried on comes out of Tonic
Sol-fa profits, and that fully half of our living expenditure
year by year comes out of the same source.

The other error against which I would guard you is,
that all this is my doing, or that I have ever been
anything but a co-worker with others.

First, there is Miss Glover.   The philosopher who
first discovered the lever said : If you will give me where
I can stand I will move the world.   It was Miss Glover,
with her simple, truthful, yet philosophical way of looking
at things that gave me where to stand, and the lever with
which to work.   Then, sir, there are my literary helpers,
the good and learned G. F. Graham, Mr. W. E. Hickson,
the father of English school music, and General Perronet
Thompson.   Then there are those who filled Wales
with Tonic Sol-fa.   Mr. Eleazer Roberts was the first
to translate it into Welsh, and close after him was the
Rev. J. Roberts, who extended the work, so that now
I think there is no country so forward in Tonic Sol-fa
work as Wales is.   (Cheers.)   And now, turning to
Scotland, I am reminded of my honoured friend Rev.
Alexander Lowrie, who came and took a little draught of
the Sol-fa water, and then spoke of its beneficial effects
throughout the whole of Scotland.   Wherever he might
go, at every soiree at which he was present you would
find him speaking of the advantages of the system.   Then,
again, there is Mr. Colin Brown, who by his readiness
to perceive what I wanted and what I was aiming at, and
by his sympathy and practical business way of looking at
things, has been a continual help to me for many years.
Then there was Mr. W. D. Read, Mr. James Heriot, and
Mr. Miller, of Glasgow, the largest teacher, by which
I mean the teacher of the largest number of children
in the kingdom, who has done more than any other man
in this cause.   Then coming back to poor England
(laughter) we have Mr. Alfred Brown, of Plaistow, my
first helper in the *Tonic Sol-fa Reporter*, Mrs. Stapleton,
the first teacher in London, my dear old friend Mr. Linder,
of whom I have before spoken, and Mr. Sarll, who is
prevented from being with us only by a bereavement
in his family, and who by his glorious energy in days gone

by filled this hall with his pupils. Then there is
Mr. Ashcroft, of Stepney, noted for his large-mindedness,
his great grasp of things and business ability, and my dear
friend and old secretary Mr. William Thodey, who helped
me during my weakness and the period of my eclipse.
There is also Mr. Powell, the apostle of the midland
counties ; Mr. Robert Griffiths, the apostle of Lancashire,
and Mr. Longbottom, the apostle of Yorkshire ; all of
whom have rendered invaluable service. Then we come
to Mr. James Stallybrass, my first analyst of harmony, and
Mr. George Oakey, by second analyst, and known also
in connection with the Composition Club. Next, we have
the originators of the instrumental movement, Mr. Cowley,
Mr. Kennedy (the young professor to whom I wish all
success ; may he have such pupils as I have had), and my
young friend Mr. M'Naught, all of whom have done much
for the cause. Then among the apostles of the art of
teaching we have Mr. Alfred Stone, of Bristol, Herr
Behnke, of Birmingham, Mr. Callaway, of Men's Voice
Music, Mr. John Evans of the School Board, the brothers
Venables, of South London, and Mr. Proudman. People
speak of Dr. Sandwith, *of Kars*, and I think we might
call the last gentleman, Mr. Proudman, of Paris and the
Crystal Palace. But I think the greatest victory Mr.
Proudman has achieved has been the teaching of ragged
school children. In this his versatility is displayed, for
he is as much at home in training a choir for delicate
singing, as in teaching a number of ragged school children
to sing the "burlesque band." And now it would be
an injustice if I were not to name my eldest son, who has
really been a co-worker with me for many years past.
You have not known the work he has done. I think it is
somewhere said, " It is a great honour for a man to have
descendants ; but it is a greater honour for a man to see in
those descendants successors in his work," and that I have

the happiness to find not only in my eldest son, but in the others also. These are only some of my helpers, and I feel already that although I have mentioned many names, there are many more left out from whom I never fail to obtain assistance.

Finally, a proof of the solidity of our movement I have already given you in the history of its steady growth, and in the fact that many publishers now print our music with simple business aims, and with a fair expectation of business returns, and that a large amount of money capital is thus engaged in our Tonic Sol-fa enterprise.

More serious than this, as a proof of our solidity, is the fact that a number of educated and competent gentlemen in England, Scotland, and Wales, have risked their whole livelihood on the truth and usefulness of our method.

But more hopeful far than any amount of money or personal responsibility, is this other fact that our method is rooted in the great voluntary movements of our kingdom. The great Temperance movement, the grand and merciful Ragged School movement, and all the youngest and most vigorous movements for Singing in Schools and Homes and Congregations cannot do without us.

With your help — with many a hard hour's work which you have all given — we have established our great system of certificates. Those who wear them, especially the higher ones, do them credit. They are recognised by School Boards, by the Managers of Denominational Schools, and by Churches, as recommendations for the post of Teacher or Precentor. We are hoping to make them National.

By your industry and success we are raising up a new school of Harmony and Elementary Composition.

Through your zeal in striving to do your work well, we are hoping to establish a course of systematic training in the great and blessed Art of Teaching.

And now by your bounty, and by your campaign for five thousand pounds, we hope soon to rear a People's College for Music ; a College to which the friends of every good movement that can be promoted by music shall come and learn to teach ; a College from which a new Musical Profession shall go forth, a profession of music teachers for the people.

I have only one promise to make to you. Those who have known me longest have found me ever ready to adopt improvements, have sometimes been a little annoyed by my doing so; well, I promise you that whenever a better method of teaching the people of England to sing is discovered than that which I got from Miss Glover I will adopt it. It will not only be my pleasure but my interest to do so. My brother-in-law, who had a cotton factory, long ago taught me that it always answered to use the best machinery. When a better loom was invented he turned the old ones out and installed the new. I should never have won your fellowship in labour —the personal affection which you show to-day—if the Tonic Sol-fa method merely, or the sale of Tonic Sol-fa books had been my object in life. My object is to make the people of this country and their children sing, and to make them sing for noble ends.

The spirit in which Mr. Curwen accepted the testimonial is shown by the following letter to Mr. Joseph Proudman, who acted as organiser and secretary of the movement :—

Southend, January 30, 1875.

DEAR MR. PROUDMAN,—In acknowledging the balance of the Testimonial Fund I wish to say how strongly I appreciate your personal kindness in the matter. I am told that the largest share of the work fell upon you; and I was gratified to notice how everything was managed with the greatest appropriateness and delicacy, from the conduct of the public meeting to the engraving on the purse. I hope and believe that you will have the satisfaction of seeing that the testimonial movement has done something more and better than do honour to a man. In view of the opprobrium which Government has poured upon us, the Testimonial was very timely; and I think it will remove prejudice, encourage our friends, and bind us together for work. Hoping that we may both live to see " the People's College for Music" well established and widely useful,

I remain, cordially yours,

JOHN CURWEN.

The *Freeman* newspaper, in its report of the meeting, said :—" Mr. Curwen's speech is worthy of being preserved, both as a chapter in the history of music in England, and as the record of what one earnest soul can achieve under the impelling power of a spiritual motive."

During 1874 and 1875 Mr. Curwen's literary time was spent upon his " Teacher's Manual of the Art of Teaching as applied to music," a most exhaustive work, laying down in its opening chapters the principles which are common to the teaching of all subjects, and then applying these principles to the teaching of music. Much space is devoted to the process of development through which the Tonic Sol-fa system had passed in the course of thirty years. The educational reasons for changes and additions are stated, and snatches of autobiography and experience mingle in a most interesting way with the text. Mr. Curwen wrote this book *con amore*. It deals with educational principles ; in the study of which he had always had such delight. The young man's heart stirred within the veteran's as he remembered his early Sunday school lectures and lessons, his fondness for teaching and talking with children, his study of Stowe and Abbott. The larger part of this book is as interesting to teachers of all subjects as it is to those who only teach music.

The following is a letter to a young friend, a girl of twenty, who was dying, written at this time. It shows very clearly Mr. Curwen's simple faith, and his power of sympathy :—

Manchester, September 16, 1875.

Your kind note has been sent on to me here. I am glad you are at home and able to write. I hope that home peace and home love will revive you.

To me, at nearly fifty-nine, it seems natural and proper to think of the nearing time when I shall pass away into another world. But it gives me a shock (I do not know why), when the Lord lays his hand on the young, and brings them near to the verge of this life. And yet why should I wonder, for in both cases it is the same Jesus who holds "the keys of death and the unseen world." What a blessing that He holds the key, and His will be the first face we shall see. I often think of Mrs. Cecil in her last illness. When her son, who was a wild young man then, though afterwards the great and good Richard Cecil, said to her, "Mother, aren't you afraid to go into another world? Who knows what you will meet there?" She answered, "Yes, Richard, I know. I know that I shall meet my Saviour there, and that is enough for me."

Dear child, Jesus the Christ is precious to you and to me. To me the world's cares and the world's work, and my own forgetfulness of God come in between me and Him. But I know that when these clouds are removed (which I hope will be before I go hence), and I see something of what Jesus is, and what heaven is, I shall long to be there.

Whether He is only giving you a near view, and means to bring you back to earth's work and earth's loves again, or whether He is taking you soon to Himself, to dwell where the best things of earth cannot be forgotten, He is yours, and you are His for ever.

Your affectionate friend,
JOHN CURWEN.

The strong sympathy of Mr. Curwen's nature, and the emotional effort which a letter of this sort cost him, is shown by the following passage from a note to Mrs. Curwen, written immediately after the above :—

I have just written to C——— R———, but it has quite overcome me to get so near to the eternal world, even in the company of so sweet a child.

CHAPTER XIII.

1875—1878.

FOUNDATION OF THE TONIC SOL-FA COLLEGE—LECTURES IN
ENGLAND AND SCOTLAND—SOUTHEND—INCORPORATION OF
THE COLLEGE—BEGGING MONEY—THE FIRST SESSION—
CRIEFF—MIXED SCHOOLS—WORDS FOR MUSIC—KARLSBAD
—TREATMENT OF STRANGERS—FORMS OF PRAYER—VISITS
TO PORTSMOUTH AND HALSTEAD — MEETING AT EXETER
HALL FOR THE COLLEGE—TRICYCLE RIDING—IMPRESSIONS
OF A GERMAN LADY—INFLEXIBLE SPIRIT—MR. THOMAS
CURWEN—HOME LIFE.

MR. CURWEN was now launched upon a responsibility
which followed him for several years—the foundation of a
College for the training of Tonic Sol-fa teachers.   He set
to work lecturing .in aid of the scheme, offering to go
wherever £10 could be guaranteed, and speaking on
various subjects.   The following passage from a letter
to Mrs. Curwen, written after one of these lectures,
will [remind many hearers of Mr. Curwen's animated
and telling speeches :—

Hillhead.

The chairman last night [at Paisley] was quite
enthusiastic about my lecture.   I thought he was praising

the choir, and I answered " Yes it was admirable, it
would be difficult to match it." But he said " No, not
the choir, but your lecture." And yet my lecture was
nothing but a set of plain statements of facts, and
then dropping them like hot coals.

In one lecture, delivered in various towns in England
and Scotland during the autumn of 1875, Mr. Curwen
pictured the fruition of his work :—

The masses of the people are not wealthy. They
cannot pay for costly pianos, for soloists, for operas. The
music which they enjoy must be chiefly made by themselves. It will not only be for the people but by the
people. When the work of our Tonic Sol-fa College is
done, the little children will hear it everywhere. Their
rising will be gladdened and their going to rest will
be soothed by the voice of song. There will be a
lark and a nightingale in every nursery. The school
children will rejoice in it. It will brush off the
cobwebs of thought ; it will cheerfulise the whole school
by its strains of soft sweet sounds ; and it will cultivate
and train the affections by pure and beautiful songs. The
churches will be made glad ; " young men and maidens,
old men and children " will each take their part " with
one consent," and with an ease, beauty, and power, of
which we have, at present, no conception ; and homes will
be made more attractive and more happy when there is no
one unable to join in the pleasant recreations of social
music. There is no music in the world like that which is
made by one's own wife and children, especially when we
ourselves can join in the loving harmony.

In February, 1875, Mr. Curwen spent some time at
Southend, in Essex, a watering place within easy reach of

his home, which he usually visited in spring. Here he met his friend the Rev. J. T. Feaston, and joined with delight in some " Psalmody exercises " which Mr. Feaston had organised in the town. In the same month he addressed a meeting of Sunday school teachers, called by the Sunday School Union, in the Weigh House Chapel, London, and lectured also on behalf of the College at Huddersfield and Stanningley.

On June 19th, 1875, the Tonic Sol-fa College was incorporated, and the movement took a permanent and impersonal shape. The College had been in existence, as a voluntary association, for some years, and its organisation had been most carefully elaborated by Mr. Curwen. The Council, with whom the administration of its affairs rests, had been imitated from that of Anderson's College, Glasgow. It was divided into several classes, corresponding with the occupations of the members — teachers of music, clerks, ministers of religion, schoolmasters, merchants, &c. Only a certain number in each class could be elected. Mr. Curwen saw that there would be danger to the College if it got into the hands of any one class, and this arrangement prevented it.

The Council thus elected was, however, a council in the literal meaning of the word only. It was characteristic of Mr. Curwen that he reserved to himself for life the right, in the new College, to veto any resolution he chose.

Q

During the winter of 1875-6 Mr. Curwen made two lecturing tours in Scotland in aid of the College. He held meetings at Newcastle, Edinburgh, Paisley, Glasgow, Aberdeen, Inverness, Dundee, Arbroath, Perth, as well as at Manchester and Ashton. At several of these places he gave two lectures—one on "The Human Voice," and the other on "Music for the People," which we have already quoted. In speaking to his Sol-fa friends we find him holding invincibly to the certificates, without fear or favour.

The work of begging money for the College was a very hard and disappointing one. The response was small, and though Tonic Sol-fa teachers and pupils worked nobly, scarcely any impression was made upon the rich and liberal class which support philanthropic movements. We find Mr. Curwen giving expression to his disappointment, and trying to account for it, in the *Reporter* for June, 1876 :—

Our Tonic Sol-fa movement permeates other movements. It works quietly. The great world does not see it. And this would be the best possible state of things, both for ourselves and for the world, if we were not eager to do more work, and did not require more money than our workers can themselves supply, to do it with. In order to get this money we *must* talk of our work. I went to a wealthy friend the other day asking for help in training music teachers for the people. Just as I was going away (unsuccessful) this gentleman, whose mind is crowded with great schemes and bountiful works in religion and politics, said : " Well, but, Mr. Curwen, *what is* your work ?" So little do our best friends know of our Tonic Sol-fa movement.

This question, "What is the College?" we find Mr. Curwen answering as follows :—

The college is a society of earnest men who desire to spread the pleasure and the blessing of music among the people. They are the men by whose exertions it has already reached even to *the lowest* in Ragged Schools and Reformatories, and to the most distant in Mission Stations. They, for many years, bore the obloquy and did the work which at last brought the power of singing *to you.* They use the Tonic Sol-fa method only as an instrument—the best they can find—for this end. They have themselves at least taken its Member's Certificate, and now they are setting to work *to train music teachers for the people.* Precentors, day school teachers, and Sunday school teachers are to be better fitted for their music work, and a new "profession" of people's music-teachers, skilled in the art of teaching, is to be raised up. Their efforts to spread music among the people, they say, have been constantly hindered and discredited by the want of *trained* teachers, and now that the School Boards of London, Glasgow, and Birmingham have adopted the Tonic Sol-fa method, the demand for *such teachers* has greatly increased.

On the strength of a few scholarships, which, except the two "Glover" scholarships, had been raised by his lectures, Mr. Curwen organised, in July and August, 1876, a Summer Term of study for young teachers. It was held in the temporary offices of the College at Plaistow, and

lasted six weeks.   The session was founded on an idea of
Mr. Scot Russell's, that the best way to learn engineering
is to spend six months in the lecture-room, and then
six months in the shops.   The students were nearly
all acting teachers ; they came to learn more, and went
back at once to apply what they had learned.   Here
is Mr. Curwen's description of them :—

There are no idlers allowed in the College.   All
are workers.   Class succeeds class as regularly as the
clock records the hours.   All day long the steady work
goes on, with scarcely any intermission, except for meal
times and sleep.   So close and trying are the studies that
none but earnest men would endure them, and none
but well-seasoned and well-prepared Sol-faists could
stand them.   Yet there is no sign of weariness.   Why ?
These forty students are here to equip themselves for
their chosen and loved vocation.   They are the pioneers
of a new profession — Music Teachers for the People —
and they exult in being students at the first term of
the incorporated Tonic Sol-fa College.

Mr. Curwen was much interested at this time in
a "Voice Harmonium," patented by his friend Mr. Colin
Brown, of Glasgow, and designed to solve the problem
of perfect intonation.   He contributed to the expense
of bringing it out, and wrote articles upon it in the
Reporter.

The " Summer Term " was but just ended when Mr.
and Mrs. Curwen started for Crieff, where they stayed at

the Hydropathic House.   Mr. Curwen carried his mission with him here :—

TO MR. D. FERGUSON, GLASGOW.

Crieff, September 12th, 1876.

If you see Mr. Colin Brown tell him that the visitors here (always some 180 in number) have twice invited me to give drawing-room lectures, and that in consequence I have had several lady pupils anxious to sing in order to do good among the sick and the ˌpoor.   It has been very pleasant to help them.

In the *Reporter* he writes :—

I had to give a great many private lessons in corners of the drawing-room.   These were very pleasant to me because my pupils were eager to learn, and anxious to do good with their knowledge.   One lady wished to sing in a village choir.   Another who could sing well with the piano desired the power of reading music without it.   She could not take her piano to the cottages of the poor and the sick, and she found that the singing of hymns was always welcomed there.   A clergyman wished to provide singing classes for his parish as a counter attraction to the public house, and a clergyman's wife, whose solo singing was of the finest quality, wished to use what she modestly called her " one gift," in teaching the children of her husband's school to sing.

About this time Mr. Curwen lifted his voice for the last time in the Educational affairs of the Parish in which he lived.   The schools at Plaistow, which he had founded in 1844, had been transferred to the School Board in 1871, but had hitherto been continued as mixed schools.   The School Board now, however, acting under Whitehall

influence, determined to organise them in the ordinary
English fashion of boys, girls, and infants. Mr. Curwen
did nothing more than protest, in a letter to the *Stratford
Express*, against the change. He says :—

It is rather difficult to explain the intellectual
advantages of the mixed system to persons who are not
practically acquainted with the art of teaching. They
cannot understand why anyone should take so much
trouble about the question whether children above seven
are to be divided into boys or girls or into senior children
and junior children. They think that the promoters
of the latter division have got hold of a crotchet, or are
indulging a fad. They have never had to teach a class
containing pupils of widely different attainments and
abilities. They do not know what it is to feel that you
are wearying and discouraging the forward and bright
while you are labouring to elucidate and force your
teachings on the dull, or that you are confirming the
dulness of the dull while enjoying yourself in teaching
the bright. They have never had the pleasure of bringing
forward a class of pupils who stood together on the same
intellectual level.

Suppose two instructors can teach arithmetic to
thirty children. On the *separate* plan each instructor
would probably teach twenty who were about to go
through addition, subtraction, and multiplication, and
a separate twenty who were able to take division, rule of
three, and fractions. If the first instructor took the boys,
then the other would take the girls — double work ; so
that we should have two teachers each doing two things.
On the mixed plan one teacher would take all the forty,
whether boys or girls, who were going through the rules
of addition, subtraction, and multiplication, and another

teacher would take the forty who had to be helped in working through division, the rule of three, and fractions; so that we should have two teachers each doing one thing. The advantage to the children would be that they would get the whole of the teacher's time to themselves, instead of half of it having to be given to those who belonged to another stage, besides the glorious stimulus of always working with your equals; the advantage to the teacher being that having fewer subjects to teach he can teach them better. Anyone who considers the concentration of the teacher's time and attention which is thus gained will not wonder at the strong language of Dr. Morrison, the rector of the Free Church Normal School, Glasgow, when he said to me "I cannot understand you English people in not adopting the mixed system of education. Why, it just doubles our teaching power."

Mr. Curwen does not here dwell upon what he always felt to be the best argument for mixed education— *i.e.*, that it follows the order of nature and of the family. He had a great belief that constant intercourse, under proper supervision, was the healthiest thing for both sexes. Attempts to improve upon Providence by separating boys from girls or men from women brought about, in his view, the mischief they were supposed to prevent. He was fond of quoting the reply which an English visitor received when he was being shown over a mixed college in America. "Don't the young men and the young women flirt?" asked the visitor. "Oh, no," was the reply, "they see far too much of each other for that." Mr. Curwen felt that time was on the side of mixed education, and that sooner or later public opinion would swing round.

"The Harmony Player for the Harmonium," a little manual in which Mr. Curwen, with the help of Messrs. Fisher and Oakey, endeavoured to systematise the art of fingering, was produced at this time.

Mr. Curwen was always very scrupulous about the *words* of music that he published or recommended his friends to sing. He believed in sincerity always accompanying the singer. He did not see how Protestants should sing "Ave Maria;" and songs in praise of drinking, in which the old glee music is so particularly rich, he proscribed entirely. There remained, however, many cases in classical music where the question arose "how far is it right to lend oneself to a dramatic situation which is part of a larger scheme." Handel, in describing the power of music over revellers in "Alexander's Feast," is an instance in point. Mr. Curwen was consulted about this, and we find him replying :—

Many things are not absolutely right or absolutely wrong. The circumstances and the persons make the difference. There are two safe rules in such cases. 1st. If we ourselves are doubtful about the rightness of a thing, leave it alone and go to something else. 2nd. If our friends are made unhappy by it, never let *our* pleasures cause *their* pain ; for mere amusement is a small thing, and easily sacrificed by us.

Mr. Curwen continued his appeals for the building fund in 1877. The following letters refer to this subject :—

TO MR. D. FERGUSON, GLASGOW.

St. Leonards, March 6th, 1877.

I am very greedy for money just now, but your letter gratified me as much as the cheque. I am very grateful to have friends who desire and strive to keep our College in religious hands. Our best security for that is that, with only very few exceptions, we know our supporters, all over the country, to be not only Christians, but decidedly evangelical Christians. Our certificates are granted by Christians of the Sunday school teacher type. I think we may safely say that all (or very nearly all) our Member's Certificates, are taken by Christians. These elect the Council and rule the College. I intend, also, this next term to announce distinctly a *precentor's* class. But we could not have set up a creed. We must help all singers of God's praises. How large is the fellowship of singers ! Some of the best used hymns in England, and Scotland too, are known to be the composition of Roman Catholics, Jews, and Unitarians. People of all creeds come closest together when they sing.

Tonic Sol-fa College, June 13th, 1877.

I think that we may next winter hire rooms in different districts of London to do part of our work. Only fractions of it can be done in this way. But we *must* have a centre. A better, for our main purposes, I cannot find anywhere. The accident of its being near my home enables me to work in it, which I could not do daily, as I do now, if it were in London. I may be spared long enough to make that a consideration of value to the College — of value sufficient to pay for the building.

Do I overvalue my own work ? Well, I mean to make it as valuable for the public good as I can.

In the autumn of 1877 the liver disease which had been slowly and surely stealing upon his wife took Mr. Curwen to Karlsbad. Even amid the anxieties of illness they enjoyed the life, and made many friends. Wherever he went Mr. Curwen used to speak to strangers among whom he was thrown. He thought that English people lost much by their reserve and the " stony British stare." Mrs. Curwen, writing from Karlsbad at this time, says :—

A great many English people have thanked father for speaking to them, and then introducing them to others. Some of them say they will try to imitate him when they come again.

Here are some passages from Mr. Curwen's letters during this visit. The speculations about forms of prayer were set agoing by his attendance at the Church of England service at Karlsbad :—

Karlsbad, August 11th, 1877.

I try to make the best of the forms of prayer ; but they do not lay hold of the heart so easily as less perfect extempore prayers. The prayer-meetings we have had, in our own rooms, with young ———, some Scotch friends next door, and a nice Methodist bachelor from Newcastle, were very delightful. Only I am sorry to find Mr. ——— and our Scotch friend running off the rails of usefulness about the Personal Reign, and the world getting worse and worse till Christ comes to destroy the wicked—most

unspiritual and un-Christlike doctrines as they seem
to me.

Karlsbad, August 26th, 1877.

Forms of prayer have their advantage. They *might*
be made to secure variety and fulness and clearness. But
they cannot, I fear, be made to carry brightness and force
and life to any great extent. I think the Holy Spirit
loves to play on the Eolian harp of a *free* worshipper's
soul. Could we not combine both plans in our services?
A short and variable set of prayers with free prayers and
preaching? As for liturgy and responses by the people of
all sorts, I am sure they should be *muiscal*, however
simple. I would let the people's verse in the psalms
be monotoned on G, and the amens given humbly by all
the people on E. I think I should enjoy half an hour of
such a service on Sunday mornings, followed by an hour
of our own sort of service.

Karlsbad, September 1st, 1877.

We should not like our children to spend luxurious
idle lives like those of many of the rich folk who come
here. Some of them must be very rich. They have no
work in the world—nothing to live for. Their characters
grow flabby. They are always looking out for a sensation,
and when it comes it goes. Poor things!

The following passage from a letter of Mrs. Curwen,
gives a glimpse of their life at Karlsbad :—

Father wishes me to tell you of a poor woman in
whom I became interested at the Sprudel. She looked so
wretchedly ill and so poor that I could never get her
out of my mind. So at last I got Miss M—— to speak to
her for me. We found she was a Russian Jewess suffering
from dropsy. She had no hope of cure, but the doctor had

told her that she would be much relieved by these waters, and so she had come here, and was going back to her home, 300 miles away, yesterday when we spoke to her. So you see if we had let another morning pass the opportunity would have gone. She was so poor that she could only afford herself soup twice a week, and her clothes looked very thin. Dear kind father let me have five florins for her, which brought the first bit of brightness I had seen to her face. Oh, she always looked so sad as I nodded to her each morning at the brunnen.

At Karlsbad Mr. Curwen visited schools, choirs, and churches to hear and study their music. He came home with the opinion :—

We believe that whatever may be said of orchestras and pianos, for the wide diffusion of *musical knowledge*, and for the common enjoyment of the *gift of song* old England will soon be at the head of the nations.

On his return he entered with renewed vigour into the campaign for money to build the Tonic Sol-fa College, offering £1,000 himself if £2,000 more could be raised. Land had been purchased a year before, at Forest Gate, and it was now planted with trees, the occasion being made a friendly ceremony.

Mr. Curwen was much interested, at the close of this year, in visits which he paid to Portsmouth and Halstead. At Portsmouth Miss Robinson, the soldier's friend, had written to him several years before :—

I most thankfully feel that my power of singing is entirely due to Tonic Sol-fa. A person could scarcely be more naturally deficient of musical taste and talent than I was till your system gave me the power to sing and teach, and enabled me readily to lead the soldiers' singing at my lectures and meetings with them.

He now visited her Institute, and lectured to an audience of soldiers and civilians.

At Halstead he met with Miss Greenwood, and saw her reformatory girls. She told him that in the early days of her work, before authority was established, she could conquer the girls by singing, when every other means of checking their lawlessness had failed.

A demonstration on behalf of the Tonic Sol-fa College was held in Exeter Hall in April, 1878, at which Mr. Curwen was able to announce that in little more than three years £4,780 had been raised for the various purposes of the College. This had been chiefly contributed in small portions, and these were specimens of the contributors :—

A workman in a Welsh colliery sends us a thank-offering, and says that the Sol-fa class kept him from bad company ; he took to teaching his five brothers and three sisters, and their singing in temperance and other circles won them the name of the "happy family." (Cheers.) A young man in London writes that it was the singing class which brought him among religious people, which led to his conversion, and opened to him a life of usefulness. The teacher of an industrial school says that his own home has been made brighter and happier, and the choirs of two churches have been strengthened by members of his Sol-fa family. Better still, the seventy girls of his industrial school "are losing some of their sadness and gloom through the power of Sol-fa songs."

The following passage from a letter to his brother, Mr. Thomas Curwen, shows Mr. Curwen in a lighter mood :—

Southend, June, 1878.

Moreover I have hired a tricycle on which I can already ride a little, and hope to ride more. I have not found myself so well exercised since we turned over the gymnastic poles together. I have made Mr. ——— (a clergyman) quite a proficient in tricycling ; he beats me, for I don't try how much I can do. And Mrs. ———, Mrs. ———, Miss ———, and ——— can all do better than I. It was quite a pleasure to teach them — to see how they enjoyed learning.

The following impressions of Mr. Curwen are written by a German lady who made his acquaintance at this time :—

I had but few opportunities of seeing Mr. Curwen, and was, of course, greatly prepared to like him, having for a long time heard so much good about him. It was in April, 1878, that I saw Mr. Curwen for the first time. He was then to me most genial and most kind, asking me about the pupil I then had ; my way of teaching her ; her capacities ; and my difficulties in dealing with her morally and intellectually. He listened with the greatest interest to all I had to say, speaking words of encouragement and giving me then even the impression, so strongly confirmed on subsequent occasions, that he was a man of the largest sympathies, who might have taken for his life motto the words of the Roman poet, "I am a man, and nothing human is without interest for me." There was a wonderful combination of tenderness and strength in Mr. Curwen. So loving and gentle as he was, one yet felt intuitively that he possessed much firmness to guide ; much strength to support ; that he was a man to be relied on, to be leant on.

He inspired me with much veneration, and when one day, on my saying good-bye to him, he took both my hands in his, saying with his own warmth and heartiness of manner, " Blessings on you ; " I felt that these words, coming from such a good man, were a patriarchal blessing indeed.

Another feature in his character that attracted me was this : His nature was more open to the harmonies of life than to its dissonances. I am sure he was never distracted by the doubts and questionings, the thousand whys and wherefores that harass less healthy minds.

His was the serenity of an assured faith — all is working for good, all will be well. I doubt not but that he also had felt the mysteries and contradictions of life, but whenever I spoke to him I felt that these were no difficulty to him, that they did not vex him ; his " heart was established with grace ; " his foot was firmly set on the rock of faith ; his views of life were healthy and hopeful.

To come in contact with such a man must soothe and calm and encourage those who find it often hard to hear the harmonies among the jarring discords ; to see the lights beyond among the present darkness.

I fancy that Mr. Curwen was not much of an abstract thinker, but preferred practical realities. He was a *worker* in the full sense of the word. I shall never forget how he laughed at me because I complained to him that in Dr. Guthrie's biography the inner life of the man reveals itself so little. Mr. Curwen thought that a true German's complaint and criticism. What need to ask to see the inner workings of the soul if their manifest outcome consisted in such noble deeds, so beneficial to mankind! Herein, of course, I could not agree with Mr. Curwen.

We have spoken of Mr. Curwen's inflexible spirit, and his determination to carry out his plans without modification or delay. In a private letter, written about this time, he says, speaking of some differences of opinion in the Tonic Sol-fa camp :—

The way to reconcile these men is to be *strong.* A strong centre is what they need—a centripetal force which they cannot resist.

The German lady, whose letter we have just quoted, was riding in the train with Mr. Curwen one day, and he told her that he was going to a meeting of the Council of the Tonic Sol-fa College, and that he meant a certain resolution to be carried. He knew they were almost all against it, but said that they would have to yield to him. "Why, Mr. Curwen," she said, "you are just like Bismarck." He smiled, and said, after a pause, "Am I? Well, perhaps I am."

Between Mr. Curwen and his only brother, Mr. Thomas Curwen, there existed through life an attachment that in its tenderness and unruffled sweetness was almost womanly. Mr. Thomas Curwen, though he lingered until the close of 1879, was at this time suffering from a fatal disease. The following is one of many letters written to him by Mr. Curwen, and it breathes characteristic gentleness and love :—

Upton, February 26th, 1878.

DEAR PRECIOUS BROTHER,—We heard of your illness. I wish we could do something for you, dear boy ! You should not be discouraged. See how wonderfully the Lord has helped you hitherto—you and your tribe of dear ones. How good and patient and forgiving and bountiful he has been to us two motherless boys all our days ! He has been answering our mother's prayers for us all the time. And then our dear father's memory, what a power of blessing that has shed into our lives ! Then, dear brother, what wives God has given us—each wife so well suited to her own husband ! Seldom have two brothers been so greatly blessed. The children ! You are so rich in them, and they are each a separate joy. Our Heavenly Father cares for each of them just as he has cared for you and me. Let us not distrust Him. What is your care and mine compared with this ? Dear Brother, of late you have been doing harder and more exciting days' work than I have done. It is not unlikely that you will outlive me. Let us both learn to look in Jesus' face, and " cast all our care on Him who careth for us."

Here a sketch of Mr. Curwen at home may be introduced. It is contributed by a relative :—

In private life, amidst the surroundings of a very happy home, Mr. Curwen's gentleness and loving disposition were well known. Although the voice might be

R

raised but slightly above a whisper, and the action as gentle as if it were for a little child, there was no evidence of weakness, it was rather the calm of reserve power. His will was law.

Mr. Curwen was a wise and patient adviser as well as a loving friend. When heavy cares and weighty responsibilities fell upon me I could always turn to Mr. Curwen for sound advice, and for cheer on my way. Very many can speak of the generous hospitality always freely offered under his roof, and that as much when he felt the need of rigid economy as when that necessity had gone. Like the patriarchs of old he regarded hospitality as a privilege as well as a sacred duty ; and in proportion to the increase of his means his gifts became more bountiful. The love of such a man was most precious, for when he loved at all it was deep and true. Alas ! that it is removed from us for ever, and that the world is made so much poorer.

The Rev. W. Dorling, in an obituary notice in *The Christian World*, describes very happily Mr. Curwen's person and manner :—

Mr. Curwen was very widely known as the leading promoter of the Tonic Sol-fa method of teaching music in England, but a large number of Christian people cherish a true affection for his memory for reasons which concern his personal character, and as belonging to a high type of Christian gentleman. Those must have been cold and dreary cynics at heart, who did not feel that something like sunlight fell upon them when they were in the presence of John Curwen. His manners were quiet and yet thoroughly genial, to a very great extent representing the tone of the refined English society which was found in most country towns some fifty and more years ago. His venerable head and face, his pleasant, touching, and cheery voice, his very dress and external habit, at once made you feel that you were near to a man who claimed your respect, and would sooner or later win your affection. The "sweet reasonableness of Christ" found gracious expression in his words and actions. It was not in Mr. Curwen's way to scale the heights or fathom the depths of modern controversies, but his eye was open to the light of truth as it touched the varieties of human work and thought in our age, and he rejoiced in it with thankfulness and hope.

It was a pleasant privilege — one not to be forgotten by any who have ever enjoyed it — to see him and his beloved wife in their own home. The hearts of loving survivors will picture them in a truer and dearer home, near to their Father's presence, and in the companionship of the "just made perfect." Such lives bring only blessing to the world, and leave memories behind fragrant with gratitude and joy.

CHAPTER XIV.

1879—1880.

DOMESTIC ANXIETY — ILLNESS OF MR. T. CURWEN AND OF
MRS. CURWEN — LETTERS TO MR. T. CURWEN — BAZAAR FOR
THE TONIC SOL-FA COLLEGE — FOUNDATION STONE LAID —
MR. CURWEN'S SPEECH ON THE OCCASION — OPENING OF THE
WING OF THE COLLEGE—SUMMER TERM OF STUDY—VISIT TO
BRENTWOOD — LECTURE IN LIVERPOOL—DEATH OF MR. T.
CURWEN — LECTURES AT FOREST GATE — UNVEILING OF
MISS GLOVER'S PORTRAIT—VISIT TO NORWOOD—LIFE THERE
—LETTERS—ANECDOTE — PSALMODY—LITURGIES—DEATH OF
MRS. CURWEN—SKETCH OF HER CHARACTER BY MR. CURWEN
— HER CHARITIES — HOUSEKEEPING SKILL — TREATMENT
OF SERVANTS — HOSPITALITY — QUOTATIONS FROM FRIENDS'
LETTERS.

In 1879 Mr. Curwen was harassed and torn by domestic
anxiety and grief. Mrs. Curwen's illness became gradually
more serious, while Mr. Thomas Curwen, his brother, was
dying a lingering death. The responsibility of building
the College was enough to have filled his mind and
occupied his energy, even if these two disturbing causes
had been absent. As it was he had no rest ; he passed

from one sick bed to the other, and tried to fix his thoughts upon public work while his heart was sore. During this year he went always twice and often thrice a week to Hampstead, where Mr. Thomas Curwen lived—a journey which occupied an hour and a half each way. During these visits he sat an hour or two by his brother's bed. Several times one of his nieces entering found the brothers hand in hand, in silence. When Mr. Curwen's regular visit was interrupted he would write a letter to his brother, such as the two which we now quote :—

Upton, Sunday morning, February 23, 1879.

The dear Lord send you some text to comfort, to strengthen, to fill with sweet hope. A happy, a blessed Sabbath morning to my dear brother. I don't know who you have to preach to-day, but I trust the congregations will not be smaller, and God will "prosper the work of your hands" in trying to gather a new Christian brotherhood in Hampstead. It is a great honour to have the smallest share in the spreading and strengthening of the kingdom of Christ upon earth; and God has given you much of this honour. For how many years, at Clapton, you "used the office of a deacon well." Dean Alford reads the text in I Timothy iii. 13—"For they that served well as deacons obtained for themselves *a good standing place*, and great boldness in the faith which is in Christ Jesus." A good standing place before their fellow Christians — respect, confidence, love. A good standing place before our Heavenly Father, near to His pity, near to His pardon, near to His sheltering love, near to His all-sufficient grace. It is not in our works but in His free mercy that we trust. But our Father, who forgets all our sins, remembers every "cup of cold water" we have ministered to his children—even to the least of them. So He gathers my brother into His arms, and draws him very near.

Upton, Sunday morning, April 6th, 1879.

My Precious Brother,—Very sweet to me when we slept together as little boys—never so sweet and dear to me as now. I am staying at home with my dear Mary, who is suffering from faceache. In choosing my book to read I was thinking of you and *your* dear Mary and the children. I found nothing so likely to help out my thoughts as Dr. Raleigh's last sermon in the "Quiet Resting-places." The text is "In my father's house are many mansions. If it were not so I would have told you." "Death is the passing of a pilgrim from the winter to the summer residence—to the Father's home." He shows the variety of employments and sympathies in heaven, and the homeliness (the *Father's* house) of that resting-place. "It may be the common life of heaven, just like the sweetest of our common days of earth, is made up of gentleness and tenderness and love. Then he shows the reality of heaven. All hangs on the Saviour's word—"I would have told you so"—and that is enough. You said to me "It is very sweet to think of them (our precious father, our sweet young mother, and other dear ones) as living." Yes, because Christ lives, we shall live also.

I do not think it matters to us *where* our dust is laid. The same miracle which raises us from the dead will bring us at once together, and let us "sit together in heavenly places." But it matters something to those dearest to us whom we may leave behind for a time. *They* will wish to visit the spot, and to have quiet thoughts and sweet memories and dear hopes and trustful prayers there.

The following, written to a member of his family, shows how acutely Mr. Curwen felt the gradual parting with his brother :—

Upton, August, 1879.

I saw dear uncle last night after we got home. He is sinking. I came away with a heavy heart. I wonder that I can care about this world and its work while my brother is passing to another. It is not wrong, when duty requires it. But such an experience ought to make one truer and purer and more " other-worldly " in a better sense than Mr. ————'s.

Notwithstanding all this sorrow the year had its bright side, for Mr. Curwen saw at least the partial realisation of his hopes in regard to the Tonic Sol-fa College buildings. In April a bazaar was held, which added £500 to the funds, and made a start possible. On May 14th the walls had begun to rise, and Mr. Curwen laid, in a prominent place, a stone in memory of Miss Glover. His speech on this occasion shows a softened and retrospective mood. He said :—

It matters nothing to Miss Glover that we should write her name on stone. She worked for her Master, and is now receiving the reward she sought. Our remembrance and our praises cannot reach to her. But it is *much to us,* that we have done this thing. It is much to our own character, because the recollection of those who have aided us, and on whose foundations we have built, helps to keep us humble. It does more ; it gives us a sense of fellow-

ship with our fellow labourers, and this strengthens us
and makes us go on joyfully. It does more still ; it
makes us feel that the work is the Master's — a work
which He will carry on by the hand of many labourers—
and it makes us thankful that He has given it to us to do
our little share. I believe that in heaven they do ever
praise the Lord ; and as churches become more pure, and
reach a higher standard, they will praise more ; they will
sing with the heart and with the understanding, and
they will sing more skilfully with their voices. Every
emotion is made deeper and stronger by being expressed,
and this of joyfulness in God is among the number. It is
as servants of God that we are trying to train teachers of
singing for the people. Miss Glover laid the deep
foundations. I do not mean that all was unknown
before, but she put the most useful scientific knowledge
into workable shape.   Copies of her works will be in the
library of the College ; and none of our students will read
them without being struck by the high intelligence of the
writer, and the earnestness of her purpose to bring great
truths within the capacity of the lowest.   I was anxious
to link the name of the Tonic Sol-fa Association with that
of Miss Glover on the foundation stone.   That name
represents many fellow-workers who laboured with me in
promoting this popular movement, for a long series of
years, when we were more despised and less influential
than we are at present.   They helped me to fight against
prejudice for purity and truth of teaching. But the
Finance Committee, including some of the oldest members
of the Association, decided that it would be better to have
in the new building, when the front with its entrance hall
is completed, large tablets on which shall be entered all
the names of the officers of that Association. It was right
for us, in laying this first stone, to remember those into

whose labours we have entered.   As to the building, we now have as much accommodation as we immediately require.   But we shall work hard to make the accommodation too narrow.   I feel almost inclined, like Lord John Russell, to say "let us rest and be thankful."   That veteran reformer was much laughed at by his younger friends for quoting this phrase before even his own aspirations were accomplished.   At Karlsbad, in one of the climbing paths, a good way (if I remember rightly) before we come to the top of the hill, they have a seat which they call the Russell Seat ; and I might be content like his lordship to linger there.   But nothing will satisfy the young people short of *the top of the hill,* so young and old must still bestir themselves.

The ceremony concluded with a devotional meeting, to which all who were inclined were invited to stay.   It was held, by permission, in a Methodist Chapel hard by. A *Te Deum* was sung, and prayers were offered for the usefulness of the College.

On July 5th the wing of the College that had been erected was publicly opened by the late Earl of Kintore, amid great rejoicings.   Mr. Curwen spoke of the day as one of thanksgiving and joy.   He saw the opening of a building of which he had often dreamed.   He was chiefly glad because the College was now placed in a safe position. He dwelt on the need of trained teachers of the Tonic Sol-fa system, and spoke of the injury done to it by unworthy teachers.

" Your father's heart," he wrote to one of his sons on the following day, "is very full of gratitude to God this morning for this great lift forward with his work of making music useful in church and school."

The usual Summer Term of study began a few days later, and the new rooms were filled with young teachers from all parts of the kingdom.

Mrs. Curwen was ordered by Dr. Kidd to have change of air, and they went to Brentwood, in Essex, taking lodgings in a cottage facing Shenfield Common—a high and healthy spot. Brentwood is about half an hour's ride from Forest Gate, and Mr. Curwen breakfasted at seven each morning in order to take his "Art of Teaching" class at nine o'clock at the College, returning to Brentwood, or going on to Hampstead, when it was over. This travelling imposed on him much additonal fatigue, and the shortness of breath, which marked the progress of his own disease, began to trouble him seriously. He took care of himself, however, walked slowly, and never ascended a hill on foot.

In September he snatched a day from Mrs. Curwen's bedside in order to lecture at Liverpool, where a Tonic Sol-fa Council was being established. In October Mr. Thomas Curwen died. Mr. Curwen speaks in the *Reporter* of his life-long counsels, the keen interest with which he followed the Tonic Sol-fa movement, shrinking always from publicity, and " doing good by stealth."

During the winter classes were held at the College for London students, and Mr. Curwen lectured on Saturday afternoons on the art of teaching, for several weeks in October and November.

On November 29th a portrait of Miss Glover, which Mr. Curwen had caused to be painted, was unveiled at the College. It was enlarged from a photograph, and painted most successfully in oils. He spoke in terms of affection and admiration of Miss Glover and her work, and hoped that the portrait would always remain in the principal room of the College, that students might point to it and say " this is our foundress."

At the end of November Mr. and Mrs. Curwen went to Beulah Spa, Upper Norwood, in order that she might take electric and chemical baths. They stayed there several weeks. At first there was improvement, but gradually Mrs. Curwen grew worse. The following passage from a letter to his daughter gives a picture of their life at Norwood :—

Beulah Spa, Upper Norwood, December 15th, 1879.

Dear mother — so unspeakably precious — is lying on the sofa, on the other side of the table, I hope sleeping. I write very silently. She said to Mrs. Sowter to-day: " We have had many happy times in this room (turning to me) haven't we, dear." The " happy times " are those in which, with tears in our voices, we have spoken together of the unchanging love of Christ, and our own experience of his love and pity. It is a comfort to think that the tears are not wrong. They are *due* to that God-given earthly love which has been ours so long. They have indeed been happy times." I join with my darling when she repeats tenderly and earnestly such hymns as "Just as I am," "Jesus, lover of my soul," "Guide me, O Thou great Jehovah," "Lord it belongs not to my care," and "I do not ask." Every verse, almost every word, has a newer and fuller meaning. So my dear wife is teaching me. Two thoughts about God often recur to her mind and comfort her. 1st. That in offering salvation He makes no bargain, but simply provides the feast of mercy and bids us come. He does not build on our weak faith or our joyfulness or our experience of any kind, but only on His own great personal love to all who will have it. 2nd. That *of late* (taught in part by her affliction, and chiefly, she trusts, by the Holy Spirit) she has had a clearer view of God as *love*, and not as an object of fear and dread. She says I have taught her to look at God "in the face of Jesus Christ." O.may I be taught so to look at Him.

The following, to a member of his family, shows the tender and dependent side of Mr. Curwen's nature :—

Beulah Spa, Norwood, November 21st, 1879.

It was very kind of you to write to me. I have often — in my selfishness — wished for you during these late months, that I might tell you my troubles and get one more bit of sympathy from loved and true and loving hearts. M—— and the two A——'s have been most kind all through. But I felt that my circle of sympathy was not complete without you to speak to.

When we have to "bow ourselves beneath the mighty hand of God," only that same heavenly Father can comfort and heal. But He employs *human* sympathy as His ministering angel. And a word, a look, a *tone* of

" fellow-feeling with our trouble" is a wonderful help
to us.

But it is very selfish of me to want to engross your
thoughts with our troubles. You, dear girl, are at a
different end of life from us—and it is enough for you to
carry your own cares and joys.

I was reading this morning — out of mother's Bible,
by-the-bye — the last chapter of Proverbs. What a
beautiful picture of womanhood. That "virtuous woman"
must, however, have been very strong in the arms, and
must have had plenty of maidens to help her. The
chapter made me look back over many years and think
what mother has been to me. Looking forward, in the
light of the same chapter, I think of what you will be
to S——.

Connected with the life of Mr. and Mrs. Curwen
at Norwood at this time an interesting story has been told.
Some months after, when both were dead, the conversation at the dinner table at Beulah Spa ran upon the
question whether marriages were often happy. A man of
the world, who professed little sympathy with religion,
and took rather the cynical view of the question, said;
" It may be that marriages are generally unhappy,
but there are exceptions. There was a couple here before
Christmas, white-haired people, who behaved to each
other as if they were in their honeymoon. I never saw
anything like the devotion of the husband, or the
unfeigned love of the wife." This was told in the
presence of a friend of Mr. Curwen's, who chanced to

be staying at the house, and who enquired the name of the couple in question.

The following is from a letter, written from Norwood at this time, to his son, who had been reading a paper at a conference on Psalmody :—

Sabbath morning, December 14th, 1879.

The conference shows what a long way we are from a real "*people's* service of song in the house of the Lord." May *your* life bring it nearer. School singing throughout the country will make it physically possible, but there is wanted, also, a *public opinion* in its favour, and more *religious fervour* among the people.

At Mr. Tipple's Baptist Church here they have a liturgical service, which I am trying to get. A quiet old bachelor here (in the house), Mr. D——, bred a dissenter, goes to church "for the sake of the quiet prayers and liturgy." He likes Mr. Tipple's service, and his quiet preaching much. But our good Baptist, Mr. C——, who went with him, recoils from the read prayers and responses even in a Baptist church! Of the two men the Baptist is the more living Christian, but should not the quiet, self-contained bachelor also be suited?

Dear mother is not so low as on Friday. How glad she will be to see you all! To-day we are expecting Dr. Kidd and S——. On Monday we shall be packing, and perhaps taking another electric bath. On Tuesday we shall want rest to gather strength for Wednesday. On Wednesday, the journey. Our Father in heaven will guide and help us.

Just before Christmas, as the above letter anticipates, they returned home, Mrs. Curwen being carried and lifted from train to carriage. After this she gradually sank, and died on January 17th, 1880.

The following sketch of her character and her last days was written by Mr. Curwen at the time, for circulation among private friends :—

MARY CURWEN.
(DIED, JAN. 17TH, 1880.)

Her only surviving brother describes her in his letters as " gentle, helpful, and always at hand with much love for all who wanted her," and her *life* as " one continued example of devotion to duty." Her husband and children bear the same testimony. There was in her manner a sweet quiet dignity, and a watchful sympathy which acted like a charm on those who came near to her.

She engaged herself much in Sunday school work, and the management of Penny Banks and of Dorcas Societies, as well as in private and personal attention to the poor. She often regretted that she had not attained the power of *speaking* much for Christ ; but since her death there have come many testimonies that *God was speaking* to many souls through her life. She was naturally very timid. And yet there were occasions on which she was able to throw aside her natural timidity and stand up boldly for the right. Once, when she thought that the poor of Sun Row—a district near her home—were suffering great injustice, she went and herself appeared before the Board of Guardians, and pleaded their cause. The Sun Row people were chiefly Irish agricultural labourers, and Roman Catholics. She never made a difference in her works of mercy between Catholic and Protestant, Churchman and Dissenter ; and on the Sunday morning, the day after her death, there was a crowd of poor people outside the door of the Catholic Chapel speaking tenderly of her who had helped them in so many sicknesses, and had so often made, with her own hands, clothing to keep them from the cold. In her last illness, speaking to her old and faithful servant, she said, in momentary depression, "I shall never be able to work for the poor again," but then, looking up with a radiant light in her face, she continued, " Mary, God does not *want* me to work for the poor in heaven. In heaven there are no sons of need. But I *loved that work.*"

In addition to her natural timidity, the nature of her lengthened illness was, in itself, exceedingly depressing, and all her lifetime she had had very humble views of her religious condition, and much fear of death. This made those who loved her very anxious lest she should suffer distress towards the close. But prayer was fully answered ; the fear of death was quite taken away from her, and " an entrance was ministered unto her abundantly into the everlasting kingdom of our Lord and Saviour Jesus Christ."

During the last four or five months of her illness there seemed to be a marked development of the spiritual sense, a manifest growth in grace as she came nearer the gates of heaven. From thoughts and words of repentance, she went on to those of faith. From faith she went on to a full assurance of the living, present Christ. And from this the step was easy to thoughts and hopes of heaven. At first, with great conscientiousness, she searched the *grounds* of her faith. She found them not in herself but in Christ. She had always been in the habit of committing to memory hymns and texts of scripture ; and now, when mind and memory were growing weak, the hymns especially (with their soothing rhythm and their gospel truth) were very comforting to her.

For some time nothing would satisfy her but hymns of penitence. Very often she was overheard pleading with the Lord in the words of the hymn

> Just as I am without one plea,
> But that Thy blood was shed for me,

and a poem in " Christian Lyrics " which describes the pleading of the Saviour before the throne for those " worthless ones " whom He brings to the Father, was frequently on her lips.

Her next favourite was the 1153rd in the " Congregational Hymn Book "—

> I do not ask, O Lord, that Thou should'st shed
>   *Full* radiance here ;
> Give but a *ray* of peace, that I may tread
>   Without a fear.
>
> I do not ask my cross to understand,
>   My way to see ;
> Better in darkness just to *feel* Thy hand
>   And follow Thee.

But soon she passed out of this trembling frame into one of greater confidence, and she delighted in such hymns as " Jesus, lover of my soul " and " How sweet the name of Jesus sounds," and the 1135th in the same book, which contains the verse—

> Thou, blessed Jesus, Thou didst *me*
>   Upon the cross embrace ;
> For *me* didst bear a crown of thorns
>   And manifold disgrace.

During her stay at Norwood she said that God had been teaching her much by this illness. He had done it through various instruments, but it was chiefly, she

s

believed, the Holy Spirit who had been teaching her not to look at God with fear, but to behold His glory in the face of Jesus Christ, and *only* there. From this time she had a very *realising* sense of the living presence of Jesus. She said "I had such a beautiful night, I woke up and looked into the room and said to myself, Jesus is here, I *felt* he was watching over us," and fell again into sweet sleep.

In her own dear home, surrounded by love, she spent her last days. Now her soul was ripening fast, and the hymns she repeated were chiefly those of hope and heaven. She said "I must not look at my sins now; Jesus has cast them all behind His back. I must only look at Jesus." Then she would repeat such a hymn as "There is a land of pure delight."

Reviving from one of her later attacks of suffering, when asked whether Jesus was with her she said, "Jesus!—Jesus!—Jesus! Yes! Jesus *is* precious." To her daughter, who had said, "Dear mother, you *can trust* Jesus," she answered, "Oh yes, I never knew I should find myself able to trust Him so *perfectly as I do*." She called her little grand-daughter to her and gave her a keepsake, and said, "My little girl, when your mother tells you that grandmamma is gone, you must try to think of grandmamma in heaven—never as anywhere else —not in the grave; but *grandmamma in heaven*."

At this time she sent first for one and then for another of her children and said to each of them, "I want you to know how easy it is to die with Jesus. This is not like dying. It is like going to sleep;" and then she repeated the verse—

> Jesus *can* make a dying bed
> Feel soft as downy pillows are;
> While on His breast I lean my head,
> And breathe my life out sweetly there.

"Think of it, John," she said to her husband, "one step on earth and *the next* in heaven ! How wonderful it will be !" When her husband told her that her life had been teaching them all, and that even now she was really speaking for Jesus," she answered, "Yes, I want you all to learn to *love Jesus* more through my death."

In the last attacks of her painful disease, there were moments of depression when she seemed in dismay ; but the Lord answered prayer in a very remarkable manner, and "His rod and His staff they comforted her." Her last words were to Dr. Kidd—"Dear doctor ; God bless you. Pray for me, that God will give me *patience* to wait *His* time." And he prayed. She died in her sleep, breathing her last breath softly and sweetly as a little child.

> So fades a summer cloud away ;
> So sinks the gale when storms are o'er ;
> So gently shuts the eye of day ;
> So dies a wave along the shore.

Something may be added to this sketch, which is necessarily a short one. It speaks of Mrs. Curwen's work for the poor. This was her great joy, and her constant occupation through life. She was clever with her needle, but her custom was to get others to make her own dresses, and to keep her own hands busy for the poor. She reduced this work to a system. From her Manchester friends she would buy every winter a stock of flannel and calico, and set to work to make the material into garments. These she would put by, so that they were ready when a deserving case presented itself. There was no carelessness about her charity. Strangers were never relieved until their stories had been personally verified. She would walk long distances in doing this, and come home tired and happy if a real case of distress had been found. Blankets stamped with her name were lent every winter to the poor around, and returned in spring. Packets of tea, sugar, and rice were kept on shelves, ready, like the petticoats, to be given away. Most of the old Irishwomen whom she relieved were smokers, and she was sometimes half inclined to set up a store of tobacco! One of these old women, whom Mrs. Curwen had partially supported for years, when she heard that " Lady Curwen " was dying, prayed that she might die too, for, she said, "there will be no one to care for me when she is gone." The poor old creature had her prayer answered ; she died on the day that Mrs. Curwen was buried.

Dinners were sent out to invalids, and a home soup-kitchen was established in severe seasons. Her fingers were always busy ; if she felt that she had enough clothes in store for her poor she would set to work for the hospitals. She was always attentive to the self-respectful poor—those who suffered in silence, and needed to be found out and helped. She relieved them quietly and delicately. Her Christmas hampers were a serious business, which occupied her thoughts for several weeks. At Norwood, in the last few weeks of her life, she wrote down in bed the names of those whom she wished to be remembered in this way.

Charities were managed with much less expenditure of money than would be imagined, owing to her skill and carefulness, and her strict accuracy in account-keeping. Mr. Curwen used often to tell how when they were first engaged to be married he asked her if she thought she could live on £150 a year. She replied that she did not see how they could possibly spend so much. Such was the state of innocency in which she entered on house-keeping.

Mrs. Curwen was the envy of all the housewives who knew her, because of the way in which she kept her servants. They very seldom left her except to be married. Her general treatment of them was sympathising and firm. She understood their work, and followed it closely, allowing no negligence to pass. At the same time she took an almost motherly interest in them. She appreciated and praised good work. She persuaded them to save, and kept their money for them, adding interest to it until the amount was large enough to go into the bank. "Followers," if their professions were ascertained to be sincere, were welcomed to the house, and invited to pay regular visits. On two occasions servants were married from her house, and she herself superintended the arrangement of the wedding breakfast in her dining-room, and then gave it up for the day to their friends. All this kindness was mixed, as we have said, with discipline ; no servant was allowed to be out late at night, and in one or two cases idlers were speedily dispatched.

All her life Mrs. Curwen was mixed up with Dorcas meetings and mothers' meetings. In these she always took the lead, and is remembered for her skill in restoring harmony if there was any tendency to discord, for her pleasant voice as she read aloud while the ladies were at work, and for her diligence and method.

Her hospitality is remembered by many, especially at those times when parties of friends interested in some public work, such as the Tonic Sol-fa movement, gathered at her table. She was not gifted much in music, and her interest in Tonic Sol-fa was, as Mr. Curwen said in his Exeter Hall speech, chiefly interest in him. But she threw herself into all his activities, and strengthened him at every point by her thoughtful love. A friend contributes the following reminiscence of a conversation with the Rev. Spedding Curwen, Mr. Curwen's father, which bears upon this point :—

Mr. Spedding Curwen said, " I thought at one time John was spending too much money in his psalmody ventures, and I took it for granted that I should find his wife somewhat in sympathy with me on the question of expenditure. So I was bold enough to ask whether she did not think he was laying out too much money in that direction. Did not I find that I had put my foot in it ? For she exclaimed, " Let John do what he likes with his money. Nobody shall interfere with him ! "

The Rev. Andrew Reed writes :—

Mr. Curwen was very fortunate in his partner in life. She was very different from him in the very particulars in which difference was desirable, but she entered heartily and loyally into all his life objects. Eminently pious, but yet of a self-depreciating temperament ; warm hearted, but yet with a critical and cautious element of character which modified sanguine impulses ; penetrating in discernment of character, but yet animated by tolerant charity ; at times reserved in manner to strangers, but able to throw off all such reticence in real and proved intimacy ; Mr. Curwen's wife was the attraction of his home hardly less than himself.

A cheerful humour, and a faculty for seeing the droll side of things were not the least pleasant of Mrs. Curwen's traits. Even in her long last illness, weighed down by the depression of spirit that liver disease causes, her gentle pleasantries did not altogether forsake her, and she retained her interest in all that was going on around.

A member of Mr. Curwen's family writes :—

Such was the wife whose love followed Mr. Curwen for thirty-seven years, and whose gradual fading out of life he watched with an intensity of loving care that seemed to take something daily from his own strength, as though he had indeed

> . . . Lent her half his powers
> To eke her living out.

At no time, perhaps, did the beautiful unselfishness of his character show itself more than now. He ever brought into the sick room a bright face and a cheery word, and would win a smile from the invalid by some tender little joke, when those around him knew his heart was breaking. He would snatch sleep when she slept, that he might be ready to read to her or wait upon her when she woke ; and when she spoke of her death with the calmness of one drawing very near to it, he too would face it with apparent calmness, and would read to her the hymns she loved with a voice that sometimes faltered, but never failed. As the end drew nearer the various little offices which he loved to perform for her had to pass into other hands, and every "giving up" was a fresh grief to him ; but thinking only of her comfort, he always made way so cheerfully that it was only from some words accidentally dropped some time afterwards, that his family learned how keenly he had felt it. During all these most trying weeks no *murmur* ever escaped him ; the inward pain that was sapping his very life, the "pressure on the heart," as the doctors called it, was known to none but God.

CHAPTER XV.

1880.

HIS BEREAVEMENT — STRUGGLE WITH HIMSELF — LETTERS
FROM NEWCASTLE — VISIT TO BRIGHTON — REV. A REED —
LADIES ON SCHOOL BOARDS — UPTON CONGREGATIONAL
CHURCH — LETTER OF SYMPATHY — CARD PLAYING AND
DANCING — LECTURE AT DUNDEE — LETTER FROM THENCE —
WEDDING OF HIS SON — PARAGRAPH ON DR. HULLAH —
WALTHAMSTOW SCHOOL — DR. KENNEDY'S RECOLLECTIONS
— CONCERT AT ST. JAMES'S HALL — OVERCOME BY MUSIC —
HIS FONDNESS FOR IT — EUING LECTURES — EXPERIMENTS
IN JUST INTONATION — THE GOVERNMENT AND SCHOOL
SINGING — DINNER OF COWARD COLLEGE STUDENTS —
RECOLLECTIONS BY FRIENDS.

THE death of his wife robbed Mr. Curwen of half his life,
and utterly broke his spirit. Yet he struggled against
himself with an iron resolution, and sought relief in
companionship, not solitude. Mrs. Curwen died on
Saturday morning; on Sunday he took his accustomed
seat at church, and brought home to dinner an old
friend, the Rev. Dr. Green, who happened to be preaching.
Dr. Green writes :—

When I review that short visit, I cannot but feel, in the memory of his beautiful, pathetic serenity, that he already felt himself to be patiently awaiting, but for " a little while," the hour of reunion.

From the day of Mrs. Curwen's death Mr. Curwen surrounded himself with friends, as the best escape from preying thoughts. Never was his manner more bright and cordial, never was his laugh heartier than in these few last months of his life. To avoid catching cold he allowed his white hair to grow long, and this gave him a venerable and more aged look. But, except when tired, his fresh complexion retained its glow, and to all outward appearances he was in good health. Alas.! the very glow of his face was a mark of disease !

The following passages from letters written at this time show the desolation which was concealed by Mr. Curwen's cheerful exterior :—

1, Jesmond Gardens, Newcastle, January 28th, 1880.

They are all very kind to me, and I am getting to sleep better. So, among you all, I am enfolded by all the loving kindness that dear mother could have wished. Of course her presence would be better than all, but how long I enjoyed her love ! and how sweet it was ! Not to find a letter, in the dear handwriting of home love, on the breakfast table the first morning, was a trial to me. For, for thirty-five years that home love has followed me wherever I went. I have quite decided to appropriate dear mother's insurance money, in her dear name, to the new church. If she had died twenty years ago I should have been suddenly reduced to half my income. It was her loving wish to shield and help me in such a difficulty which caused the life insurance. It is not needed now. But it comes to me as a love token from her hand, and where could I place it better than in the new church. The Lord own and bless it.

Jesmond Gardens, Newcastle, Sunday morning.
January, 1880.

It is 11.30. They are all at church. I sit at the table, near the fire, and look out on the sunshine. I have just read a beautiful sermon on "The white-robed throng," Rev. vii. 13. Read the text, and think of your sweet mother going on "loving and serving" as she always did, but with new faculties, and under glorious new conditions. She does not trouble about us. She *knows* how Jesus will take care of us, and how the Holy Spirit will guide and influence us—if we only ask |Him. Having been the close companion of her true spirit so long, the companion almost of her thoughts, I have had, since the 17th, a constant *longing* to carry on that companionship, and to know what she is doing, and to stand by her side. But now I am more satisfied. She is *serving* and *loving*, as she always did. The only difference is that she is better and happier, and we shall follow her, through the blood of the Lamb. Oh! to love with a deeper, truer faith than we have felt before, the once suffering, now reigning Christ.

Upton, E., March 14th, 1880.

DEAR H——,—I have been reading your brother's "Ode to Mary"—yes, I could not help it—with streaming eyes. You know, dear H——, you helped us to come together, and for thirty-five years our lives have been fully blended. We have lived in one another, more, perhaps, than is commonly the case, so you see nature will have her tears, though I can indeed say that I " thank God at every remembrance " of my Mary, and I know that in her death He has revealed Himself to the children and to me very, very mercifully.

The Rev. Andrew Reed writes of a visit which Mr. Curwen paid to Brighton with a daughter-in-law at this time :—

Every friend supposed that John would not very long survive his beloved wife. They were so intimately bound together that either apart from the other seemed out of an accustomed element. I was at Brighton when John was there, and by a happy accident was recognised in passing their window, and so had another opportunity of seeing my friend. I was shocked at his bodily emaciation and feebleness, but there was all the old heartiness and sympathy. He would first know all about me and my ministry and my literary work, before he would open up about himself. Then he told me in all naturalness—mixed with sobs and silence—of his wife's decease; of her happy tranquillity and clear trust at the last ; and he closed by saying, with his hand in mine, "Andrew, I could wish to follow her ; my work is done ; I have not the least fear about dying ; Jesus has taken her, and before long He will take me. There is more to draw me to heaven than to keep me on earth."

Yet he spoke most tenderly of the love and care of his children, and even playfully alluded to his new home with his ' dear son and daughter, who had given up their own intended abode in order to come and live with him. " They are so good to me." " Ah, John, you were always so good to everyone ; even to me at College, when you made me sick and nursed me in the small-pox." " Ah, so

I did," he replied, "but I have had sorer nursing since then, and it has pulled me down, for it was in vain. 'Tis so hard to nurse and be beaten," he added, in an emphatic whisper.

The following is from a letter written by Mr. Curwen, at this time, to his daughter, who had just been elected on the West Ham School Board — the same on which her father had served nine years before :—

Upton, February 17th, 1880.

In recalling the memory of School Board work, I think that where womanliness could best come in would be :—

1st. Generally. To soften the dry officialism of the work by sympathy and helpfulness.

2nd. In visiting schools. Not to go as an Inspector (for they have plenty of that—Government Inspectors and Board Inspectors, who do their work efficiently) but as a teacher's friend ; as a sympathiser and helper. Such visits would be very welcome and very useful.

3rd. In the work of the Compulsion Committee to help (sometimes) in investigating the cases of parental neglect, or of real distress which come up there, and to bring some cases to the notice of the various voluntary societies likely to assist them.

The Lord guide you, sweet child, and make your life a useful and a happy one.

Mr. and Mrs. Curwen had interested themselves in the formation of a Congregational Church near their home. Mr. Curwen had, in fact, held a site for some time in readiness for the purpose. The following letter to

Mr. Henry Cook, treasurer of the building fund, shows how, after Mrs. Curwen's death, her interests and wishes became to Mr. Curwen the most sacred of duties :—

Upton, E., February 20th, 1880.

DEAR MR. COOK,—I think it better to send you our quarter's subscription to the Upton Congregational Church at once, so that you may have something in hand at the committee to-night.

I have also the pleasure—to me a most deep and sacred pleasure—of handing you, for the same object, a claim on my dear wife's life insurance for £999. The Insurance Companies take three or four months to pay the claims. But I think the enclosed will give you the right to receive the money, even if I should be taken away before that time, and my dear children all know and approve the gift. Enter it, in your accounts, in the name of "the late Mrs. Curwen," or simply " Mrs. Curwen, Workington House, Upton." I hope this will enable us to go on with the work without borrowing.

You know how my dear wife loved the work, and longed to see the foundation stone, and I know how carefully she husbanded our "giving money," so that little surplusses might be left for Upton. May the blessing of her Heavenly Father rest upon her gift.

The words "If I should be taken away before that time" are no mere formal reference to Providence; they express the eager desire of Mr. Curwen's spirit, which was tempered only by his love for his family and his work. From the time of the loss of Mrs. Curwen, he looked forward to death as the goal of happiness.

In a letter of sympathy, written about this time, to a lady who had lost her husband, Mr. Curwen speaks to himself as well as to her :—

For yourself, dear madam, an old minister, himself tried in like manner, may say that he knows of no cure for the wound which *must abide*, no *relief* even, but creeping nearer to Jesus, and telling Him all. But He who thus wounded you is your Heavenly Father.

He has left you children, and bids you throw your affections into their affairs with a redoubled carefulness. And He has ordained that *time and duty* shall be healers.

On the death of Mrs. Curwen it was arranged that a son, who was about to be married, should live with his father. This was in accordance with the dying wish of Mrs. Curwen.

At the end of March Mr. Curwen went to give a lecture, for the Tonic Sol-fa College, at Dundee.

The following letter, written from here, show how his thoughts were ever turning to his great loss :—

Perth Road, Dundee, March 30th, 1880.

Here we were three years ago—sweet mother and I—enjoying the hospitality of as good and kind a little lady as you can find anywhere. Mother and she were great friends at once. She has been talking of dear mother in a very true, simple, affectionate way.

Last night Mr. Adamson met me and went with me to Lamb's Temperance Hotel, at the head of Reform Street, in a sort of central square with public buildings all about. Coffee and poached eggs and a fire soon made me very comfortable and sleepy, though the dust had got into my throat. This morning, at nine, chops and tea had a reviving effect. The dining-room walls were covered with good oil paintings, and the place looked bright. The commercial gentlemen were very quick over their breakfast, but pleasantly talkative without bounce. A car (after I had watched the judges pass in great state, with trumpets and soldiers, on the first day of the sessions), brought me to this house.

Opposite my bedroom window runs the Perth Road, and below that, at the bottom of the hill, the Dundee and Perth railway—Dundee being to the left, and Perth to the right. Beyond the railway stretches, far and wide, the great mouth of the Tay. It is here two miles wide. Looking down stream to the left I see the Tay Bridge and its eleven ruined piers. It is very sad to see. Three years ago it looked beautiful in its engineering pride and promise. Now the crown of it has gone, and it lies a broken thing. How like the change in my life! Although *that* never looked beautiful, except that the companionship of mother made it so. It is very sweet to find how much she was honoured and loved.

Mr. Curwen broke the journey at Glasgow, where friends noticed his enfeebled condition. He did no public work here.

Five days after leaving Dundee he was due at Newcastle, for the occasion of his son's marriage. He returned, however, to London in the interim, in order to record his vote in the general election, which was pending.

At the wedding his resolute brightness and self-control were more touching even than if he had given way to the feelings which he was hiding. He bade his children put off their mourning dress, and threw himself with all his old geniality and freedom into the engagements of the day. Two days after he wrote the following letter, strange and dreamlike, to the newly-married couple :—

Newcastle-on-Tyne, April 7th, 1880.

I went to a wedding on Monday. It is only two days ago, but it seems like a dream.

When I woke in the morning I remembered who would have wished me to be happy that day, and to diffuse happiness about me, and I had great reason for being happy, so I threw myself with all my heart into the great tide of peaceful joy which was flowing around me. I remembered, also, the bride's mother, and thought how she was living out of herself that day. Thus by God's help I got courage and grace.

* * * * * *

Both bride and bridegroom spoke out their words of troth and plighting distinctly and clearly, so that all might hear. It was not observed by the congregation that the old minister, their father, omitted a word or two from the service. " Till death us do part " were words too terrible, in his fresh grief, to trust his lips to utter, and he dreaded lest by any emotion in his own |voice he should put even a momentary tremble into the voice of the bride—his own son's bride. So he read her out her words with force and firmness, and she responded bravely and truly. It was delightful to hear her and see her.

* * * * * *

At the breakfast all, without exception, were happy and thankful. Old friendships were renewed, and new

T

ones made.   To me they were mostly new, but being old friends of the bride and her family, they seemed like old friends to me.

The bridegroom, in his speech, which was full of humour and good fellowship, made also reference to the sacred memory of his mother, who had "desired to see that day," and whose last days were comforted by the sight of his bride, and by the loving assurance that the two would willingly give up their own bridal home, and come to take care of the old father.   She knew that, in his quickly-coming bereavement, there could be no human help for him like children's love.   And so the last earthly burden was lifted from the heart of the dying mother and wife.   This reference was very touching, but all felt it to be right and just, and beautifully done, and it did not stop the flow of happiness, in which her spirit joined.

To finish this episode—when the bride came down dressed for her happy journey, it was seen that she wore a jet necklace with a pendant, and that that side of the pendant was shown which bore the photograph of her husband's mother.   So neither of them had forgotten, in their joy, the precious memory.

At night, as I retired to rest, I thanked my Heavenly Father for his gift of two dear children for my house.   I shall now call it "home" again.

In the *Tonic Sol-fa Reporter* for April appeared a reply, by Mr. Curwen, to one of the periodical attacks upon the Tonic Sol-fa system by Dr. Hullah.   There is nothing at all in the article exceeding the ordinary limits of criticism; it is, indeed, rather mild in its language. But after writing it Mr. Curwen heard a rumour of

Dr. Hullah having been attacked with a fatal illness, and sent the following postscript to the sub-editor. The rumour proved to be exaggerated, and the postscript did not appear, but it was accidentally preserved, and is now given as showing the spirit of the writer :—

As we go to press we hear with great regret of Dr. Hullah's sudden and serious illness. Although our "movement" has suffered severely through his opposition, and we have several times had to reply to him, we have never been moved by any sort of personal animosity, and have never thought him moved by anything worse than a strong and rare professional prejudice. We shall gladly hear of his speedy recovery, and welcome him back again to his own proper sphere of usefulness in the promotion of music among the people.

On April 15th Mr. Curwen gave away the Tonic Sol-fa certificates that had been earned by girls of the School for Missionaries' Daughters at Walthamstow, under the teaching of Mr. McNaught. On the 23rd he presided at the quarterly meeting of the Council of the Tonic Sol-fa College. A resolution of sympathy on the death of Mrs. Curwen was passed at this meeting, but he was quite unable to make any reply. When business began he was himself again, and succeeded in persuading the members to give way to him in a point on which he was almost alone in opinion.

Mr. Curwen had spent some pleasant hours in the society of his old friends Dr. and Mrs. Kennedy (of

Stepney) at Brighton, during the visit already referred to. At the end of April he had the pleasure of receiving them for a few days at his house. Dr. Kennedy, in a funeral sermon preached on Mr. Curwen's death, thus spoke of this intercourse :—

In the end of April I had another precious opportunity of converse with him on these and similar themes, while spending two days under his own roof. But being myself much occupied in preparing my May-Day Lecture, my other self had more leisure with him than I had, and she has given me these notes. "The last time my dear friend Mr. Curwen and I conversed together, he told me of the physician having ordered him on the Continent for the winter. But he said, ' Where is the use? It is a long time now since I have done any work, and I do not wish to prolong my life if I cannot work.' I told him what a blessing his presence would be to his family and to his friends, much more than he knew or thought of. Physically, I think, he was much depressed, and his mind reflected his bodily state. As to the future life he had a childlike trustfulness that he would be in the Father's keeping. I spoke to him of a passage in Isaiah, which I told him had often been my stay in times of darkness— "Who is among you that feareth the Lord, that obeyeth the voice of His word, and that walketh in darkness, and hath no light. Let him trust in the name of the Lord, and stay himself on his God." He was much pleased. We then spoke of the passage in the 14th of John—"If a man love Me he will keep My words ; and my Father will love him, and we will come unto him and make our abode with him"—and of its beautiful meaning, of the holy soul being at home with God even in this life. I wish I had

known (oh! vain wish) that that was to be our last meeting on earth, for then we should have prayed together. I
believe we did so in spirit. And the remembrance of his
sweet, holy, most Christian-like spirit will ever be a
joy to me; and now the knowledge, too, that his weary
soul is so entirely at rest, and satisfied in the presence of
Christ. The trials of life only mellowed and chastened a
naturally bright and sanguine nature, and to the last one
sometimes heard that cheery laugh of his." And never
was that laugh more cheery, more like his former self,
than when we parted with him at his own gate on the
first of May; and she whose notes I have quoted said
to him, pleasantly, "Now, don't you say any more that
your work is done."

On May 11th Mr. Curwen attended a concert by
the South London Choral Association—a Tonic Sol-fa
Society—in St. James's Hall. His nerves, since the death
of Mrs. Curwen, were quite unstrung. On this occasion,
at the thrilling passages in the songs and choruses, he held
the book of words to his face to conceal his emotion. This
loss of self-control was not usual with him, nor did he
show, as a rule, any signs of being overcome by music.
One exception to this is recalled by his family. It was a
month or so before the death of Mrs. Curwen, when he
knew that her illness must be fatal. His daughter-in-law
was singing Mr. Weatherley's pathetic verses "Darby and
Joan." He sat listening, enjoying the song until the last
verse :—

Hand in hand when our life was May,
Hand in hand when our hair is grey ;
Shadow and sun for every one,
As the years roll on.

Hand in hand when the long night tide
Gently covers us side by side—
Ah ! lad, though we know not when,
Love will be with us for ever then !

As these words reached him he rose from his chair, and abruptly left the room.

Mr. Curwen was fond of music, and his taste for it was very discriminating. In his own house he enjoyed most of all duets for pianoforte and harmonium, played by members of his family. For one of these duets, an arrangement of " O du mein holder Abendstern," from *Tannhäuser*, he was never tired of asking.

Shortly before Mrs. Curwen's death Mr. Curwen made an attempt to proceed with his " Euing Lectures." He was anxious to complete the teaching of composition by adding a book on orchestration. True to his practical ways, he determined to deal first with brass and reed bands, as being more common than full orchestras. Proceeding on the same lines as he had followed in writing his other instrumental books, Mr. Curwen searched for a practical man, and found Mr. Kappey of Chatham. He went down with his son and spent a morning with him. Mr. Kappey made several arrangements for bands of different sizes, to be used as illustrations in the book.

But Mrs. Curwen's death interrupted this new effort, and it was never completed.

Mr. Wilfrid Ferguson, a young friend who acted as Mr. Curwen's secretary after Mrs. Curwen's death, says :—

Impaired health compelled Mr. Curwen to put aside "Orchestration," as he said he had not strength to work at it. But he could not be idle, so as "light work" he turned his attention to an old idea—that of perfecting a keyed instrument tuned on the principle of Just Intonation. There was correspondence with a Paris firm to manufacture the instruments, and with some of the leading scientific men on special points. Three of the latter were so taken with Mr. Curwen's new ideas, that they each ordered the new harmonium to be sent to them as soon as made. Of course there were also many discouragements, but these only made Mr. Curwen more determined to complete what he had commenced. We paid frequent visits to London in connection with this enterprise. I remember that on one occasion Mr. Curwen was accosted by a musicseller in a shop, who blamed him for publishing an *unmusical notation.* "Your Tonic Sol-fa," said the man, "is not music at all, but (pointing to a book printed in the Staff notation) *that* is music." "Oh, indeed!" said Mr. Curwen (picking up the volume and holding it to his ear), "I don't hear it!" Although he gave the same course of lessons at the Tonic Sol-fa College term after term, Mr. Curwen always carefully revised and improved upon his notes, commencing to do so in good time—about three months before the beginning of the session. The reason he gave was that "he never risked trusting to dry bones." I remember that one evening, when we happened to be alone, he asked me to stay to tea, and he talked to me for an hour or two about Mrs. Curwen, relating to me the whole story of his first meeting with her, and describing her character and her work. The act of telling this seemed to cheer him.

At this time the Government were about to require "singing by note" to be taught in every school, and there seemed some doubt as to whether they included the Tonic Sol-fa notation in this term. Mr. Curwen felt that something must be done to ascertain the intentions of the Education Department, but he found it hard to rouse himself for action. One day his son went to talk the matter over with him, and suggested that a memorial from professional musicians favourable to the Tonic Sol-fa system should be circulated and signed for presentation to Mr. Mundella. "The musicians!" he exclaimed, and as he paced the room all his old.fire seemed to return to him, "do you think the *musicians* have placed us in our present position? Where should we be now, I should like to know, if we had been dependent on the musicians. No, it is the politicians, the philanthropists, the educationists, the clergy, the religious people who have been our helpers all through, and we must appeal to *them.*"

Mr. Curwen went up to town with his son, a day or two after, and saw his old friend Sir Charles Reed, who promised to put a question on the subject in the House of Commons. The two friends met at the School Board Office on the Victoria Embankment. The interview was very touching ; for some minutes Mr. Curwen could not speak. Afterwards he walked with difficulty up the slight incline into the Strand, pausing several times for breath. ·

On May 15th Mr. Curwen was present at the annual reunion of " Coward College " students, held at Dr. Reynolds' house at Cheshunt. The College had ceased to have a separate existence in 1857, and thus the students met in steadily diminishing numbers. The meeting was, however, a very happy one. Several fellow students who were present at it speak of Mr. Curwen's manner. The Rev. T. Fison says :—

We were, I think, all struck with the overflowing joy which Mr. Curwen manifested in meeting with his old friends, and with his tender affection for them. He impressed upon us that the meeting next year must be at his house, and he was apparently so well that, to me at least, it did not seem improbable that this wish would be fulfilled.

The Rev. Andrew Reed says :—

I saw him once more at the Coward dinner at Cheshunt College, where he was very bright, though we all shook our heads sadly at his low physical condition. But he abated nothing of concern and love for us all individually, and in a short speech he said he had hoped to have entertained us that year, but God had been pleased to bereave him sorely. Still he had meant to have gathered us together and done his best to make us

happy though alone, only good friends had advised him
against making the effort, and he supposed they were
right.   But (and his eye kindled) he never liked flinching
from duty (here I seemed to see him again at College
standing up against "hated expediency") nor did his
good wife, but he hoped he should have strength to face
all life's duties while they lasted, nor was he afraid or
reluctant to face their end.

Rev. H. Griffith, F.G.S., writes:—

We last met on May 15th, at a gathering of Coward
Students, under the hospitable roof of Dr. Reynolds, at
Cheshunt.   Though sadly broken in health, Mr. Curwen
appeared in such capital spirits that we all ventured to
hope his valuable life might yet be prolonged for many
years.   It was to me, and I am persuaded it was also to
him a matter of unspeakable joy that on our way home
we agreed to spend together a fortnight of the following
month at the Wells of Llandrindod.   The conditions were
that each was to have a thick pair of shoes and a strong
hammer, and that although an occasional episode of
geology might be tolerated, the burden of conversation
was to be "Auld lang syne" and how to improve and
enrich our psalmody.   They were bright pictures we drew
for each other, with fond anticipations of renewing our
youth, while rambling over those glorious old mountains
and revelling in their bracing air.   Alas! it was otherwise
ordained!   That dream is past for ever!   "I shall go
to him, but he shall not return to me."   "Here we have
no continuing city, but we seek one to come, eternal in
the heavens."

CHAPTER XVI.

1880.

JOURNEY TO MANCHESTER—MRS. BANKS'S NARRATIVE—WITH
THE SUNDAY SCHOLARS—GOES TO HEATON MERSEY—SUDDEN
ILLNESS—HIS CHILDREN SUMMONED—HE RALLIES—FEVER—
LAST HOURS—SYMPTOMS GROW MORE SERIOUS—DEATH—
FUNERAL—DR. MACFADYEN'S ADDRESS—THE SERVICE—
MONUMENT IN ILFORD CEMETERY.

THE only surviving brother of Mrs. Curwen was at this
time lying ill at Manchester, with little hope of recovery.
It will easily be understood that in Mr. Curwen's state of
mind, the welfare of every one connected with Mrs. Curwen
became a sacred charge. He wished to satisfy himself
that his brother-in-law was receiving the best nursing and
medical attendance. With this view he started on the
morning of Wednesday, May 17th, for Manchester. His
friend, the Rev. J. Richardson, of Madagascar, who had
been staying with him, saw him off at St. Pancras
station.

From this point we may quote an account of Mr. Curwen's last illness and death written at that time by his daughter, for circulation among friends.

He saw my uncle on the Thursday, and ministered to his comforts in many ways ; returning to Mr. Macfadyen's by noon. The day was warm and sunny, and later on about 400 of the Sunday scholars came and sang some of their Whit-week hymns in Mr. Macfadyen's garden. My father sat, warmly wrapped, listening to them for some time, until at last he grew so interested that he went and stood on the door step, by the side of the choirmaster, beating time with his hand, and encouraging the children to sing. The superintendent and many of the teachers knew him, and when the singing was over, after they had given three cheers for their minister, they gave three more for Mr. Curwen. The same day he wrote to tell us how he found the invalid, and what the doctor's opinion of him was. In the same letter he says of himself, " Oh ! with what a leaping, joyful heart I used to look down from the railway as I came into grimy, smoky Manchester, and thought *what a jewel it held for me !* All those happy years are gone, *and I live !* But I should not touch that subject." He little knew when he wrote it that he was within a week of his death.

Ever since my mother's death he had been simply waiting. He never made himself miserable, and was ever ready to take interest in his children and grandchildren, and all his many friends. But through it all we could see the far-away look in his eyes, and we knew that he had, as he once expressed it, an "infinite longing to go to heaven."

His health was feeble, but as we knew of no organic disease we all hoped that as time healed his sorrow, he would regain spirit and strength.

On the Friday he again saw my uncle, and as it was Whit-week, drove to the field where the Sunday school children were romping, but not feeling very well he soon re-entered the carriage and returned.

On Saturday morning he conducted family prayers, taking on his knee a little fellow of three, who looked round in a helpless kind of way, as if he wanted to be nursed. Then he wrote some letters, one to Mr. Ferguson about the new harmonium; one to Sir Charles Reed, giving the exact terms of the questions he wished asked in the House of Commons; and one or two to members of his family. With all his old art of advising faithfully and kindly he talked with a little girl of the house who spoke indistinctly, and showed her how to open her mouth and articulate more clearly. Then, after an early dinner, he drove to the Chorlton Station to get the train to Heaton Mersey. Here, at the house of his nephew, Mr. Edward Coward, another nephew and niece, just about to start for Canada, were staying with their children. Through Mr. Coward's absence in London the letter intimating that my father was coming was not opened, and no carriage met him. The five minutes' walk against a north wind was quite too much for him, and when he reached Heaton House he could hardly walk to a seat. His breathing was very laboured, the hands and feet were deathly cold, while perspiration stood in great drops on his forehead.

The doctor was sent for, and every means used for his restoration, but they feared it was too late.

After about two hours he began to revive, and was carried to bed. About eight o'clock that evening a telegram was received at home, but as his son was out it was not opened until his return, a little after nine. The message was: "The doctor has been; come at once;

expect the worst." J—— and S—— started off without any delay, and M—— came round, after seeing them off, to tell me the sad news. My desire was to go, and my husband said it was right, so in a few minutes we were out of the house. The trains were late with holiday takers, and it was with very great difficulty we caught the midnight train at St. Pancras. My husband ran along the platform to try and find if my brothers were in the train, but could not see them, so I travelled down alone.

It was a sad, strange journey, through that beautiful moonlight night. Praying, hoping, despairing; thinking that even then my darling father was most likely gone from me.

At Stockport, in the early morning, I found a man cleaning out a cab yard near the station, and persuaded him to drive me the two miles to Heaton Mersey.

When my cousin met me at the door I could hardly ask for news. Oh! what mercy to know he still lived, and was better. I found him propped up on pillows looking very near death. Such a marble brow, such short laboured breath, and the perspiration standing on his forehead.

An hour afterwards J—— and S—— came, having gone round by Manchester. They went up, one at a time to see the dear father, but found him so anxious to talk that they soon left him, fearing the excitement for him.

The doctor put dear father in my charge at breakfast time, and warned me to keep him quiet, and not let him see even my brothers again till afternoon. It was a wise precaution, for very soon he sank to sleep. He slept for an hour, then half an hour, and once for two hours, waking each time for nourishment. Every time he woke he was better, his breathing quieter, his face a more natural colour, and the perspiration less profuse. Towards afternoon he was so much better that the doctor said all immediate danger was past, so my brother J——· decided to go back by the night train to London.

S—— and I divided the night between us. Father slept a good deal, but was nervous, and 'dreaded a return of the exhaustion in the early morning. It did not come, however. The breathing was so far natural that he could lie on his side and sleep. Early in the morning our old nurse, Mary Perry, for whom we had sent when we found two nurses would be needed, arrived. S—— left at nine, quite content, I promising to stay as long as the dear one needed me, and J—— or S—— to come down and fetch him home whenever he could be moved.

Mary and I then settled into the routine of nursing. How the little details of such work help one to bear the pressing anxiety !

Several friends who had heard of the illness called that morning, but I kept the dear father quiet, and did not let them see him.

It was in the middle of the morning, while washing him that I found a rash on him. When the doctor saw it he said that that altered the case. There was evidently poison in the system. He could never give the fever a name, though saying that in many respects it was like scarlet fever, but there was an absence of any throat affection, no dry fever and no delirium. Whatever it was the doctor said the danger would be when the fever left him, lest his strength should fail.

Throughout Monday the fever was very high. Father did not talk much, only telling his wants. All through the illness he was perfectly content, without the weary longing there had been since mother's death. He had every comfort, and accepted all his nephew's great kindness as simply as a child, knowing well how much he was loved. Once when I said " I don't know how we shall repay all this kindness." He answered, " We *can't*, and we don't *want* to, Edward (Mr. Coward) likes to do it for us."

He was always very grateful and patient, and it was very touching to see how all the little things we thought a privilege to do for him he received as a favour conferred. He was pleased to hear parts of the letters read, and when he was ready to listen would say to me, " Now, dear, read slowly and softly."

On the Tuesday he felt better ; the pulse had gone down. He said, when he felt himself gaining strength, " I don't know why I should live, I can't put my life to any use." My answer was, " But your children know, darling father; what would they do without you!" "Oh! well," he said, " if I can be any comfort to them I am quite willing to wait God's time, but for *myself* I should not chose to live !" Several times he said " I am too weak to listen to texts or hymns." Once, after having his brow and hands bathed, he said, " Now read me a few verses of a hymn or some texts." I repeated—

> One sweetly solemn thought
>   Comes to me o'er and o'er,
> I'm nearer home to-day
>   Than e'er I've been before.
>
> Nearer my Father's house,
>   Where the many mansions be,
> Nearer the great white throne,
>   Nearer the jasper sea.
>
> Nearest the bound of life,
>   Where we lay our burdens down.

Then he broke down and said, "That is enough, you shall finish it another time."

On Tuesday night he did not sleep so well, and at three in the morning insisted on dictating a letter on Sol-fa business. When I wanted him to leave it, he said, "No, my mind will be more at rest when this is done." But he could not sleep again till between five and six.

On Wednesday morning the doctor said that he had not one bad symptom, and the fever had left him. He gave us leave to use quinine and champagne, with all the nourishment he could take. There was great weakness, but not more than the doctor expected, and we were very hopeful that the increased nourishment and stimulant would strengthen him. Towards noon it seemed to have taken effect, and he revived a little. Every time he woke we had food ready, and when awake gave it every ten minutes or quarter of an hour. Eggs beaten up in wine, jelly, custard, milk and soda water, oysters, all that we could think of to nourish and to tempt.

Towards evening he was more restless, the breathing not quite so easy, and at eight, when the doctor came, the fever had returned, and we learnt afterwards that the pulse was intermittent. The doctor stayed to write to Doctor Kidd, and then left saying he would return at eleven and stay the night. When waking about half-past eight dear father said, "Oh! how sweet it would be to sleep away like this."

After nine the heavy breathing increased rapidly, and father said, "I am much worse. I feel as ill as when I first came here. Perhaps I shall be with my Saviour to-night."

He complained of coldness, and we put hot water bottles to him, gave the exhaustion medicine, raised his

U

head, but nothing gave relief. Mr. Coward went off to try and find the doctor. Mary and I stood helpless, knowing that the end was very near. Four or five times I bathed the precious face and hands, this always refreshed and gave him pleasure. Then I took his hand in mine and prayed silently that he might be released. Oh! to stand and *let him go !* when in my selfish love I would have done anything to keep him ! At last the breathing grew feebler ; he gazed upward as one who already was conscious only of heaven ; then his eyes gradually closed, and a few short gasping breaths ended, on this Wednesday evening, the 26th of May, 1880, at half-past ten o'clock, the most lovely, perfect life I ever knew.

The funeral of the late John Curwen took place at the City of London Cemetery, at Ilford, on Thursday afternoon, the 3rd of June. A very large concourse of friends assembled, estimated at from two to three thousand persons. Besides the children and relatives of the deceased, and many local and personal friends, the following were among those present :—

Mr. Colin Brown of Glasgow, Dr. Stainer (organist of St. Paul's Cathedral), Mr. Vernon Lushington, Q.C., Mr. Godfrey Lushington, Mr. A. J. Ellis, F.R.S., Sir Charles Reed, M.P., and Lady Reed, Mr. J. Sarll, Mr. J. Proudman, Mr. A. L. Cowley (Dublin), Rev. G. M. Murphy, Rev. R. Ross (vicar of Forest Gate), Mr. and Mrs. T. Warr, Mr. W. M. Miller (Glasgow), Mr. W. R. Bourke, Mr. A. P. Burr, Mr. and Mrs. G. F. Treverton, Herr Behnke, Mr. A. T. Jones, Mr. L. C. Venables, Mr. and Mrs. G. J. Venables, Mr. S. R. Rolfe, Mrs. Stapleton, Mr. and Mrs. M'Naught, Mr. Ashcroft, ·

Mr. and Mrs. R. Griffiths and family, Mr. A. Lussignea, Mr. G. R. Darby, Mr. G. Merritt, Mr. G. Oakey, Mr. and Mrs. W. H. Bonner, Mr. Wilfred Ferguson (Mr. Curwen's secretary), Mr. W. Boyd, Mr. H. Stevenson, Mr. J. Evans, Mr. Alfred Brown, Mr. R. D. Metcalfe, Mr. and Mrs. Parish, Miss Clements and the Choir of St. John's, Highbury Vale, Mr. and Mrs. A. Hamilton, Mrs. Ellis, Mr. and Mrs. H. Taylor, Messrs. J. N. Cullingford, W. Green, James Thomson, G. J. Chapple, John Nicol, E. G. Hammond, W. R. Phillips, J. Ruddock, J. W. Glover, F. H. Rooke, H. Sampson, F. M. Gordon, W. Crouch, W. C. Harris, A. Bond, T. R. Rayment, J. Youens, W. Moody, J. Woodard, F. T. Brooks, F. A. Bridge, H. Selfe, R. H. Gowan, J. Garwood, W. Weller, E. Locke, A. S. Lupton, T. H. Warner, B. C. Laycock, T. R. J. Ames, S. J. Robinson, J. E. Costello, G. F. Wates, J. Sarll, jun., W. Bond, E. Lock, H. W. Penn, G. E. Hart, Fitzsimmons, J. Courtney, Misses Bennett, Badcock, Evans, Marks, and Ford, &c., &c. The road through the Cemetery was lined by sympathising friends, while a large body of stewards, under the control of Mr. George Venables, kept order and space for the chief mourners.

The service in the Chapel began with the hymn "Come let us join our friends above," to the tune "St. Bernard," after which the Rev. J. Knaggs read the service. The Rev. J. A. Macfadyen, M.A., of Manchester, next delivered the following address :—

It was but the other day that many of us were gathered here as mourners to consign to the grave the body of our dear friend Mrs. Curwen. We are here again on a similar errand to-day, but there is one of that company absent. That beautiful face on which we looked, and which we wondered to see so placid, " its composure the outward and visible sign of an inward and spiritual grace," is not here. The voice which then mingled so distinctly in our hymns is silent. That place, to which we turned with so much interest and anxiety, is empty. We felt that then we were burying the larger half of his life. We feared that he would find the rest of his days very lonely. We hoped for our own sakes (in these matters we are very selfish) that nevertheless he would be with us for many years. But God has seen it better to disappoint us, and to gratify him. He always seemed to live on the border of the other world since I knew him. "It seems natural and proper to me," he says in a letter written some time since, to a young friend who was leaving this world, "to think of the nearing time when I shall pass away into another world;" but ever since that service he has lived more in the invisible world than in this world. If ever man could say with the apostle "I am in a strait betwixt two, having a desire to depart and to be with Christ, which is far better, nevertheless to abide in the flesh is more needful for you," "what I shall choose I wot not," he, during these last few months, could say it. Willing to stay if it were the Lord's will, he was anxious to go.

And we can see more clearly than we usually can in such cases, that the stroke has come at the right time for him. There were not many incidents in his life; yet few lives are so perfectly rounded and completed as his. His ministry over, his family settled happily and usefully, the great political questions in which he was most deeply interested in a fair way for solution, the education questions of the Sunday and day school raised to a higher level, the important movement to which he devoted his later days, and by which he has made the nation and the church so deeply his debtors, piloted safely out of the difficulties which surrounded it in its beginnings, and admitting of being entrusted to other hands, the books he meant to write nearly all written; the College he wished to establish, founded and at work, others raised up in large numbers to enter into and carry on his labours, it *was* better for him that he should rejoin the partner of his life. They were lovely and pleasant in their lives, it was fitting that in their deaths they should not be divided.

But for us this death is breach upon breach and sorrow upon sorrow. We are losers, and what a loss it is!

Some are here to whom this day is in a sense in which it cannot be to most of us, a day of gloom and bitter sorrow. Those of us who had any opportunity of seeing and sharing in the beautiful family life, of which their father was the centre, can enter in part into their grief. But we can do no more. We have often envied them the privilege of having such a father. The greater the privilege, the heavier the sorrow. Emphatically here "the heart knoweth its own bitterness." None of the stereotyped forms of sympathy are of avail in the shadow of such a grief. We can but pray "the Lord bless them and keep them; the Lord make His face shine upon them and be gracious unto them; the Lord lift up His countenance upon them and give them peace."

Many of us mourn the loss of a dear friend. The older and more intimate the friendship has been, the greater the reason for the lament "I am distressed for thee, my brother, very pleasant hast thou been to me, thy love to me was wonderful." For myself, words cannot convey my sense of indebtedness to my friend for the past, and my consequent sense of loss. He was the most intimate friend I had among my fathers in the ministry.

If he was beloved and venerated as a patriarch in my
house, he made me feel as a son in his house. For years
I have gone in and out at will, revering his pure and holy
character, his saintly life, his unselfish affection, his frank,
childlike, and sympathetic manner, the blending of love
and intellect "by which he seemed to think with the
heart and feel with the mind," his steady attachment to
principle, an attachment that made him in all matters
pertaining to conscience as much of the oak, as in all
things that seemed to him nonessential he was of the
willow, one of the noblest and most chivalrous natures I
have known. To use the language of another who cannot
be here to-day, "He was such a man, so quiet and firm,
so manly and childlike, so full of noble purposes and so
patient in regarding the smallest matters. He was so
forbearing, so hopeful of the bad, and so appreciative of
the good amongst men. How little children loved him,
and strong-willed men submitted to him!" In one word,
he was a friend to be trusted utterly, an adviser to be
consulted in any difficulty, into whose ungrudging ears
one might pour any story one had to tell of success, and
whose prayers made the heart strong when called to plead
for God with man. The last act of his life was typical to
all who knew him in this relationship. He met with
death in the performance of a friendly duty, a duty which
he would have performed all the same had he known before
he set out that death awaited him in the act.

But the large concourse that has assembled here this
afternoon, the wide-spread circle who heard the news of
his death with deepest regret throughout the country, the
thousands who are with us this moment in spirit, knew
him mainly as a public man. This aspect of his character
was directly due to his religion. There are many who
seem to think, and when Mr. Curwen began his ministry

there were more than there are now who thought that Christianity could and ought to be separated from daily and from public life. They thought of it as a species of angel neither marrying nor giving in marriage, a kind of Elijah appearing upon earth and as mysteriously disappearing, a species of Melchisedec without beginning of days or ending of years. Wherein the Christian man stood on common ground they reckoned him nothing. Wherein he rose above mundane matters they did him homage. To this school our departed friend never belonged; we might say, from the very constitution of his mind and the strong sympathies of his heart could not belong. In all personal questions he was a John who lived near his Saviour—might almost be said to recline on His bosom. But when conscience was touched he had the spirit, if not the presence and the voice of a Boanerges. The older he grew, the more decided his political opinions became, and the more disposed was he to lift up his testimony against any legislation that violated the wise man's proverb "Righteousness exalted a nation." By birth and education a Nonconformist, the chance associations of his youth became the deliberate convictions of his mature years.

Alike from the sympathy of his nature, from his public spirit and from his ecclesiastical preferences he became in early life an ardent educationist, at a time when it was a grave question with no unimportant section of the community whether any education was desirable for the children of the poor. It was in the exercise of his mission to children that he discovered his life work. He approached music from the side of education. Music must have had many charms for him. It presented so many attractions to him as a young minister, that lest he should be drawn away from his Church, his Sunday School, and his Day School (he regarded these departments of work as coming in that order in importance), he would not learn to play on an instrument. Circumstances, as men would say, Providence, as we say, mastered his resolution. Indeed, he could do no otherwise than he did. Bodily and mental force failed him, and he was compelled to turn to business. "I have sometimes been blamed for this by those who think that once a minister always a minister. I do not remember the time when I believed that doctrine. When I went to college at 16 years of age I certainly dedicated myself to the service of what I thought good and right in the world. But I said then as I say now, there are many ways of serving the holy and true beside that of the pulpit. I think that indeed the highest service. But a man must serve as he can. If he is shut out from the higher offices, he must be glad to take the humbler part." At a conference of Sunday School teachers in the autumn of 1841 he was solemnly charged to make this the mission of his life, and he accepted the commission in no half-hearted fashion.

How well he discharged it there are many here who could tell far better than I. Suffice it to say that he caught the first hint of the system with which his name is identified from Miss Glover. But he elaborated the system till it fulfilled the conditions desired—a method which could teach to sing in half the usual time, and a notation which could supply music at half the usual cost. In the conduct of the enterprise our friend developed a resolution and strength of will with which few would have credited him. The institution of the necessary propaganda called for a faculty for organisation which is unrivalled so far as I have heard in the musical world. His devotion to the work inspired with his own enthusiasm a band of co-workers of whom he seemed to feel that he could never speak highly enough, while his simple-hearted docility prompted him to entertain any suggestion of improvement from any quarter. "Those who have known me longest have found me ever ready to adopt improvements. My brother-in-law once said that in a cotton factory it always answered to use the best machinery. When a better loom was invented he turned the old ones out and installed the new." The system has made its way through many difficulties, and to-day it is confessedly the cheapest, the easiest, the truest way of carrying music to the people. In England and America, on the Continent and throughout the stations of all our missionary societies, the testimony is borne by all who have given it a fair trial, that it is by far the most effective instrument yet employed for the purpose. In connection with this work the name of Curwen is destined to go down to future generations, as it is to-day in England a household word.

But pleasing as it must have been and was to him to see the system spreading (and there is no worker amongst men who does not find in such a result his reward), this was not the primary end for which he laboured, this was not the result that brought him his highest pleasure. The most interesting feature about the history of this movement so far, to an outside observer not competent to speak on musical questions, has been its benevolent and religious aspect. When Miss Glover was in her 82nd year Mr. Curwen visited her, and when in conversation he referred to some charges of plagiarism made by a French musical journal, she replied "Do not concern yourself to vindicate my originality, let the question be, not who was the first to invent it, but is the thing itself good and true and useful to the world." The mantle of the inventor of the system descended in this respect upon its perfecter and apostle. He was never tired of impressing upon his co-workers that their success was due not so much to the fact that new and popular music had been introduced, that the means put forth had called for diligence and self-sacrifice, as that they had sought and had received the blessing from on high. It was as an educationist that he first took up the subject, and from Sunday school teachers that he received his first commission. To the last his joy and crown of rejoicing was that the Church of Christ was enriched in the present and for the future by his mission; that in the assemblies of God's people he had been the means of promoting the service of song in the house of the Lord; that there could scarcely be a gathering of little children to whose love of praise he had not ministered; that there was not an important philanthropic movement that did not find its right hand in him and in his labours; that homes in countless numbers were happier for his work, that lives were brightened, that hours of sorrow were made less dreary, that hearts which had become impervious to other holy influences were touched and opened through the love of music he had fostered, to the spirit of God.

Surely it is no mockery, no delusion to say that this life so nobly lived is not ended. "Better is the day of death than the day of one's birth." In words with which all here are familar Wordsworth sings :—

> Our birth is but a sleep and a forgetting
> The soul that rises with us, our life's star
> Hath elsewhere had its setting
> And cometh from afar.
> Not in entire forgetfulness
> And not in utter nakedness,
> But trailing clouds of glory do we come,
> From God who is our home.

Some might deny the statement of the poet, some have challenged it as meaningless. But all will agree in this, that what the poet saw in the infant's birth, the eye of the Christian sees more truly in such a death. "What seen from one side is the setting of the life, seen from the other side will be its rising. If the man has lived truly, he does not lose in death one of his treasures. Learning, wisdom, experience, ripe culture, exquisite susceptibility to beauty, truthfulness, generosity, gentleness, unselfishness, humility, reverence, nothing is lost. It is all precious to Him. There are other and grander spheres of effort, other and greater work to be done in worlds unknown, to which our best and bravest are called away. We speak of their sun as having gone down while it was yet day—they have begun to shine already as the stars for ever and ever."

And surely in that bright land to which our friend is gone, that world of song and music and joy, there is a noble mission, a glorious work before him. "And I saw as it were a sea of glass, mingled with fire, and them that had gotten the victory over the beast and over his image and over his work, and over the number of his name, stand on the sea of glass having the harps of God, and they sang the song of Moses the servant of God, and the song of the Lamb. After this I beheld, and lo, a great multitude, whom no man could number, of all nations and kindred and people and tongues stood before the throne, clothed in white robes and palms in their hands, and cried with a loud voice, saying, Salvation to our God who sitteth upon the throne, and unto the Lamb." We know that he is among them. If he is among them there will be work for him to do. We will not mourn as they that have no hope. Rather we will tune our dirge into a hymn of praise. "Blessed are the dead which die in the Lord, they rest from their labours and their works do follow them." "God will redeem my soul from the power of the grave. He will swallow up death in victory." " Thanks be unto God Who giveth us the victory through our Lord Jesus Christ." " Blessed be the God and father of our Lord Jesus Christ who hath abolished death and hath brought life and immortality to light through the Gospel. Praise our God, all ye His servants, and ye that fear Him both small and great. Thanksgiving and honour and power and might be unto our God for ever and ever.

At the close of the address the Rev. Dr. Kennedy offered prayer. The procession then moved to the grave, which is beautifully situated at the eastern edge of the cemetery, beneath a clump of trees. The hymn " Servant of God well done," strikingly appropriate in its pourtrayal of finished work and 'sudden death, was sung to Dr. Gauntlett's tune " St. George." The Rev. J. Knaggs then read the concluding portion of the service, after which the hymn " Go forward, Christian Soldier " was sung to an old German Chorale. The Rev. T. W. Davids then pronounced the benediction. A lark, rising close by at the moment that the last line of the hymn died away, poured out a stream of melody that pierced the air during the uttering of the benediction, and continued during the impressive stillness which followed.

Among those who wrote expressing their disappointment at not being able to be present at the funeral were :—Rev. E. P. Cachemaille, Vicar of St. James's, Muswell Hill (who, it was hoped, would be able to take a part in the service), Rev. C. Livermore, Rev. P. W. Jones

(Penygroes), Rev. A. J. D'Orsey, Rev. J. Richardson (of Madagascar), Rev. W. F. Callaway (Birmingham), Professor Kennedy, Mr. J. A. Brown (of Paisley), Mr. J. S. Crisp, Mr. F. Coventry (Manchester), Mr. John Dale (Macclesfield), Mr. R. Anderson (Glasgow), Mr. W. C. Jones (Chester), Mr. W. M'Kendrick (Newcastle), Mr. W. B. Harvey (Frome), Mr. R. B. Litchfield (of the Working Men's College), Mr. W. L. Carter, Mr. J. Hooper, M.A., Mr. J. J. Stuttaford, Mr. W. Anderson (Perth), Mr. Brinley Richards, Mr. Tom Parry, Dr. W. M. Cooke, Mr. W. Dobson, Mr. M. S. Dunn, Mr. J. Hatch, &c.

The monument erected over the grave is an obelisk of red granite, bearing the following inscription :—

In affectionate remembrance of
JOHN CURWEN,
Born November 14, 1816, Died May 26, 1880.
He developed and promoted the Tonic Sol-fa method of teaching music.

"Let the people praise Thee, O God ; let all the people praise Thee."

And of his loving wife
MARY CURWEN,
Born March 24, 1819, Died January 17, 1880.
"They were lovely and pleasant in their lives, and in death they were not divided."

CHAPTER XVII.

Home Life. By his Daughter, Mrs. Banks.

STUDY—WITH HIS CHILDREN—CONVERSATION—MECHANISM — MARRIED LIFE — MONEY MATTERS — FESTIVALS — DICTATION—NEW IDEAS—POLITICS—LOVE OF CHILDREN —LETTERS TO HIS GRANDCHILD.

My earliest recollections of my father are in the Minister's Home at Plaistow. I remember, wherever we lived, the quiet study, sacred from all noise and disturbance, and, for that reason, always far off from the nursery. It was the privilege of each child by turns to knock at the study door, and call the dear father down to meals. This was done because he seldom heard the sound of the bell. I can picture now the room; the table, the floor littered with books, the walls lined with them. If in the midst of some thought he would quickly say " wait a minute, my darling," and then as he finished his sentence he would turn with a bright smile and a kiss to take his child by the hand, or to mount it on his shoulders, and so go down to the family meal.

A sunny room was always chosen for the study, for my father greatly loved the sunshine. When weak in health he would sit for hours basking in it. The blinds were never dropped in his room, and he would glory in the hot rays of a summer sun pouring in at the window.

As a family we saw no more of him than if he had been a business man in the city all day. The study engrossed him all the morning, and, during the first part of his ministry, visiting in the afternoon, and meetings in the evening. It was only on rare occasions, such as birthdays, and on Christmas day that we children claimed him for our own all the evening. Then, indeed, we had grand times; father on his hands and knees making believe he was a bear bent on catching and eating up us children. How he growled till he was hoarse, and how we jumped about half in delight and half in terror till we were caught and cast into the den! But these unbendings were few and far between. Even when going to the seaside he would come, generally at the last moment, with a huge pile of books, to my mother saying, " Dear, can you make room for these," and while there several hours of each morning would be given to study and writing.

The absent-mindedness and absorption in work which prevented his hearing the dinner-bell, was characteristic of him all his life. He would, if left alone to a meal, forget altogether to eat, or put two or three mixtures on his plate. He would sit in the room quite lost to all that was going on around him, and we might speak several times before he heard or answered.

My father always had a hearty appreciation of humour, and made a capital listener to a good story. He had no memory for these things, and we children had a number of riddles which we asked over and over again at intervals of a few months, always saying, "Did you ever hear that before?" and when the answer came "No," greeting it with laughter which betrayed to him the truth, when he would join in, often adding "I don't know how it is, I have no fun in my character; your Uncle Tom has inherited all the stock of family fun."

When speaking of the art of conversation he said, "Most people like best to talk of their own affairs. To listen to them, now and then putting in a sympathising word, will give them more pleasure than anything else." At another time he said, "If I want to talk to anyone I try to find out their favourite subject. Every one, even the apparently reserved and shy people will have some one question on which he can talk, and talk well. If you want to please try one subject after another till you discover *the* subject." His was truly "a heart at leisure from itself to soothe and sympathise."

With these rules of conversation, guided by a tender heart, no wonder that his friendship was much sought and prized. One characteristic of his conversation was its perfect freedom from all exaggeration. In the present day when the fashion is to assume an intense interest in the commonest occurrence; when superlative adjectives are ʼused to express even every-day commonplaces, this simplicity was the more remarkable. Should one or other of the family be talking rather largely he would say "adhere strictly to the truth." And this he did himself, neither at any time "colouring" his picture, nor affecting interest or emotion which was not natural to him. Neither did he ever *pretend* to a knowledge he did not possess. He knew and appreciated so thoroughly the pleasure of imparting knowledge that he was never afraid of saying, "I don't understand." He would in such cases ask question after question, many a time puzzling his informer, but not satisfied until he had mastered the subject for himself.

It was his very attitude of learning that made him so successful as an educational writer. He placed himself in the position of the youngest learner, and wrote for that one. Had he taken up any other subject than music there is little doubt but that he would have been equally successful. That others were of the same opinion is proved by the fact that a large publishing firm asked him to write elementary reading books. He often wished in later times that he had had time to do so.

x

The " art of teaching " was one of the subjects in which he took a very special interest. Soon after starting the public British Schools at Plaistow he undertook a training class for teachers. I remember, as a child, often going with him to those schools, and the great interest he took in the Bible lessons and the gallery lessons. In those days object lessons were something quite new. These voluntary schools were very successful, and were supported without any assistance from the national funds. Upon the formation of the School Board they were handed over to it.

My father was much interested in mechanism, and entered as enthusiastically into the merits of a new printing machine, as he did into the analysis of a chord in music. As all the different household machines came out he would study their merits, choosing the best 'of each he could find, and bringing-*it* into household use. If any prejudice was shown against it he would try it himself, were it for boiling coffee, washing, or for sewing. We children were always ready to help in any of these innovations. Very often the machine was pronounced useless, but my father was never discouraged, and only set to work to find a better.

My father's married life is a subject so sacred that it is most difficult to calmly tell of it. As has been said earlier in this volume it was not without opposition that his wife was won. As years went on their lives were closely welded together, each filling up what the other lacked. Only those who saw them in their happy home can realize what they were to each other. Some have said that my father was too demonstrative, but those who knew him best understood that it was only that he expressed in actions and words a depth of affection which many stifle. The very expression of it made it grow. This, together with his gentleness of manner, made him a most attentive husband. His daily letters when from home would have rivalled Carlyle's in expressions of affection.

He was ever most thoughtful to my mother, sparing no expense where her health and happiness were concerned. She relieved him of every household care, managing his income with economy and wisdom. This he appreciated fully, praising her for all she did. Small acts of kindness which usually go unnoticed he would receive most gratefully. In philanthropic and church work they had great mutual interest, but Sol-fa notation was a dead letter to my mother, so in that he could only count on her general sympathy.

To his home circle he was always as polite as he would be to a stranger. He was ever more ready to recognise the well doing by praise than to condemn the wrong doing.

In money matters he was always generous and often lavish, though never for his own purposes. My mother dreaded to have a request for charity made to him. She feared his giving without any regard to the purse. His usual practice, however, about every donation, from the smallest to the largest, was to consult with her. Often, when asked to give, he would playfully say, " I must consult my Chancellor of the Exchequer, and then I will send you an answer."

All festivals and anniversaries were observed in my father's house. The arrangements for the day, and the choice of gifts mainly fell into my mother's hands ; but his gift was always added. He it was who supplied the nursery with pennies on the 5th of November. In early days his gift was a book to each of his children as the birthdays came round, and in after years a gift of money with the condition attached that it must be spent on books, the books to be our own choice. In this way he cultivated our taste for books, and enabled each of us to form the nucleus of a library. The wedding-day and my mother's birthday were never forgotten. On the latter day it was his custom to go up to town with my mother, and together choose some present for her. He had a not-to-be-shaken belief that " surprizes were disappointments," and so rarely ventured to choose a present alone for his wife.

His mind was always full of the many schemes he had on hand. In the small affairs of the houschold he never interfered, except when appealed to as a higher authority. My mother often called him a "helpless man," and so in many ways he was, liking to be waited on ; to have everything packed for him, and his clothes laid ready to his hand.

Until the last few years he seldom wrote a letter with his own hand. He had acquired the habit of dictating. This habit often called his wife or one of his children to his side. Before a private secretary had become necessary to him many an hour was spent by them in this pleasant service. He was very exact in his directions, dictating slowly, pronouncing distinctly, and often spelling any word that was likely to be mistaken. The amanuensis was never allowed to begin writing a phrase till the whole of it was dictated. It was an education to act in this capacity when any books were in hand, especially in the later and more scientific works. Where any point had to be made certain, instances and examples were searched out, and in this the amanuensis was allowed to help. Sometimes this patient investigation of, for example, some question in harmony, would last for days, and perhaps in the end lead to the abandonment of that theory. At other times the plan of chapter determined on, and the subject mastered, the dictation would go on briskly, the dear father sitting in his easy chair, with his notes before him, or marching about the room. At these times he was ever absorbed in his work, and never seemed to have any difficulty in fixing his attention or in keeping his thoughts from wandering, he would often, on winter days, after pacing the room, sit down with his feet on the fender and quite absently poke and poke the fire until reminded of the destruction he was making.

I never knew a mind so thoroughly without prejudice. Were it a new doctrine, a fresh cure for disease, a new system of medicine, a scientific truth, a fresh aspect of politics, or a new acquaintance, his mind was ever ready to investigate, and then accept all that was good. New things had a charm for him because of the possible truth he might find in them.

He early studied Homœopathy, and used it in the village as well as in our own family, and afterwards amongst his work people. He was a firm believer in it to the day of his death. One of his presents to each of his children when they married, was a case of homœopathic medicines and a Ruddock's Manual.

When any one of us was ailing at home he would come to the bedside, and, book in hand, would ask the symptoms with a grave face, and then prescribe the medicine. We all had faith in our dear doctor, although sometimes, for the fun of the thing, we would pretend symptoms we had not, often repeating word for word the descriptions of the symptoms in the old manual of which he was so fond.

All through life he was an ardent politician, only abstaining in later years from large gatherings on account of the excitement. From the time when, as a boy at Frome, he mounted the hustings, he took a most active part in every struggle of right against might, his sympathy being ever with the oppressed. Every new struggle for freedom that was fought out he watched with intense interest. During the American, Franco-German, and Russo-Turkish wars he would pin a war-map on the wall and follow the course of events most carefully. He liked to get some one to whom he could explain it, and then with the newspaper in his hand he would read, pointing out each change in the position of the contending armies, and the effort to make it clear to his listener made it doubly plain to himself.

The newspaper was always read and discussed at the breakfast table, his wife or one of his children reading aloud the summary, Parliamentary news, and often one or more of the leading articles.

His love of children and his sympathy with them have been referred to elsewhere. It was seldom he failed to win a child's confidence, and that not with presents, but by his loving ways and tender smiles. This was particularly noticeable as his grand-children gathered about him. How he enjoyed them even as babies! Watching their physical and mental growth, very anxious that they should be trained and nurtured rightly. He liked to have the children all to himself, that he might the more easily win their hearts. Many a time he would take them out of the nurse's arms, and seating them on his knee, whistle to them or show them some little thing of interest. As they grew older he would take them by the hand and show them some picture or tell them a story. Often might the dear grey head be seen moving quickly about as he played some game with the little people in the garden. They all looked on grandpapa as a friend, and in their hearts he is even now loved and reverenced above all others.

In talking to children his language was studiously simple, and easily understood by them. He himself looked on Jacob Abbott as the best writer for young children. His own writing for them was based on the same lines. Graphic picturing — laying hold of small incidents to complete the picture—leaving nothing to be guessed at. But my father went beyond Abbott in one respect, in the simplicity of his language, never using a two-syllabled word if one syllable would answer his purpose. As far as possible he used the simple expressive Saxon, rather than the longer though more polished Latinised words.

The following letter to his eldest grand-daughter will serve to show his manner with young children :—

To his Grand-daughter Winnie, aged 4 years.

St. Leonards, March 10, 1877.

Dear Winnie,—Grandpapa wishes he had your little hand in his, and he could look into your dear eyes, and take you on his knee, and kiss your sweet lips. Dear grandmamma and I hope to come home soon—to their dear grand-daughters Winnie and Chrissie.

In these lodgings there is a little black kitten, full of life and fun. Her name is Topsey, and sometimes she amuses us very much, and sometimes she is a great teaze.

When I am sitting reading in an arm chair Topsey will climb up on to my knee and poke her nose between my book and my face. Then she will look at me with both her eyes and put out her paw to scratch my beard. I feel afraid lest she should put out her paw into my eye, so I push her down.

Then she will fall on her four feet and look round to see what there is to play with. One day she saw the hearth brush lying down, and the bristles sticking out, so she made a jump upon them, as much as to say, "I don't know what you are, but I like you." But the bristles did not like Topsey; they pricked her, and she bounded back with all her might. In doing this she fell on the tongs, and the tongs made such a rattle on the fender as frightened Topsey terribly. So off she flew to the very farthest end of the room. Poor Topsey! that all came of embracing a brush.

She soon got over her fright, and was found on my knee again, darting her paw at my watch key, and biting at my tuning fork. She could not make the fork sound, but I think we may call her a musical kitty.

Topsey is very fond of jumping on to the tops of the chairs and the highest part of the sofa, just to have a peep round the room. Yesterday she got under grandmamma's shawl, and began biting the buttons on grandmamma's dress, and at dinner time I saw her climb up Mary's back and stand on her shoulder and look over just to see what Mary was eating. I think she meant to say

" Mary, please give me a bit, just a little bit, and then I'll come on to your shoulder again, Mary." So Mary gives her a little bit, and walks about the room with Topsey on her shoulder.

One morning grandmamma was having her breakfast in bed. So Topsey jumped on to the bed for company. She soon saw something moving under the clothes at the bottom of the bed. So pussy made a jump at it ; it moved again ; and again Topsey jumped at it and tried to bite it. She could not tell what it was. It was only grandmamma's toes moving about to play with Topsey. I wish I could show you our bright little black kitten Topsey.

Upton, E., February 14, 1880.

My Own Sweet Winnie,—Mary brought a letter to me at breakfast this morning. I laid it on the cloth and looked at the direction. Then I said, " Who can this be ? I have never seen this hand-writing before. Let me open it." So I opened it and found a pretty little girl come to me as a valentine ! Who can it be ? I said again ! Then I read dear mamma's letter, and found it was my own little Winnie.

Who is Winnie ? Winnie is a little girl with two grandpapas. Do you know another little girl with two grandpapas who love her as much as Winnie's grandpapas do ? I don't. I was delighted to hear of your digging in the garden with your dear Cumberland grandpapa. I love him very much because he is so kind to Winnie, and to Winnie's mamma. Chrissy came in yesterday. She is as bright and happy as she can be. She looks about with her merry eyes as if all the world belonged to her.

Cologne, Sept. 25, 1878, Wednesday morning.

Dear Winnie,—I am glad you have been praying to God for grandmamma and grandpapa. I think God has heard your prayers, and is bringing us safe home again.

Just now we are in a railway carriage—very comfortable. Coming fast to Winnie. On our right hand is the river Rhine — very large and beautiful. At Cockermouth you have the river Cocker, and its waters run into the river Derwent. And I think you have seen the river Thames in London. That is a great river. It runs all the way to Southend, and there it goes into the sea. Well the river Rhine is greater than the Thames, and it is much longer. On the banks of it, in some parts, there are beautiful hills and castles, like the castle at Cockermouth. The hills are like those at Keswick. Many of them have grapes growing all up their sides.

Just as I look out of the window I see a pretty castle in the middle of the water on a little island. We have just passed the place called Bingen. There is a red flag flying on the top of the castle, and there are two other castles on the opposite hill. On we go. Again I see a larger castle on a larger island—all rocky. The stream of the Rhine runs the same way that we are going, but it does not run so fast. There is a steamer going the same way. It goes with the stream, and the stream helps it, but steam and stream and all do not go so fast as the train which brings grandmamma to Winnie. I see another steamer. It is coming the opposite way to us. It is coming against the stream ; so it is very slow.

Thus we go—more steamboats—more islands—more hills—more castles—more hills—more grapes. Some day Winnie must come and see the Rhine.

Oh ! how we long to see Winnie and Crissie, and little Lewis and Nina ! Many kisses.

Your
GRANDPAPA.

АДVERTISEMENTS.

THE CHILD'S OWN HYMN BOOK.

Edited by JOHN CURWEN.

The first of the Penny Hymn Books. Prices:—

THE HYMN BOOK. Paper cover, 1d.; cloth, 2d.; large type, in cloth, and with biographical notes on authors of hymns, 6d.
THE TUNE BOOK. Staff notation; cloth 1s.; paper, 6d. Tonic Sol-fa, same prices.

MUSICAL THEORY.

BY JOHN CURWEN.

Price 3s. 6d., postage 3½d.

TOPICS—

THE COMMON SCALE AND TIME.
THE MINOR MODE AND TRANSITION.
MUSICAL FORM.
EXPRESSION.
HARMONY AND CONSTRUCTION.

From *THE ORCHESTRA.*

"In this book all the illstrations are printed in both notations. Leaving the symbols, we can only stop to allude to the symmetrical and systematic arrangements of the subjects discussed in this book; to the excellent way in which essential principles and facts are prominently put forward; and to the interesting comments and elucidations which supplement the main definitions."

STORY FOR CHILDREN.

HISTORY OF NELLY VANNER.

BY JOHN CURWEN.

Bound in cloth, ONE SHILLING; cheap edition, SIXPENCE.

A TONIC SOL-FA PRIMER.

(No. 18 of Messrs. NOVELLO, EWER, & Co's Music Primers, Edited by DR. STAINER.)

BY JOHN CURWEN.

The PREFACE says:—

"This work is not intended to teach those ignorant of music how to sing, but to explain the Tonic Sol-fa Notation and Method of Teaching to those already familiar with the established method of writing music by means of the staff. A knowledge of that notation is taken for granted, and it will be mainly by comparing the two notations that the various points of the new notation will be made clear."

Second edition now ready. Price 1s.; postage, 1d.

www.ingramcontent.com/pod-product-compliance
Lightning Source LLC
Chambersburg PA
CBHW030926050726
47498CB00003BA/909